POE'S FIRST LAW

A MURDER ON MAUI MYSTERY

ROBERT W. STEPHENS

For Felicia Dames

1

YOUR HONOR – PART 1

I THOUGHT ABOUT CALLING THIS TALE, *UNINTENDED CONSEQUENCES*, FOR never have I seen so many well-intentioned gestures go so spectacularly wrong. I was guilty of some of them but not all.

I have a rule, although it's certainly not my main rule, to never get involved with crumbling marriages. Unfortunately, as an occasional private investigator, that is often unavoidable. Many criminal acts have their beginnings in adultery, which always spins into a web of lies and can even lead to murder.

Before I go much further with this mystery tale, please allow me a moment to introduce myself and tell you how I got into this mess. My name is Edgar Allan "Poe" Rutherford. I put "Poe" in quotation marks since it's a nickname of mine. My parents, God rest their souls, were huge fans of the legendary mystery writer, and they assumed that naming their only child after him would be a great honor.

It was a challenging name to have, as I'm sure you can imagine. Fortunately, my best friend started calling me Poe in the high school years and the name stuck. Most people still call me Poe these days. However, you may call me Edgar if you wish. I'm no longer embarrassed by the name. It's purely your decision and I will answer to either.

After graduating from the University of Virginia, I went to work as an architect until that career was stalled during the Great Recession. I was summarily dismissed from my job, but I really didn't mind. The architecture gig wasn't what I imagined it would be. Unfortunately, I was at a loss as to what new path I wanted to forge.

There was also my failing romantic relationship with a woman named Dorothy, who I caught cheating on me with a BMW car sales-man. As I look back on those days, it's obvious to me that Dorothy was mainly motivated by money, and she assumed that a man peddling used Beamers had more of a future than an unemployed and unenthusiastic architect.

What she didn't know, mainly because I never told her, was that I am loaded. Forgive me if that sounds obnoxious. Actually, I know it sounds obnoxious, but I don't mean it to, nor do I take credit for my wealth. Much of that money came from my grandfather, who passed it to my mother, and then it made its way to me. I will take credit for some sound investments I've made over the years, but the seed money for that certainly didn't come from my hard work.

After the loss of my job and my girl, I was lured to the tropical island of Maui by my friend, Doug Foxx, the same friend I mentioned above who'd given me the name of Poe. Foxx was a professional foot-ball player with the Washington Redskins until a nasty knee injury ended his career after two short seasons.

Foxx came to Maui to heal his injured body and mind. He never left. After a good deal of badgering by him, I finally accepted his invi-tation to hop on a plane and fly six thousand miles to the island. I'd hoped that after the trip I'd figure out a new direction for my life. That actually happened, but I would have never guessed that direc-tion in a million years.

During my first night on Maui, Foxx was arrested for the murder of his girlfriend, a successful artist who he'd planned on proposing to during my trip. I was in Foxx's house when a beautiful half-Hawaiian, half-Japanese detective slapped the handcuffs on him. The Maui detective's name is Alana Hu and I spent the next several days trying to prove Foxx's innocence, while at the same time convincing the good detective to help me search for another suspect.

In fairness to the Maui Police Department, Foxx looked guilty as hell, but I finally managed to wear Detective Hu down and together we caught the true culprit. I wouldn't dream of giving you more details of my first island adventure, a tale I dubbed *Aloha Means Goodbye*, but it's all there for the reading.

After wrapping up that case, I made the decision to stay on the island and continue to pursue the Maui goddess called Alana. Today, we are married, and we live in an oceanfront home with our dog, Maui, a ten-pound mix of a Maltese and Yorkshire Terrier.

The new dog breed is called a Morkie. I've had a few readers write me and accuse me of making that up. To those suspicious ones who think I bend the truth from time to time, I encourage you to google the term Morkie. You'll find dozens of images of cute dogs, although none of them are as handsome as my Maui.

Now, let's get back to my introduction and the use of the term *Unintended Consequences*. It's how I ended up sitting on the witness stand in a Maui courtroom. My tales always involve a murder, and to date, I've successfully resolved them all. That doesn't mean, of course, that the guilty ones all went to jail. The criminal justice system is deeply flawed, although I probably don't have to tell you that.

My tales rarely show what happens after the bad guy or bad guys are caught. In some ways, that is just the beginning of the process, as talented Maui prosecutors take over the case and do their best to get guilty verdicts. I'm sometimes called to testify during these trials and believe me when I say that it's my least favorite part of the process.

For one thing, I have to lose my customary t-shirt, shorts, and sandals and wear something more presentable. For another, I hate sitting in front of a crowded courtroom and having to perform. And that's exactly what a court appearance is. We're all there to put on a show for the judge and jury and convince them that our version of events is the true one.

It's probably best that I give you a brief rundown of the case in question. Guy Livingston is a photographer who specializes in taking photos of tourists. He has arrangements with several of the large hotels in Kihei, Wailea, Lahaina, and Kaanapali. They feed him customers, and in return, he gives them a share of the profits.

His wife, Lucy Livingston, used to be a teller for a bank in Kahului. I say "used to be" since she's no longer with us. Hence, my reason for being in the courtroom.

"Mr. Rutherford, can you tell us when you first met the defendant, Guy Livingston?" Piper asked.

Piper Lane, with her short black hair and dark eyes, is probably Maui's toughest prosecutor. I've had the misfortune of being on the wrong end of one of those prosecutions in the past. Fortunately for me, I wasn't guilty. Even more fortunate, I was able to prove it.

"I met Mr. Livingston in my bar, Harry's," I said.

Harry's, by the way, is a Lahaina-based bar that I co-own with Foxx. It's a few blocks off of the famed Front Street – the tourist strip known for a fascinating and fun collection of art galleries, shops, and restaurants. Harry's is loved by both locals and tourists. Locals love it because they get to escape the crazy crowds on Front Street.

Tourists love it because it makes them feel more like locals. Both groups are fond of the lower-priced drinks and food. There's also Foxx, the main attraction of the bar. He excels in entertaining guests with tales of the NFL, as well as his involvement in many of my criminal investigations.

"What did you and the defendant discuss while he was at your drinking establishment?" Piper asked.

I smiled.

"Is something funny, Mr. Rutherford?" Piper continued.

"Sorry, I don't mean to appear to make light of these proceedings. But your use of the words 'drinking establishment' is a bit too nice for my bar. It's more of a dive. In answer to your question, Mr. Livingston said that he'd heard that I was a private investigator, which I am, on a part-time basis."

"Did the defendant ask to hire you?"

"Yes. He told me that his wife had been mugged and her diamond necklace and tennis bracelet had been stolen. He said that they were anniversary gifts to his wife. He was very upset."

"Objection, your Honor," Livingston's lawyer, a short, stocky man named Henry Mitchell said. "Does Mr. Rutherford really assume to know how my client felt that day?"

"Sustained," the judge said.

"Mr. Rutherford, did you take his case?" Piper asked.

"I did. I don't normally take theft cases, but I had some free time..." Okay, this wasn't exactly true, but I'll explain more in a minute. "...so I told him I'd do my best to find the missing jewelry."

"What happened next?" Piper asked.

"I checked with my wife who is a Maui police detective and verified that a police report had been filed. I then talked to the officer who'd made the report."

"What did you learn?" Piper asked.

"They had no leads. There was no security camera in the shopping plaza where the robbery took place, and Mrs. Livingston's physical description of the suspect fit hundreds of men on Maui, if the man was still even on the island," I said.

"How do you proceed in a situation like that? It seems rather daunting."

"I met with Mrs. Livingston and she gave me the same physical description of the suspect. Then I went to the plaza where she'd been robbed. While I was walking around, something jumped out at me."

"Which was?"

"When I'd been to the Livingston's home earlier that day, I'd noticed there were several boxes of food from Nutrisystem, which is that company that helps you lose weight. I asked her about it, and she told me that both she and her husband were on a diet. She said they'd been on it for a week and both had lost around five pounds. I congratulated her."

"Why is that relevant?" Piper asked.

To be clear, she knew exactly where I was going with it, and she'd asked the question in a serious tone. Also, to be clear, the judge did not, and I thought I saw him roll his eyes at me. Yes, I know, that wasn't a very distinguished thing for a judge to do, but they're human like the rest of us.

"I'd like to know why too," the judge said in a sarcastic tone, confirming the eye roll I'd seen.

"It's relevant because of the shops that were in the parking lot where she was mugged," I said. "First, there's an ice cream store and several tourist shops that sell things like t-shirts and hats. It seemed an odd place for a local to go unless she wanted to buy ice cream. That didn't make sense since she was on a diet and doing rather well."

"Was there anything else you noticed?" Piper asked.

"I went by the shopping plaza several more times and at different times of the day and week. The parking lot was never full, not once, yet Mrs. Livingston had told both the police and me that she'd had to park to the side of the plaza since the lot was overflowing. That's how she ended up getting mugged since the thief wouldn't have been able to rob her if she'd been in the main part of the parking lot. Too many shop employees would have witnessed it."

"You suspected something wasn't quite true with her story?" Piper asked.

"Yes. I started following Mrs. Livingston, which I hate doing since I'm not the type of investigator you get to follow an unfaithful spouse. It's one of my rules."

"You thought Mrs. Livingston was having an affair?"

"I suspected it, which was confirmed two days later when I saw her with a man."

"Who was that man?" Piper asked.

"I later learned his name is Bret Hardy."

"What is Mr. Hardy's relationship with the defendant, Guy Livingston?" Piper asked.

"I was told by Mr. Livingston that they were friends, golfing buddies."

"Were you ever able to find the missing jewelry?"

"I was. I looked further at Mr. Hardy and learned he was having financial difficulties. The diamond necklace and bracelet were sold, and the money went to Mr. Hardy to pay off his debts."

"How did you determine that?" Piper asked.

"I made the assumption that the jewelry might be pawned. I also assumed that the Maui Police Department had contacted all of the local pawn shops and had learned the jewelry was not taken there. I also guessed that the thief would know not to sell the necklace and bracelet to a Maui store. So, I checked other islands and discovered the necklace was pawned at a shop on Kauai and the bracelet was sold to another store on the same island."

"Who took the jewelry to those pawn shops?"

"Bret Hardy. I saw him in the surveillance video in both shops," I said.

"What did you do then?"

"I gave the video to my wife since I knew it was a police matter."

"And what about Mr. Livingston?" Piper asked.

"He was my client and I owed him the truth. I asked him to meet me at Harry's. I told him about Bret Hardy and his wife. I showed him a copy of the pawn shop videos."

"What was his reaction?"

I didn't immediately answer. Instead, I glanced at Guy Livingston, who was seated behind the defendant's table. He didn't look defeated. Rather, he looked angry – angry with Piper, angry with the police, with the justice system, and undeniably angry with me.

"What was his reaction, Mr. Rutherford?" Piper asked again.

I turned back to her.

"He said, 'I should shoot her.' Then he left the bar."

"What did you do then?"

"I called my wife and informed her that I'd told Mr. Livingston about the affair and the recovered jewelry. I also told Detective Hu that Mr. Livingston had made a threat, but I hadn't thought he was serious."

"Yet less than two hours later, Mrs. Livingston was shot dead in her own home. No further questions, your Honor."

2

COUNTER POINTS

AFTER PIPER WALKED BACK TO HER SEAT, THE DEFENSE ATTORNEY TOOK a run at me. There was no disputing the information I'd discovered about Mrs. Livingston's adulterous affair with Bret Hardy, nor Bret's trip to Kauai to sell the stolen jewelry, which turned out to not have been stolen.

Instead, Livingston's attorney attacked my character. He claimed that I was in the police department's back pocket, especially considering the fact that I often work with law enforcement as a consultant. That was true, at least in terms of one police detective's back pocket. I'm sure you can guess her name.

That good favor didn't extend to the rest of the department, though. If you've read any of my tales before, then you'll know I often butt heads with the police when I feel they've gotten it wrong.

Livingston's attorney concluded his attack by accusing me of having told the jury selective parts of my conversation with Guy Livingston.

Here's a small snippet of his cross-examination for your amusement.

"Isn't it true that you left out a pivotal part of your conversation with my client?" Henry Mitchell asked.

"I'm not sure what you mean."

"After you informed my client about his wife's infidelity, he said, 'I should shoot her, but I won't.'"

"No, that's not what he said."

"That you remember?" he asked.

"Excuse me?"

"I contend that you simply forgot that he said the words, 'But I won't.' You were in a bar, after all. You'd probably been drinking."

"I wasn't," I said.

"You were in a bar, but you weren't drinking?"

"That's right."

"Let me get this straight. You went to your bar in Lahaina, but you didn't have a drink?" he asked, and then he laughed.

"I co-own the bar. I frequently go there to check on the business, and that sometimes involves me having a drink. Often, I don't have one. I didn't have one on this occasion. Furthermore, I thought Harry's was a good location to meet. I was worried about how Mr. Livingston would respond to the news of his wife cheating on him with his friend. I thought it was better to deliver that information in a public place. I felt terribly awkward about it and I thought it less likely he'd cause a scene at the bar."

"So, you're admitting that he might have said the words, 'But I won't.' That is what you just said, isn't it?" Mitchell asked.

"No. That's not what I said."

He went after me from several different angles, all of which were designed to trick me into admitting that I'd recounted the conversation incorrectly. It didn't work. Of course, there's the tried and true theory that if you repeat a lie many times, people will start to believe it. I'm not foolish enough to think that all of the members of the jury saw through his little act.

After leaving the courthouse, I walked outside and climbed into my silver BMW Z3 convertible. I'd bought the car from Foxx shortly after moving to Maui. I popped the top back to take in some sun and then selected music by Oscar Peterson, the Canadian pianist and composer.

The first song that came on the playlist was "Lush Life," sung by the incomparable Ella Fitzgerald. That was followed by "Just One of Those Things" by Oscar Peterson and Louis Armstrong. I didn't start playing air keyboards, at least with one hand, until "Love for Sale" came on.

The music certainly isn't island music, but it's nourishment for my soul. That is the point of music, isn't it? The songs also blended in nicely with the blue sky and blue ocean one sees while driving down the coast. Before I knew it, I was pulling into my driveway and all the negative thoughts of Guy Livingston and his attorney, Henry Mitchell, had washed away.

I parked inside the garage to keep the sun from melting the car's black leather seats. When I opened the door to the kitchen, I was greeted by my dog, Maui. He was sitting by the kitchen island, his tail wagging a million miles per hour.

"Hey, Maui. It feels like several months since I've seen you," I said.

In reality, it had been all of four hours.

Maui trotted over to me and did his world-famous tuck and roll. This is basically when he transitions from his happy-you're-finally-home dance into a position on his back for the expected and demanded belly rub. I kneeled on the kitchen tiles and scratched away.

Maui wasn't the only thing I noticed when I walked in the house. Those lovely and calming tunes from Oscar Peterson had been replaced by Britney Spears' music blaring from every room. We have a high-end entertainment system that can play music throughout the house. It's all controlled with an app on our phones.

I don't mean to sound disrespectful to Ms. Spears. I'm sure she's a lovely woman, but the presence of her music in my house told me one thing. Alana was stressed since she only tends to play pop music at that volume when she's upset.

I found her apparent distress kind of ironic considering that she'd just started a two-week vacation. Her sister, Hani Hu, was due to be married soon, and Hani had asked Alana to take some time off to help her with last-minute details.

You may suspect that I immediately went looking for Alana. I didn't. We've been married for a while and I've learned to give her some space during times like this. Instead, I walked over to the refrigerator and grabbed a Negra Modelo, one of my beers of choice. I popped the top and took a long drink.

"Any more of those in there?" Alana asked.

I turned and saw her walking down the stairs. She was dressed in a white tank top and white shorts. The shorts were a little shorter than usual, which showcased those long, tan legs of hers. I couldn't help but wonder how I'd landed such a hot wife, but that's usually what I think of when I set eyes upon her.

"There are a few more beers. Want just one or should I hand you two?" I asked.

"Why would I want two?"

"What's that? I can't hear you over the loud music."

"Oh, yeah," Alana said, and she pulled her phone out of her pocket. She adjusted the volume to a level that didn't make my head want to explode.

I handed Alana her beer as she walked into the kitchen.

"How did the trial go?" she asked.

"Fine. I'm still in one piece."

I gave Alana the rundown on the defense attorney's cross-examination.

"He really accused you of forgetting what was said? Wait. Forget I asked that question. He's a defense attorney."

"Sure, but what else was he going to do? His client's obviously guilty."

"Sounds like we both had rough mornings," she said.

At this point, I secretly congratulated myself on predicting Alana's foul mood. There were very few people who could get her upset. I'm one of them, but I felt pretty confident I wasn't the offending party in this situation. That left two likely suspects. Hani and Ms. Luana Hu, Alana's mother. My money was on the mother.

"Hani came by this morning."

And there went my perfect record of predictions for the day.

"Oh, what did she want?" I asked.

"You know about the party Yuto is throwing."

I did and I found it rather odd. Hani and Yuto's wedding was just two weeks away, yet Yuto had decided that he wanted to throw a party for Hani a week before the big event. He'd said that he had a surprise for her. No one knew what that surprise was, though. I certainly didn't, which had offended me slightly. Why? Because Yuto had asked if we could have the party at our house. You'd think he could have at least let me in on the surprise, but he'd refused.

"What about the party?" I asked.

"Well, Hani came by this morning to talk about the catering."

"I thought we had that settled. We're using the same company we used for the last party."

"That's what I thought, but apparently Hani wasn't happy with them," Alana said.

"That's a surprise. Everyone seemed to like them."

"Exactly. She told me that she's already hired a replacement, but we're going to lose the deposit I put down on the first one."

"How much?"

"Five hundred dollars. Can you believe that?"

"I'd just drop it. It's not worth the argument."

"It's five hundred dollars, Poe."

"I get it."

"Your problem is you have no sense of money because of how much you're worth."

"First of all, we're worth that much. Your name is on all of those financial accounts. Second, I do know what things are worth, and five hundred bucks is a steal if it keeps your little sister happy."

"When you put it that way."

"Was that the only argument? Something tells me there was more to it," I said.

Alana took a long drink of her beer.

"That good, huh?" I said.

"We argued about Foxx."

"Let me guess. You told her that she should invite Foxx to the party, and she said no."

"Well, Mr. Investigator, you're exactly right."

"I thought things were getting much better between the two of them."

For those new readers, Foxx and Hani had a fling a while back. Foxx had ended the brief relationship, only for Hani to realize later that she was pregnant. Everyone thought they would give it another shot, but Foxx was convinced it would never work.

After Ava was born, their relationship continued to have its ups and downs. They'd hit a seriously rough patch for a while where they wouldn't even acknowledge the existence of the other person.

That changed after Foxx had suffered a near-death experience. I won't say their relationship was great now, but at least they were talking again. I hadn't heard about a fight in a few months, which was a world record for them.

"I thought so too," Alana said. "But she won't invite him. She said she's worried he'll drink too much and say something to offend Yuto."

"And Foxx lives a few houses down from us, which means he'll see and hear the party and wonder why he's not here."

"No, he won't wonder. He'll know exactly why he's not here and I worry it will wipe away any gains they've made. I told her that Ava deserves parents who aren't at each other's throats."

"What did she say to that?" I asked.

"She told me to mind my own business. Then she stormed out."

And that's when Britney Spears started singing, I thought.

"I can talk to Foxx if you like and explain the situation to him. He might be secretly happy that he doesn't have to come to the party," I said.

"I don't believe that for a second. Foxx puts up a good front, but you told me he was hurt the last time he wasn't invited."

"What would you like to do then?"

"Maybe I should call Mom. Maybe she can talk some sense into Hani."

"Your mother hates Foxx. She hates me too."

Alana said nothing.

"You're not going to even try to deny it?" I asked.

"I'm sorry I even brought my mother up."

"There is one thing I could do."

"What's that?"

"Talk to Yuto. He's having more and more sway over Hani these days and I really think he and Foxx have put their differences aside for Ava's sake. He might be willing to convince her to invite Foxx."

"If you asked him, he would," Alana said.

"What's that supposed to mean?"

"It means Yuto follows you around like Maui does. He looks up to you."

"Looks up to me? He and I are the same age."

"That has nothing to do with it. He envies your personality."

I wasn't sure what she meant by that, so I said nothing.

"You'll make the call then?" Alana asked.

"I'll call him after lunch. I'm starving right now."

"You know, this is my first day of vacation. I'm supposed to be relaxing. I was hoping we could go upstairs and relieve some of my stress. But if you're too hungry..."

"Who said I was hungry? Lead the way," I said, and I smiled.

3

A NEW FRIEND

I SPENT THE REST OF THE AFTERNOON HANGING OUTSIDE BY THE POOL IN my backyard. Maui came with me and he alternated his time between exploring every inch of the yard for possible intruders and snoozing in the shade under the patio umbrella. He snored for about an hour until I dove in the pool to swim a few laps.

I think he sometimes feels left out when I'm in the water and he's not. Often, I'll put him in the pool with me so he can swim around for a while. Then I place him on top of my raft so he can float. I'm convinced the neighbors think I'm nuts for doing that.

The evening was just as productive. After lovely blackened tuna steaks and glasses of white wine, Alana and I retired to the living room to watch television. I won't mention the programs we watched since I'm too embarrassed. I'm pretty sure we managed to kill a few brain cells. Eventually, I had to put my earbuds in and listen to Oscar Peterson again. I simply couldn't stand the screeching of the reality show cast members yelling at each other anymore.

The next morning, I awoke a bit earlier than usual and did my morning ritual of a swim in the pool, followed by a three-mile jog around the neighborhood. I then took Maui on a long walk. The weather was perfect, as it usually was – seventy-five degrees, sunny, and a nice breeze coming off the ocean.

I was almost back to my house when my phone vibrated in my pocket. I pulled it out and saw the name Mara Winters on the display. Mara's my personal attorney and sometimes employer. She represents some of the wealthiest clients on the island who are often in need of a private investigator who can keep his mouth shut.

"Good morning, Mara. What can I do for you?"

"Mr. Rutherford, how are you doing today?"

We'd known each other for years, yet she still insisted on calling me Mr. Rutherford.

"I can't complain. Just walking the dog and taking in this fine weather."

"Say hello to Maui for me," Mara said.

"I will. He sends his best as well."

"A friend of yours called me this morning. She wants to know if we can meet as soon as possible."

I searched my mind for who she might have been talking about but came up empty.

"Who is it?" I asked.

"Mele Akamu."

I didn't respond, mainly because a million questions raced through my mind. The prime one being, how can I get out of this?

"Not who you were expecting?" Mara asked.

"No, can't say it was. Did she tell you what she wants?"

"No. In typical fashion, she asked that we come to her home to meet. She said she'd explain everything there."

"Doesn't Mrs. Akamu already have an attorney?"

"Yes, and I know the man. He has a reputation for being ruthless."

"I would expect nothing less from her lawyer."

"Mrs. Akamu specifically stated that I need to bring you, which tells me one thing. She needs an investigator."

"Or more likely her grandson does," I said, referring to Tavii Akamu, a man I'd met in my last major investigation.

"That's certainly a possibility. Is there a specific time that works best for you?"

Had I actually agreed to the meeting? Apparently.

"How about eleven this morning?"

"That's good for me. I'll phone Mrs. Akamu and suggest that time. I'll text you to confirm everything."

"Thanks, Mara. I guess I'll be seeing you shortly."

I ended the call with Mara. Things were about to get interesting. By the time I got out of the shower and had put on fresh clothes, I saw that Mara had texted to confirm the meeting.

Although I'd lived on Maui for several years, I hadn't heard of Mele Akamu until recently. As I mentioned before, I'd met her grandson Tavii during my last case. Tavii is the Mayor of Maui County. His term was up soon, and I'd heard that he didn't intend to run again for reasons that are obvious if you've read my tale *Rich and Dead*.

When I'd asked Alana if she knew who Mele Akamu was, she'd responded with shock that I'd never heard of the "godmother" of Maui. I'd driven to Mrs. Akamu's home during that case, expecting to find an intimidating woman. I don't mean to imply that she doesn't instill fear in many people. She apparently does, but she reminded me of my grandmother on my mother's side.

I couldn't help but take a liking to the woman, and for some unknown reason, she seemed to like me as well. She'd ended our last encounter by informing me that she believed, "You and I will be friends." Perhaps she'd decided to cash in on that friendship already.

Mrs. Akamu lives in Kula, which is one of the areas in Maui's upcountry. Her house sits on the slopes of the famous Mount Haleakala, and it has breathtaking views of the valley and the ocean beyond that.

I stuck with Oscar Peterson for the long drive from Kaanapali and got through his songs, "Georgia On My Mind," "Almost Like Being in Love," "I Was Doing All Right," and "There Will Never Be Another You."

I spotted Mara's car as I pulled onto the turnaround in front of

Mrs. Akamu's house. She climbed out of her vehicle and walked over to me as I turned off the ignition. Mara is a tall woman with dark red hair that is almost always pulled back. Even the attorneys in Maui dress casually but not Mara. She was wearing her customary business suit.

"Hello, Mara."

"Was that Oscar Peterson I heard?"

"It certainly was," I said, and I got out of the roadster.

"Excellent choice."

"I thought so. Ready for our meeting?" I asked.

"As ready as one can be."

We walked toward the house and a moment later, Mrs. Akamu's elderly butler opened the door. I'd met Samson on my previous visits. I'd also learned the man had a vicious streak and sometimes worked as Mrs. Akamu's muscle. The lesson? Don't underestimate the elderly.

"Good morning, Samson. How are you today?" I asked.

"I'm well, sir. And you?" Samson asked in a low tone that was barely above a whisper.

"Couldn't be better."

"Mrs. Akamu is expecting you both. Please follow me."

Samson led us through the house and out the sliding glass doors in the back. They opened to reveal that spectacular view I mentioned a while back. As in our previous meetings, Mrs. Akamu was seated beside a large fire pit that was in the center of a patio. There was a tall pot on each corner that was filled with the gorgeous Birds of Paradise flowers.

Also, as before, Mele Akamu didn't stand to greet us.

"Mrs. Akamu," I said, and I nodded.

"Hello, Mr. Rutherford, Ms. Winters. Please have a seat."

"Thank you," Mara said.

We both sat down.

"Is there anything you need, Mrs. Akamu?" Samson asked.

"No, Samson. That will be all."

I know what you're thinking. Did I find it odd that Mrs. Akamu didn't offer us a drink or some other refreshment? Not at all, mainly since she'd never done that before.

"So, Mrs. Akamu, how may we be of service?" Mara asked.

"As you know, Ms. Winters, the Akamu family already has an attorney. However, it's my understanding that you have a good relationship with the police department. I've also been told that if I want the services of Mr. Rutherford, then I would hire him through you."

"I don't have an exclusive agreement with Mr. Rutherford, but many of his cases have come through me. As far as my relationship with the police department, I don't know that I have one that's any more positive than any other attorney on the island. We often find ourselves on opposite sides," Mara said.

"I understand, but it's certainly better than the relationship my attorney has with them. I'd like to hire you and Mr. Rutherford to look into a matter for me. It's rather sensitive. May I assume that attorney-client privilege applies here?" Mrs. Akamu asked.

"Of course," Mara said without hesitation.

For me, that wasn't so easy of a response. My marriage to Alana has its advantages and disadvantages when it comes to my investigations. The advantages are obvious. She often provides me with vital information.

The disadvantage comes into play during moments like this one. I'm bound to keep things I hear in client meetings with Mara a secret. In full disclosure, I've not always followed that rule. Each time I've broken that oath, though, it was to bring a murderer to justice. Does that make me less honorable in your eyes? I guess that's your decision to make.

"I have a source who informed me of a recent discovery that could have a significant impact on me and my business," Mrs. Akamu said.

How's that for vagueness? I thought.

"What is the nature of this discovery?" Mara asked.

"A body was found in north Maui in the old pineapple fields near the Jaws surf break. I don't know who found it."

"Do you know the identity of this person?" I asked.

"I was told it's Eric Ellis. He was an employee of mine," Mrs. Akamu said.

"What did Mr. Ellis do for you?" Mara asked.

"He assisted me with a variety of tasks."

"Were those tasks of a sensitive nature?" Mara asked.

"There are very few people who know my business. Eric was one of them."

"How long ago did he leave your employ?" I asked.

"It's been at least five years. Things didn't end well between us."

"How exactly did they end?" Mara asked.

"Eric got it into his head that he was going to try to shake me down. Things didn't turn out the way he thought they would."

"What happened?" Mara asked.

"After he tried to blackmail me, I sent Samson to talk to him and explain the situation. But Samson was unable to find him. I thought Eric had finally realized how foolish he was being, and he'd left the island years ago," Mrs. Akamu said, and she paused a moment. Then she continued, "I know what you're thinking. You believe I had Eric killed back then. I didn't."

"Mrs. Akamu, we both know your butler is very resourceful. Do you expect us to believe he couldn't locate Eric Ellis? I've seen Samson's handiwork up close. Is it possible he got carried away?" I asked.

"No, it's not."

"How do you know?" Mara asked.

"Because I asked Samson myself. He said he couldn't find him, and I believed him."

"If Samson didn't kill him, who do you think did?" I asked.

"It could be any number of people. Business associates. A scorned lover. How would I know?"

"But there's no one person who jumps out at you?" I asked.

"Other than me? No, I can't think of one person in particular."

"That's why you assume the police will look at you for this?" Mara asked.

"Of course. The Maui Police Department has been trying to get me for years. Trust me when I say this is not how I'm going down. I didn't have Eric Ellis killed and I want Mr. Rutherford to prove it. First, I suggest you discover what the police already know. I'll expect a report from you in two days. After that, I want an update every few days. I appreciate you both coming over here. Now, if you'll excuse me, I have an important call to make."

Mara looked at me and I knew why. She knows me pretty well by now and she was bound to think I'd have a response. I didn't want to disappoint her.

"I understand you're busy, Mrs. Akamu. I'll let you know when I've made my decision."

"When you've made your decision? I've already hired you," she said.

"No, ma'am, you didn't. Mara mentioned in the beginning of our meeting that she doesn't have an exclusive agreement with me, which is another way of saying that I don't work for her. I actually don't work for anyone. I'm not sure this is a good time for me to be taking on a new case, especially one as daunting as a five-year-old murder case."

"What do you mean?" Mrs. Akamu asked.

"My sister-in-law is getting married and she might need my help for last-minute wedding details," I said.

"People don't say no to me, Mr. Rutherford."

"I'm not saying no. I'm saying I'll need some time to make a decision."

"What do you want?" Mrs. Akamu asked. "Is it more money?"

"I like you, ma'am. But I'm also not blind to your reputation. I'm sure you understand the difficult position I'm in being married to a Maui detective. I don't want anything to blow back on her and I'm certainly not going to ask her for privileged information."

"You think I'm guilty, don't you?"

"I don't, as a matter of fact. I suspect that I would be the last person you'd call if you'd really killed Eric Ellis. Instead, I think you're deeply worried. He had way more on you than you're willing to admit."

"I've already told you that he knew my business. What else do you want to know?"

"Ah, now I've figured it out. He stole something from you, and it was almost certainly information. You never got it back, though. You're worried it was on his person when he died, or he hid it so well no one has found it yet. The killer didn't, otherwise you would have heard about it by now."

Mrs. Akamu said nothing.

"Step one of your plan. I find out what the police know, mainly whether they have this information and how imminent your arrest is or isn't," I continued. "Step two, I find a suspect for you, someone your people may have missed. Step three, you take what I've discovered and give it to your people, hoping they can find this missing information."

"It seems I've underestimated you, Mr. Rutherford."

"People tend to do that," Mara said.

"I don't know whether that's a compliment or not, but I'll take it as such," I said.

"That's the way I intended it," Mara said.

"In that case, thank you," I said.

"Eric downloaded a copy of all of my business files. If someone were to get those files, I would be finished," Mrs. Akamu said.

"That was Samson's other task when he went to see Eric. Get the files back," I said.

"We never knew what happened to Eric. I thought he was working out a deal with the police once he realized I wasn't going to pay him what he wanted. When the police never came to my door, I didn't know what to think," Mrs. Akamu said.

"Then his body appears recently, and the worry starts all over again," I said.

"Essentially."

"I'm sorry, Mrs. Akamu, but I can't take this case. It's one thing to find the identity of a murderer. It's another to inadvertently help recover these files for you. I'm not going to assist you in any illegal activities," I said.

Mrs. Akamu smiled, which wasn't the response I was expecting.

"My earlier impression of you was correct. I like you," she said.

"Thank you."

"I'll make a new deal with you. I don't expect you to find the files for me. I'll do that on my own. You don't even have to tell me what the police know, but I want you to discover who murdered Eric."

"I'll still need to think about it," I said.

"I'll need an answer by tomorrow. Is that agreeable?" Mrs. Akamu asked.

"Yes," I said, and I stood. "I'm sorry for making you late for your important phone call."

"I don't have one."

I laughed.

"I find you delightful, Mrs. Akamu."

"Delightful? I've never been called that before."

"There's a first time for everything," I said.

Mara stood.

"It was a pleasure seeing you again, Mrs. Akamu," Mara said.

"Thank you, Ms. Winters."

We turned and almost ran into Samson. I hadn't heard him walk down.

"Samson will show you out," Mrs. Akamu continued.

We followed Samson back through the house and he walked us to the front door. I'd just stepped outside when he called to me.

"Mr. Rutherford."

"Yes, Samson."

"I've only seen her husband and son push back on her like that and get away with it."

"Then I should feel honored."

"You should."

"Where are her husband and son now?" I asked.

"Sadly, they're both deceased."

"I'm sorry to hear that."

"Have a good day, Mr. Rutherford, Ms. Winters."

"Thank you, Samson," Mara said.

We both turned and continued toward our cars.

"Let's not talk here. I'll call you in a minute," Mara said.

"Sounds good."

I climbed into my convertible and started the engine. I'd just made it around the first bend in the road when my phone vibrated on the passenger seat.

"How do you think that went?" I asked after pulling over to take the call.

Mara laughed, which isn't a very common thing for her to do, at least when I've been around her.

"I wasn't sure we were going to get out of there alive."

"Sorry if I scared you," I said.

"Are you sure you want to get into this?"

"Who says I've decided to take the case?"

"A dead body recently discovered after being buried for five years. Missing files. Of course, you're going to take it," Mara said.

"It's possible. I'll let you know tomorrow."

"Thank you. I'll talk to you then."

I ended the call with Mara and continued my drive home. As I got closer to Lahaina, I decided to turn off and head to Harry's. It wasn't until I pulled into the parking lot and saw Foxx's Lexus SUV that I realized I'd completely forgotten to call Yuto the day before. I made a mental note to call him once I left Harry's.

I walked inside and saw Kiana and Foxx behind the bar. Kiana has worked at Harry's since it opened under the original owner.

There were a few other customers inside, but they were seated in booths on the opposite side of the room.

"How's it going?" Foxx asked.

I slid onto one of the barstools.

"Can I get you anything, Mr. Rutherford?" Kiana asked.

"No, thank you. I'm fine."

"You look like you've got something on your mind," Foxx asked.

"I do. A new case. Well, maybe I should say a potential new case. I haven't decided whether I'm going to take it."

"Why not?" Foxx asked.

"Two words: Mele Akamu," I said.

"Mele Akamu wants to hire you?" Kiana asked.

"She does and that goes no further than here," I said.

"Mum's the word," Kiana said.

Then she walked to the other end of the bar where two new customers had just sat down.

"What's the case about?" Foxx asked.

I gave him a general rundown on what I'd learned, leaving out my correct guess that Eric Ellis had stolen incriminating evidence from Mele Akamu.

"When do we start?" Foxx asked.

"What do you mean we?"

"Sounds like you're going to need help on this one. I think I've more than proven my worth in past investigations."

"Yes, but look what happened to you on the last case you helped with. You almost got killed," I said.

"And you would have definitely been killed had I not been there to save you."

There was no sense in denying that since it was most definitely true.

"There's one other thing you haven't thought about," Foxx said.

"What's that?"

"If this case involves Mele Akamu's business, then you're going to be dealing with some pretty unsavory types."

"I do on all my cases."

"True, but Mele Akamu is in a different league. Let's be honest. You don't exactly have a stellar track record when it comes to defending yourself."

"What do you mean by that?" I asked.

"How do I put this delicately, Poe? You've gotten your ass kicked more times than I can remember. You'll need a bodyguard if you're going to start questioning people who run in that world."

"Those weren't ass kickings. I was luring my opponents into a false sense of security."

Foxx laughed.

"Is that right?"

"So, you want to be my protection?" I asked.

"Not just that. I think we both know I'm more than brawn," Foxx said, and he tapped the side of his head with one finger. "There's a lot going on up here."

At six-four and two-hundred and forty pounds, Foxx is a physically intimidating guy. But it would be a mistake to underestimate his intelligence. He's one of the smartest men I know.

"Plus, with this Hani wedding coming up, I could use a good distraction," Foxx said.

"Is there something bothering you about the wedding?"

"No, I'm just tired of hearing Hani talking about it. Every time I go to pick up Ava, she has to remind me that she's getting married. I don't know what her angle is. She's got to know I'm not jealous."

I thought I had a decent theory as to why Hani was doing that. Foxx was right when he'd said that she must have known he wouldn't be jealous of Yuto. But I didn't think that was what she was really doing. Instead, I thought she was trying to one-up him. Sort of like, "Look at me. I've found someone to marry and you're all alone."

If that was the case, then it was a petty thing for Hani to do.

"By the way," Foxx continued. "You're not going to believe who called me this morning."

"Who?"

"What's-his-face."

What's-his-face was Foxx's moniker for Yuto. Did I also find that petty? Of course, but like the previous example, I swallowed it and said nothing.

"What did Yuto want?" I asked.

"He told me about that big party you and Alana are throwing for him and Hani."

"We're not throwing them a party. Yuto is having it for Hani and he asked if they could have it at our house."

"He said it was some kind of surprise party for Hani and he thought I should be there. Do you know what he's giving her?"

"No idea. I asked a couple of times, but he wouldn't tell me. Are you going to come to the party?"

"First, I'm mad at you for not saying anything about it," Foxx said.

"Sorry. I was going to, but Alana was trying to secure you an invitation first."

Unfortunately, that little fact came out of my mouth. I'd done one of those things where your brain is telling you it's a bad idea to say it, but your mouth keeps talking anyway.

"Oh, so Hani didn't want me to come? Is that right?"

"I wouldn't say that. I think she just hadn't made up her mind yet."

"Nice spin job, Poe, but it's not going to work. Hani says she wants things to be better between us. Then she goes and does something like this."

"Look at it this way. I'm sure Yuto didn't invite you without mentioning it to Hani first. Since he called you, that tells me she changed her mind and wants you there," I said.

"Or she decided it's another chance for me to see how great her life is without me."

"I don't know what to say."

"You don't have to say anything. I get the picture."

"I'm sorry she's acting like this."

"I'm a big boy. I can handle it. The truth is that Hani's a good mother to Ava and that's all I really care about. The rest of the stuff is unimportant. Now, let's get back to this Mele Akamu investigation. Where and when do we start?" Foxx asked.

"As far as the where goes, I have no idea. As for the when, that all depends on how my conversation with Alana goes later. I'm not going to do a job for Mele Akamu without running it by her first. This could have major ramifications for her."

"Understood, but I have a strange feeling she's going to tell you to do it. So, call me when you're ready to go. Hey, you want that drink now?"

"Yeah. Suddenly I feel like having a beer."

Foxx grabbed two cold bottles from behind the bar. He popped the tops on them, and we tapped our bottles together.

"Here's to Hani's upcoming wedding," he said.

"You really want to toast to that?"

"The way I see it, the more preoccupied she is with what's-his-face, the more she's off my back," Foxx said, and he laughed.

4

THE PHILANTHROPIST

I LEFT HARRY'S AFTER HAVING A SECOND BEER AND A HAMBURGER. MY midsection definitely didn't need the burger, or the fries, and I knew I should have opted for a salad instead. Sometimes you just feel like eating something greasy, though, don't you?

I'd planned to spend the rest of the day hanging by the pool and going over the pros and cons of working for Mele Akamu. As I approached the house, any thoughts of a relaxing afternoon vanished when I spotted Hani's and Ms. Hu's cars in my driveway. I was tempted to pull a quick U-turn and head to the farthest parts of the island.

Unfortunately, I'd already texted Alana from Harry's and had told her I was on my way home. She'd failed to mention the presence of her mother and sister. Did I suspect that was intentional? Of course, it was.

I parked my little car on the street so there would be no impediment to Hani and Ms. Hu leaving. Then I walked into the kitchen, only to almost get runover by Ava as she raced past me. Maui was just a few feet in front of her, and judging by his playful demeanor, they hadn't been at the house very long. The dog was good for about thirty minutes of playing with the little girl. Then he'd grow tired of her and he'd try to find somewhere to hide, usually under the sofa.

The three Hu women were all huddled around the kitchen table. Ms. Hu was the only one to turn to me as I entered. She took a quick and indifferent glance my way and then turned back to Alana and Hani.

Faithful readers are well aware of my strained relationship with my dear mother-in-law. I've used this description a handful of times before, but I can't think of another one that so perfectly captures our co-existence. Ms. Hu is the founding member of the "I Hate Poe Club."

I walked over to the refrigerator and grabbed another beer. I didn't usually drink that many beers, especially in the early afternoon, but one must have some level of liquid courage to deal with all three Hu women at once.

"Hello ladies," I said.

Alana and Hani looked up. Ms. Hu did not.

"Hey, Poe," Hani said.

"Maybe you can settle a debate for us," Alana said.

"What debate?" I asked.

"We're trying to work out the seating chart for the wedding reception," Alana said.

"I thought you did that weeks ago," I said.

"We did, but Mom thinks we should make some changes," Hani said, and she hit the word "Mom" a bit harder than the others.

"It's your wedding, Hani. If you're okay with making some fatal mistakes, that's fine by me," Ms. Hu said.

Fatal? What in the world did that mean?

"Well that's a morbid way to put it, Mom," Alana said, apparently reading my thoughts.

"I just don't think you want to put those two couples at the same table. You're asking for trouble," Ms. Hu said.

"Those were just rumors," Hani said.

"Sometimes the truth doesn't matter. If Natasha thinks it happened, then it may as well have happened," Ms. Hu said.

"What happened?" I asked, even though I knew I should have kept my mouth shut and made up some excuse to go upstairs and lock the bedroom door.

"Natasha's husband allegedly stepped out on her. Hani wants to put them at the same table with the woman he had the affair with," Alana said.

"It sounds bad when you put it like that," Hani said.

"How else am I supposed to put it? That's what you're doing," Alana said.

"There's nowhere else to seat them," Hani said.

"There are several places you could move them. I think you want to see fireworks, that's all," Ms. Hu said.

"That's absurd. Why would I want to encourage some fight at my wedding reception? Everyone should be focused on me," Hani said.

Her alone but not her and Yuto? I asked myself.

"It's bad enough they'll all be in the same room. You're going to push them over the edge if they're at the same table. But I'll repeat what I said before. It's your wedding. You do what you want," Ms. Hu said.

"Fine then. It's settled. I'm not moving them," Hani said.

Alana shook her head and then turned to me.

"How was your meeting with Mele Akamu?"

"You met with Mele Akamu?" Ms. Hu asked, suddenly interested in what I had to say.

"I did. It went fine," I said.

"Why did she want to meet with you? That makes no sense," Ms. Hu said.

"Why doesn't it make sense?" I asked.

"Never mind," Ms. Hu said, and she dismissively waved her hand at me as if she were swatting away a pesky insect.

I thought Alana might come to my defense and question why her mother had just been rude to me again for no apparent reason, but she didn't. I guess we all have to pick and choose our battles.

"What did she want?" Alana asked.

"A body was found near the Jaws surf break. She's worried it will be tied to her," I said.

"This is the one that was buried for some time?" Alana asked.

"I believe she said it's been there for around five years," I said.

"Who was it?" Hani asked.

"A man named Eric Ellis. He worked for Mele Akamu," I said.

"She wants you to find out who killed him?" Hani asked.

"Exactly."

"Or she wants you to come up with some other possible candidates for when the police show up to arrest her," Alana said.

"Why would they arrest Mele?" Ms. Hu asked.

"Why do you think, Mom?" Alana asked.

"Well I'm sure I don't know. That's why I asked," Ms. Hu said.

"Come on, Mom. Don't play dumb," Hani said.

"Watch how you talk to me, young lady. And I'm not playing dumb. Mele Akamu is an upstanding member of our community. The Akamu family has done more for this island than anyone," Ms. Hu said.

"Oh yeah? Like what?" I asked.

"You mainlanders are all alike. You come to Maui and you have no knowledge of our heritage or anything else for that matter," Ms. Hu said.

"Mom, don't be like that," Alana said.

"Why not? It's the truth," Ms. Hu said.

"Don't worry, Ms. Hu. I'm not offended. And you're right. I don't know nearly as much about the island as I want to. I'm also interested in why you think Mele Akamu is such a good person," I said.

"The Akamu family has donated millions to different charities, from the hospital to the arts community to the environment," Ms. Hu said.

I turned to Alana.

"Is that true?" I asked.

"I said it. Why wouldn't it be true?" Ms. Hu shot back.

"Forgive me. I didn't mean to imply you weren't telling the truth," I said.

"That's kind of what you just did," Hani said.

"I know and I'm sorry," I said.

"To answer your question, Poe, yes, the Akamu family has donated a lot of money over the years. That's probably the main reason Tavii got elected Mayor," Alana said.

"I thought you also told me that everyone knew their family business wasn't exactly on the up and up," I said.

"That's true, but no one has ever been able to prove anything," Alana said.

"People talk about the poor woman like she's a cold-blooded murderer. Mele Akamu is a philanthropist," Ms. Hu said.

I was tempted to laugh, but I managed to restrain myself.

Nevertheless, Ms. Hu must have read the look on my face for she asked, "You think that's funny?"

"I happen to like the dear old woman," I said.

"Old? She's not that much older than I am," Ms. Hu said.

"You walked right into that one, Poe," Alana said.

"I apologize again, Ms. Hu. Perhaps I should go outside to the pool before the hole I'm digging gets any deeper," I said.

"Yes, maybe you should go," Ms. Hu said.

"Before you leave, what did you tell Mele Akamu?" Alana asked.

"I told her I'd give her an answer by tomorrow," I said.

"I think you should take the case. If the police are out to get her, then you owe it to this island to make sure one of its finest citizens isn't unjustly arrested," Ms. Hu said.

"First of all, Mom, the police aren't out to get anyone. If you get arrested, then it's because we had good reason," Alana said.

"And second?" Hani asked, apparently enjoying her sister and mother going at it.

"I don't deny that Mele Akamu has done some good for Maui," Alana said.

"Some?" Ms. Hu asked.

"Okay, a lot. But that doesn't mean she hasn't also broken the law at some point," Alana said.

"Everyone breaks the law at some point, Alana. Even you," Ms. Hu said.

"I'm not talking about speeding and jaywalking. I'm talking about more serious crimes," Alana said.

"There's nothing you can prove, which means she's innocent. We do have a system in this country that says you're innocent until proven guilty," Ms. Hu said.

"Why are you defending her like she was your own mother?" Alana asked.

"I consider Mele a friend. I don't like my friends being criticized," Ms. Hu said.

"Regardless of what Mrs. Akamu is or isn't, I'm not sure what I'm going to do with this investigation," I said.

"I agree with Mom. I think you should take the case, although not for the same reasons she does," Alana said.

"What reasons are those?" Hani asked, taking the question right out of my mouth.

"I doubt Mele Akamu had anything to do with that dead body. She wouldn't have wanted to hire you if she did, especially since she has first-hand knowledge of your abilities. If you do take the case, though, I have one piece of advice for you," Alana said.

"Which is?" I asked.

"Question everything that she tells you. She'll almost certainly hold back vital information, even if it would help her case," Alana said.

I could have commented on Eric Ellis' blackmail scheme, but I decided to wait until Hani and Ms. Hu left.

"When you see her again, please tell her I said hello," Ms. Hu said.

"I will. I don't know why I'm so surprised that you two are friends," I asked.

"We both grew up on Maui, didn't we?" Ms. Hu asked.

"Yes. How could I forget?" I turned to Hani. "Good luck on the seating chart. Just do me one favor and keep Alana and me as far from those quarreling couples as possible."

"Oh, I have you two at the same table," Hani said, and she smiled. "Just kidding. You guys are near me."

"Good. Otherwise I was going to come up with some excuse to miss the reception," I said.

"Alana can't miss it. She's the maid of honor," Ms. Hu said.

"I was joking, and I did notice that you said Alana couldn't miss the reception, not me. But I'll give you the benefit of the doubt and assume you simply misspoke," I said.

"I didn't," Ms. Hu said.

"Mom, don't be rude," Alana repeated an earlier plea.

Ms. Hu said nothing.

"I'll see you ladies later," I said.

"Thanks, Poe. And good luck with your new case," Hani said.

Had I decided to take the case, though? Foxx wanted me to. The Hu women all did. Apparently, I was going to work for Mele Akamu.

I looked around the room for Maui.

"Maui, come here boy. Let's go outside," I yelled.

The dog stuck his nose out from under the sofa.

"Come on, Maui. Let's go," I said.

He crawled out and darted toward the back door. Ava was hot on his heels.

5

THE MAYOR

I EXPECTED HANI AND HER MOTHER TO LEAVE AFTER AN HOUR OR SO. I was wrong. They were at the house for another five hours. The first one or two of those dealt with wedding matters, but then Alana suggested that they stay for dinner. She informed everyone that I would be thrilled to grill steaks and vegetables. Then she turned to me and confirmed that they'd graciously accepted her offer, even though I was in the room to hear it for myself.

The dinner conversation renewed the debate about Mele Akamu. Ms. Hu continued to defend her, while Alana continued to point out that the woman was almost certainly involved in some crimes. There was one topic that evening that was noticeably absent, at least I noticed it, and it concerned me. I never once heard Hani mention Yuto's name.

I joked more than once during the runup to my wedding that I was simply a prop for the ceremony since I thought it was all about Alana. I don't mean to imply that Alana was any kind of bridezilla. She wasn't. But there's a reason they play the song "Here Comes the Bride" and not "Here Comes the Groom."

I'd had numerous discussions with Alana in the past over whether or not Hani truly loved Yuto. We both knew she liked him, and we both had this theory that Hani thought Yuto was the type of man she should marry. Still, I'd never heard her mention Yuto in any of the wedding planning, and I'd been around Hani a lot since she was using a venue I owned on the other side of the island for the wedding and reception.

I thought back to my own wedding again. I didn't go around telling everyone how excited I was to be spending my life with Alana. Of course, I felt that way. I just kept it inside of me. I'm just not the type of guy who publicly proclaims love all the time. Maybe Hani liked to keep her feelings to herself, I thought. Then I realized how stupid that was to believe. Hani never hesitated to tell someone what she thought.

The next morning, I did my customary swim in the backyard pool and a jog around the neighborhood. As I was doing my cool down, I sent Mara a text and told her that I'd take Mrs. Akamu's case. I asked Mara if she would also request that Mrs. Akamu arrange a time for me to speak in person with her grandson, Tavii. I suggested Harry's as a meeting location. I didn't think Tavii would want to see me again, especially considering how our previous interactions had gone. But I also knew his grandmother had considerable sway over him.

Without giving away too many details of my past investigation, Tavii had broken the law and I had proof of it. Nevertheless, the District Attorney had decided not to press charges. It was my understanding that they came to a gentlemen's agreement with Tavii. They would avoid the scandal of publicly charging the mayor with a crime and in return Tavii would agree not to run for reelection.

Imagine my surprise when I got a text back from Mara within the hour. She said that Tavii had agreed to my meeting and that he would see me at Harry's at three o'clock in the afternoon. Apparently, Mele Akamu was anxious to get the investigation rolling.

After showering, I came downstairs and saw Alana sitting outside by the pool. Maui was asleep under her chair.

"Any wedding activities today?" I asked as I walked out of the house.

"We're supposed to pick up our dresses today."

"Cutting it kind of close, aren't you?"

"A bit. Strange since Hani had some things planned out well in advance. I don't know why she dragged her feet on the dresses."

I sat on a chair beside Alana.

"How's Hani doing? Is she nervous?"

"She doesn't seem to be. Oh, I forgot to tell you that Foxx is invited to the party after all."

"I forgot to tell you the same thing," I said.

"Hani told you last night?"

"No. Foxx told me yesterday afternoon when I saw him at Harry's. He said Yuto called him earlier in the day and invited him."

"I guess your talk with Yuto worked then."

"Actually, I forgot to call him. My guess is that Hani mentioned her argument to Yuto and Yuto sided with you."

"Maybe, but Hani made a point to tell me that she changed her mind on her own. She said Yuto had nothing to do with it."

"The fact that she pointed that out means he had everything to do with it."

"Absolutely, but I didn't tell her that. There was no point in arguing anymore."

I was tempted to ask Alana if she'd noticed the lack of talk about Yuto the previous night, but I decided not to. I didn't want to create more drama when it might have simply been me overanalyzing the situation, as I am often prone to do.

"Hey, when do you officially start the new case?" Alana asked.

"This afternoon. I'm meeting with Tavii at the bar."

"Interesting."

"Have you heard anything from the department on the discovery of this body?" I asked.

"I heard about it the day they found Eric Ellis' remains, but I knew I wasn't going to pick up the case since I was about to leave for vacation."

"Do you know who got it?"

"I think it went to Josh."

"Josh? Who is he again?"

"He replaced Makamae."

"That's right."

Detective Makamae Kalani had recently moved back to Oahu to return to that island's police department. She'd come to Maui thinking she was going to eventually run the department. Her abrasive style quickly made enemies, my wife being one of them.

I'd worked a handful of successful cases with Detective Kalani, and her departure had come as a surprise to me, especially since she'd never told me, nor had she even sent a text message saying "so long" or something like that.

I couldn't picture Josh Parrish, the beat cop who'd worked his way up to detective, but Alana said he was a decent and hardworking guy. Apparently, I'd met him and his wife at one of the police department's holiday parties.

"Are you asking because you want to talk to Josh about the case?" Alana asked.

"No, I was more curious than anything else."

"Well, depending on how deep you get into this, I'm sure you two will cross paths. I'm certain you'll like him."

"That's good to hear."

We spent the next hour sitting by the pool and taking in the sun. Then we eventually made our way back into the house for lunch. Before I knew it, my meeting with Tavii was fast approaching. I hopped into the BMW and made the short drive to Harry's. I'd sent Foxx a text earlier to let him know about Tavii and also to invite him to partake in the interview. Foxx had quickly agreed.

As I entered the bar, I spotted Foxx sitting in one of the back-corner booths. He was writing something in a small leather notebook. I walked over to him and sat on the opposite side.

"How's it going, Foxx?"

"Good, just making a few notes for our interview."

"What kind of notes?" I asked.

"Interview questions. I don't want to forget anything. You do that, don't you?"

"Not exactly. I have them in my head, but maybe I should start writing them down. I usually take notes about what was said after the meetings."

We spoke for a few minutes about my interview style and then Foxx looked past me to the bar's entrance.

"There's Tavii," he said.

I slid out of the booth and stood to greet him. Foxx did not.

Tavii is of Hawaiian descent, although you probably guessed that from the name alone. He's of average height with short, jet-black hair. He's mostly thin with the exception of a small and isolated ring of fat around his midsection. It's quite strange looking and hard not to stare at.

"Mr. Mayor," I said.

I thought he might extend his hand. He didn't. I didn't offer a handshake either.

"Would you like something to drink or eat?" I asked.

"No, thank you. I had a late lunch," Tavii said.

"Please have a seat," I said.

I walked to the other side of the booth and squeezed in beside Foxx. Tavii sat opposite us. Then he glanced around the bar, probably to see if anyone was trying to listen to us.

"This is a pretty slow time of the day. No one will eavesdrop," Foxx said, reading Tavii's obvious concern.

Tavii turned back to us.

"You got your wish. I'm here," he said in what was clearly a hostile tone.

"Why so upset?" Foxx asked.

"I thought we agreed we wouldn't be seen together anymore," Tavii said.

"We did? I don't recall having that conversation," I said.

"It was implied," Tavii said.

"How's that?" Foxx asked.

"Look, we all know what went down. You both blackmailed me. You're lucky I'm the forgiving type," Tavii said.

Foxx laughed.

"Is that right?"

"You think this is funny?" Tavii asked.

"Yes, I do," Foxx said.

Tavii turned to me.

"Is he serious?"

"As a heart attack. Foxx generally doesn't respond well to threats, but who does? I think you have a gross misunderstanding of what went down between us," I said.

"Oh yeah? Then tell me your version of what happened," Tavii said.

"I was about to do that. We were investigating a murder, which is what brought us to you. Your corruption, and yes that's the right word for it, wasn't hard to figure out. It also wasn't our fault that you got in over your head. You're still a free man and you're still the mayor. I would think you'd be feeling pretty damn grateful toward us," I said.

Tavii didn't respond.

"Nice summary, Poe, and an accurate one at that," Foxx said.

"Why don't we agree to put all of that behind us. Let's get to the purpose you're here. What have you heard about Eric Ellis?" I asked.

"Not much. I know they found his body after he vanished five years ago. I've done my best to find what the police know so far, but I've come up empty," Tavii said.

"Is that surprising?" Foxx asked.

"Yes. The police don't normally keep secrets from the mayor. But given who Eric was, I understand."

"How well did you know Eric?" Foxx asked.

"That's a tricky question to answer. He worked for my family for a long time, but it wasn't like we were close friends."

"Were you aware that he tried to blackmail your grandmother?" I asked.

"Not at the time."

"That's surprising," Foxx said.

"Not really. I don't work for my grandmother. She doesn't share business details unless there's a need for me to know," Tavii said.

"Just curious, why didn't you go work for the family?" I asked.

"My grandmother always encouraged me to get into politics. She wanted me to be Hawaii's governor. There's no chance of that now."

"I asked your grandmother who she thinks might have killed Eric. She couldn't provide me with any specific names," I said.

"I assumed you were going to ask me the same question. I could only come up with one person. Lee Walters."

"Who's that?" Foxx asked.

"He worked with Eric. My grandmother got rid of him after everything that went down."

"He was part of the blackmail scheme?" I asked.

"My grandmother certainly thought so. Lee and Eric were best friends. No one thought it was possible that Lee didn't know what was going on."

"That includes you too?" Foxx asked.

"Absolutely. Those guys were practically inseparable."

"If they were such good friends, then why do you think Lee may have killed Eric?" I asked.

"Because Eric ruined Lee's life. Lee was making a lot of money from my family. Eric screwed all that up with his ridiculous scheme. Anyone who knows my grandmother would realize she'd never agree to a payoff."

"Is that because she'd have other ways of dealing with it?" Foxx asked.

"What's that supposed to mean?" Tavii asked.

"I think it's obvious," Foxx said.

"My grandmother's no pushover. She wasn't about to let some guy like Eric Ellis take advantage of her, especially after everything she did for him. That guy came from nothing. Anything he had was because of her generosity. That's how people are, though, aren't they? All they care about is what's in it for them."

"Do you know where Lee Walters is now?" I asked.

"He's still on Maui, as far as I know. I don't know what he does to make money."

"There's no one else you know who might have wanted to murder Eric Ellis?" Foxx asked.

"No. He's the only one. Of course, I'm not saying he actually did it. I have no idea. Now, I've told you both all I know. I trust you won't call me again."

"Thanks for stopping by, Mr. Mayor," I said.

"Any idea what you're going to do when your term is up?" Foxx asked.

"Go to hell," Tavii said.

"Go to hell? Why did you say that?" Foxx asked.

Tavii slid out of the booth and left Harry's without saying another word.

Foxx turned to me.

"What did I say?"

"The guy's ruined, Foxx. You just reminded him of something he didn't need to be reminded of."

"No, I didn't. I asked him a question."

"How do you think our first interview went?" I asked.

"We got one lead. That's better than nothing. I guess we need to track down this Lee Walters guy."

Before I could respond, my phone buzzed. I looked at the display but didn't recognize the number.

"Hello."

"I'm calling for Edgar Rutherford."

"You've got him."

"Mr. Rutherford, my name is Josh Parrish. I'm a detective with the Maui Police Department. I'm hoping we can meet."

Alana's prediction had come true, but much sooner than I'd thought it would.

6

THE DETECTIVE

Since I had some free time, I agreed to meet with Detective Parrish immediately. Okay, let me rephrase that to make it more accurate. Since I didn't want to go home and potentially get sucked into more endless talk about Hani's wedding, I agreed to meet with Detective Parrish immediately.

He suggested we meet at a coffee shop not far from the police station in Kahului. It was a bit of a drive for me, but I didn't mind considering that the gorgeous weather of the morning had decided to stick around. I hopped into the convertible (top down, of course) and threw on some music from jazz musician, Wes Montgomery.

I was obviously going through a jazz phase. If you're going to have a phase, though, it might as well be that one. Better than a tattoo phase that you'll regret decades later when you're in the nursing home and that cool tribal tattoo is now a misshapen design on sagging skin.

The coffee shop wasn't the most original of meeting places. It was a popular hangout for the local cops, and they did serve excellent coffee, or so I'm told. I'm not a huge coffee drinker, and I usually end up ordering something else.

As I entered the coffee shop, a tall man in the back corner stood and walked over to me. He was about my height at six foot two. He had sandy blonde hair and blue eyes. I estimated his age at around thirty.

"Mr. Rutherford, I'm Josh Parrish," he said, and he extended his hand, which I shook. "You may not remember this, but we've actually met before."

"Yes. The holiday party. How's your wife doing?"

"She's great. Thanks for asking."

"By the way, you can call me Poe if you like. But it's really whatever makes you most comfortable."

"Sure thing, and please call me Josh. I haven't gotten used to the whole Detective Parrish thing yet."

"Of course."

I followed him back to his table, and we sat down.

"Do you want anything to drink?" Detective Parrish asked.

"No, I'm good. So, what did you want to talk about?" I asked, although I thought I already had a pretty good idea.

"I understand that you're a consultant with the department and that detectives are free to call you if they think they might need help."

"That's right."

"This is only my second case. The first one wasn't much of a challenge and I had it wrapped up in a few days."

"Congratulations."

"Thanks. Then they dropped this new one on me. It's formidable to say the least."

"Is it the Eric Ellis case?" I asked.

"You know about that?"

"One hears things on a small island."

"What do you know about it?"

"Not much, only that Eric Ellis went missing five years ago and his body recently turned up," I said.

"His remains were found by a man hiking with his dog. He didn't have the dog on a leash and the dog took off. When he found the dog, it had a bone in its mouth. The radius bone to be exact. Whoever killed Eric Ellis dug a shallow grave. It was only a matter of time before the rain exposed parts of the body."

"How was he killed?"

"A single gunshot to the back of the head, execution style."

"Before we go any further, I need to make sure you're aware of something. I was contacted by a client to look into this murder. This could be considered a conflict of interest," I said.

Detective Parrish didn't immediately respond.

Then he asked, "Could this new client be considered a suspect?"

"Probably, but I feel confident they didn't do it. I wouldn't have taken the case otherwise."

Okay, that wasn't technically true since I've been guilty more than once of working for a crooked client. In fairness to me, I didn't know they were guilty at the time, although I'd probably suspected it on some level.

"Are you always right about your client's guilt or innocence?" he asked.

"Unfortunately, no."

"So, you have no way of knowing if this new client, let's say her hypothetical name is Mele Akamu, might be guilty?"

That was interesting, I thought. The fresh-faced detective wasn't as green as he'd initially tried to appear. Or had I simply assumed he was? One sometimes judges without realizing they're doing so.

"What makes you think it's her?" I asked.

"You're not going to confirm or deny it?"

"Not yet. I'm more intrigued as to why you tossed out that name."

"Is this some kind of test?"

"No and forgive me if it comes across that way. I enjoy learning how others solve puzzles. That's all."

Detective Parrish took a sip of his coffee. Then he put the cup back down on the table.

"I heard rumors that Mayor Akamu was somehow involved in your wife's last major investigation. I also heard rumors that his grandmother, Mele Akamu, intervened. I doubt that she went to Detective Hu directly. My guess is that she did the next best thing.

She spoke with you and you passed along whatever information she wanted to get back to the police."

I smiled.

"Is something funny?" he asked.

"No, nothing funny. I just realized the irony of this conversation."

"What's ironic about it?"

"Nothing about this conversation in general. It's a specific question you asked a few seconds ago. You asked me if I was testing you. You had a bit of aggression in your voice, as if I'd offended you."

"I'm a new detective, fresh off the boat so to speak. People are going to underestimate me."

"And that would be their mistake, not mine."

"Are you going to tell me what was ironic about my question?" he asked.

"Something tells me that you already know. You found out that I'd been approached by Mele Akamu again, and you assumed, correctly I might add, that it was about Eric Ellis. But you didn't open this conversation with that knowledge. Instead, you tested me. You wanted to see how far I'd go before letting you in on that little secret, or maybe I wouldn't have told you at all."

Detective Parrish shrugged his shoulders.

"It's a small island, but you already noted that."

"Yes, it is," I said.

"Are you willing to tell me what she said? Which choice will you make? Consultant for the Maui Police Department and husband of its best detective, or private investigator for Mele Akamu?"

"Thank you for the compliment on Alana. I happen to agree with you. Many of my cases have put me in a tough spot, especially with Alana and other detectives, but I don't believe this is one of them."

"How's that? Mele Akamu is my number one suspect."

"And I can understand how she would be. Eric Ellis worked for her and he was privy to many of the details of her business. I can see how that would make him vulnerable, but I don't think that vulnerability is just with her. There are others, perhaps Mele Akamu's enemies. Maybe Eric Ellis crossed one of them."

"What are these business details you're talking about?" he asked.

"I don't know. You may not believe that, but it's the truth."

"You're right. I don't believe you."

"I understand. We don't know each other, and I just admitted that I'm doing a job for Mele Akamu."

"Does your wife know that?"

"First of all, what is said between my wife and I is none of your business," I said.

"And second?"

"It's still none of your business."

"I'm sure you must have asked Mele Akamu who she thought had killed Eric Ellis, especially if she'd declared that she didn't do it."

"You're right. I did ask her that and she told me that she didn't have a clue."

"You bought that?"

"No, I didn't buy it, but I didn't think that meeting was the time to press her. I need to learn more about the case. You're only going to get so many shots with Mele Akamu. Better to be prepared."

"So many shots? It sounds like you're out to get her."

"I'm not out to get anyone. I'm only interested in the guilty party being brought to justice."

"And if that's Mele Akamu?" Detective Parrish asked.

"Then she should go to jail. What did you think I was going to say?"

"When word got out that I was being promoted, Detective Kalani offered to take me to lunch to celebrate. We had a long conversation about you."

He paused a long moment, apparently waiting for me to ask him how that conversation went. I didn't.

"She warned me about you," he continued. "She said that you undermined her on several occasions."

"Did she also tell you how I helped her solve some of her toughest cases?"

"No, but I assumed there was a reason she kept calling you."

"I like Detective Kalani and I don't have one bad word to say about her."

"Good. I have another question for you. Why in the world would you be willing to work for one of Maui's biggest criminals?"

"I've already answered that question. Is there anything else you want to say before I leave? It's obvious that you have no interest in working with me."

"One more comment. That's all. I'm not going to let you play me like you did Detective Kalani. You try to obstruct my investigation, I'll arrest you. I don't care who you're married to. Do we have an understanding?"

"And here I had such high hopes for our potential working relationship. But not everything is to be," I said, and I stood. "Have a good day, Detective. I'm sure we'll be talking again soon since I have no intention of dropping my investigation."

Detective Parrish said nothing.

I turned and walked out of the coffee shop. The conversation hadn't gone anywhere close to where I thought it would. Detective Josh Parrish had already decided that he'd rather have me as an enemy than an ally.

You may be wondering if I was worried about that. I wasn't and maybe that was my overconfidence talking. I was more than a little annoyed with Detective Kalani for sowing the seeds of discord as she'd walked out the door of the Maui Police Department. I knew our last case hadn't gone well, at least in terms of how we'd interacted with each other. But I didn't think she'd try to sabotage my relationship with the department.

Once again, I was reminded of my naïve nature and how I try to look for the best in others. That brought up an interesting question related to my current case. Was I committing the same mistake with Mele Akamu? As I mentioned before, she reminded me of my own grandmother, a woman I admired greatly.

Perhaps my desire to see my grandmother again had me overlooking obvious problems with Mele Akamu. Nevertheless, I'd been honest with Detective Parrish when I'd said that I'd have no problem with pointing the police in Mrs. Akamu's direction if I discovered she'd been the one to murder Eric Ellis.

Despite the hostile nature of the conversation, I did learn one new interesting fact about the case. Eric Ellis had been killed with a gunshot to the back of the head. It was a pretty cold-blooded way to kill someone, and I had no idea who'd done it.

7

THE BEST FRIEND

IT TOOK A FEW DAYS FOR US TO TRACK DOWN LEE WALTERS, THE former co-worker and friend of Eric Ellis. We discovered that he worked as a manager of a jewelry store in Kahului. Since Foxx was my partner in crime on this new investigation, we agreed to meet at Harry's for the drive north to Maui's most populous town.

Foxx barely fits in the Z3 convertible, so I climbed out of my car and hopped right into his Lexus SUV. It's a solid, comfortable vehicle, but it's nowhere near as fun as the little roadster.

"Nice job tracking down Lee, by the way," I said.

"Not a problem. I have a pretty good network on the island. I figured it was only a matter of time before I came across someone who knew him. Hey, you never told me what Alana's reaction was when you told her about your meeting with that new detective. What's his name? Parrish something?"

"Josh Parrish, and I didn't tell you anything because I didn't mention it to Alana."

"Why not?"

"Because she's been overwhelmed with the upcoming wedding and that party we're having for Hani. The last thing I want to do is drop another distraction on her and there's really nothing she can do about it," I said.

"Good point. Should we be worried about this guy?"

"In what way?"

"He might try to shut us down."

"True, but I think it was just an idle threat. My bet is that he'll come back to us for help. He wanted to establish dominance, that's all."

"Maybe. At least you got some information out of him. Gunshot to the back of the head. What a way to go. You sure it's not Mele Akamu?"

"I'm not sure of anything at the moment."

"Any more ideas as to what Hani's surprise tomorrow night is?" Foxx asked, shifting the focus of our conversation.

"Nothing, but I stopped trying to guess. Yuto's lips are glued shut."

"It's probably some fancy trip somewhere."

"I doubt it. We already bought them one."

During our last investigation, I had to deceive Hani and Yuto for my own safety, as well as Foxx's. In the process, I said some hurtful things to them that were part of the cover story. Even though I eventually came clean with them, I still felt horrible about the situation.

Foxx, Alana, and I decided to give the new couple an extravagant wedding gift, namely an all-expenses paid honeymoon to Paris. Alana tried to convince me that we should tag along, but the last thing I wanted to do was go on a vacation with Hani since she'd almost certainly want to call the shots, from where we went during the day to where we ate every meal.

"That's true," Foxx said. "Why couldn't they have picked Disney World or something like that?"

"Disney World? That might have cost more than Paris," I said.

"Any word on where they're going to live after the wedding?"

"I don't know. I heard that Yuto was going to move in with Hani and Ava, but I also heard that they're looking to buy a bigger place. Yuto said he was thinking of renting out his home versus selling it."

"Isn't that what Alana did when you guys moved in together?"

"Yeah. She still owns the place, although she was talking about selling it recently."

"Tired of dealing with renters?" Foxx asked.

"How did you guess?"

"I've heard it's a nightmare. Of course, I've only rented space to one person before and that was you. You always paid the rent on time. You know, I should have charged extra once you bought that dog."

"He more than covered his rent with the added security he provided."

"Security? That little guy?"

"I'll have you know that Maui has the heart of a lion," I said.

"Yeah, I'll grant you that."

Our conversation continued to bounce back and forth between making guesses on Yuto's surprise for Hani and whether or not Detective Josh Parrish was going to be a problem. Our consensus by the end of the drive to Kahului was that Yuto had bought a new sportscar for Hani. There was no agreement on Detective Parrish.

We found the jewelry store where Lee Walters worked. It was in a small section of shops and eating establishments. Foxx parked the SUV in the back of the lot, and we climbed outside.

"How do you want to handle this?" Foxx asked.

"Let's just be upfront about it. He may not even know yet that Eric Ellis' remains were found."

The body's discovery had made the local news, but the police hadn't released Eric's name.

We entered the shop and saw an elderly couple being helped by a female salesperson. Before we made it to the middle of the store, a short, thin man with long black hair pulled back in a ponytail approached us. He was dressed in a tan silk shirt and dark pants.

"Hello, gentlemen. Can I help you find anything in particular?"

"Yes, we're looking for Lee Walters," I said.

"You found him."

"Mr. Walters, we'd like to talk to you about Eric Ellis," I said.

His warm salesman's smile vanished.

"I don't know anyone by that name," he said.

"Sure, you do," Foxx said. "Is there somewhere we can talk?"

"I have nothing to say. I just told you that I don't know him."

"Mr. Walters, are you aware that the police found Eric Ellis' remains recently?" I asked.

Lee said nothing, and I could tell from the look in his eyes that he hadn't heard the news.

"We understand you were good friends with him. We want your help in finding who killed him," Foxx said.

"Are you guys cops?"

"No, we're private investigators," I said.

"Who hired you? Gracie?"

"No, we were hired by Mele Akamu," I said.

"Mele Akamu? Now I know you're lying."

"Why would that make us liars?" Foxx asked.

"Because Mele Akamu would be the last person who'd want to be looking into Eric's death. She's the one who killed him."

He'd said the phrase, "She's the one who killed him," much louder than he'd probably realized. The elderly couple at the other end of the store turned and stared at us.

"Perhaps we should have this conversation outside," I suggested.

"No, let's go back to my office. More privacy there," he said.

We followed Lee Walters through the store and into an office behind the sales counter. We had a seat in front of his desk. Lee shut the door and then walked to the other side of the desk and sat down.

"You said the cops found Eric's body. Where was it?" Lee asked.

"North Maui. A dog walker found it in a shallow grave," I said.

"How was he killed?"

"Gunshot to the back of the head," Foxx said.

"Poor bastard. He didn't even have a chance."

"What was your relationship with Eric?" I asked.

"We were best friends since childhood. We both grew up dirt poor, but we didn't know any better."

"How did you end up working for Mele Akamu?" Foxx asked.

"She hired us when we were kids. We'd deliver things for her on our bikes. No one stops to think two poor kids are carrying anything valuable. As we got older, she started giving us more and more responsibility."

"Mele Akamu told me that Eric knew a lot of details about her business, things she wouldn't want to get out," I said.

"Sure, he did. I did too."

"Can you tell us what changed? What made Eric turn on her?" Foxx asked.

"She paid us peanuts when we were kids, but it didn't matter to us. We had nothing in our pockets before, so to have some money, even if it was just a little, was a big deal for us. Here's the thing, though, when you start out at the bottom of an organization, it's damn near impossible to get to the top of it, especially if your last name isn't Akamu."

"It's a family business and she made it clear you weren't going anywhere," I guessed.

"She didn't have to. It was obvious. Eric got tired of it. He approached me about getting out. He tried to convince me that we should do our own thing."

"When you say, 'do your own thing,' does that mean you'd have been in direct competition with Mele Akamu?" Foxx asked.

"Yeah, and that's why I told Eric I wasn't interested. That's a sure-fire way to end up dead."

"Only he didn't listen to you," I said.

"No, he didn't. Word eventually got back to Mele. I don't know how Eric thought it wouldn't. So, she did what she always did, and she sent Samson to find him."

"What happened then?" Foxx asked.

"Samson sent the message. He beat Eric so badly that he should have been in the hospital."

"You saw this?" I asked.

"Yeah, I was the one who found him on his living room floor. I started to dial 911 but then Eric told me not to. He said he didn't want the ER doctors contacting the police. I stayed with him the rest of the day until Gracie came back. Then I left. That was the last time I ever saw Eric."

"You've mentioned the name Gracie twice. Was that his girlfriend or wife?" I asked.

"Her full name is Gracie Ito. She was his girlfriend."

"Is she still on Maui?" Foxx asked.

"Yeah, I talk to her from time to time."

"What did Gracie think when Eric disappeared?" I asked.

"The same thing that I did. She thought he fled the island after his beating. She was upset that he didn't take her with him. Then she became convinced that Mele Akamu had him killed. I didn't believe it, not at first."

"Why not?" Foxx asked.

"Because why would Mele Akamu have Eric worked over by Samson, only to go back and kill him later," I answered for Lee.

"That's exactly what I thought, but then I figured out what it was. It was Tavii."

"Why Tavii?" Foxx asked.

"Because Eric couldn't stand him and Tavii knew that. He lobbied his grandmother for years to get rid of Eric."

"Why didn't Eric like him?" I asked.

"Because Tavii is lazy and worthless, but he was still going to be handed the keys to the kingdom. That's what really pushed Eric over the edge. Tavii had what Eric wanted and no amount of hard work was going to ever pay off, no matter how long we stayed there."

"Did Mele Akamu suspect that you were in on it with Eric?" Foxx asked.

"If she did, I wouldn't be alive today. But it wasn't like she was ever going to let me close to her business again. She got rid of me and that's how I ended up in this BLANKING place."

For new readers, I usually omit the offending words so as not to upset delicate people. I once had a man threaten to sue me because he almost died while reading one of my mystery tales, which is ironic since they're always about death. Apparently, he was eating a ham sandwich when he came across a naughty word that made him gulp.

This also had the unfortunate result of him getting a piece of ham lodged in his throat. Fortunately for him, his wife was nearby, and she applied the Heimlich maneuver. He did mention in the bottom of his threatening email that he enjoyed the story, but he only gave me one star on Amazon since I'd almost gotten him killed.

"If Tavii was the one to convince his grandmother to get rid of Eric, do you think he might have been the one to kill him?" Foxx asked.

"No chance. Tavii would never have the balls to do it himself."

"Would he have gone behind his grandmother's back and hired someone else to do it?" I asked.

"Doubtful. Again, he's terrified of her. I don't think he'd risk it, but that doesn't mean he didn't help change her mind about Eric."

"Hypothetically speaking, if Mele didn't kill Eric, who did?" Foxx asked.

"There's no one I can think of. Eric didn't have a beef with anyone but the Akamu family."

"Is there any chance we can get Gracie's contact information from you?" I asked.

"Yeah, sure. I know she'll be willing to help you catch Eric's killer any way she can."

Lee wrote Gracie's information on a notepad with his jewelry store's name and logo at the top. He tore off the piece of paper and handed it to Foxx. We both thanked him for his time and exited the store.

Foxx turned to me as we climbed into his SUV.

"I don't know, pal. He made a convincing argument as to why it was Mele Akamu who did this."

"Yeah, but that doesn't explain why she'd hire me to find Eric's killer if she was behind it," I said.

"What about that comment he made about finding Eric on the living room floor after that Samson guy beat the hell out of him? Didn't you tell me that Mele Akamu said that Samson couldn't find him?"

"She obviously lied about that," I said.

"In your experience, if a client lies about one thing, do they lie about everything else?"

"Not necessarily."

"Did you buy his argument that Tavii might have had something to do with it?"

"It's possible. Tavii does seem like a sniveling weasel. But Lee also said that Tavii would be too scared to go behind his grandmother's back."

"Only we know that's not true from our own experiences with Tavii."

"Sure, it's not true now, but it might have been true back then," I said.

"When do you want to see this Gracie person?"

"I need to be getting home now. Alana wants me to help prep for this party, so maybe we can try to see Gracie tomorrow."

"Sounds good. Hey, you want to put any money down on whether or not Hani likes this surprise gift?" Foxx asked.

"She'll like it. I feel pretty confident about that."

I couldn't have been more wrong.

8

THE PARTY

MY DOG, MAUI, IS USUALLY A HAPPY-GO-LUCKY FELLOW, CONTENT TO lounge in the sun, go on long walks, and eat treats whenever they're offered. Nevertheless, he shows a different personality whenever someone he doesn't know comes to the house. Long story made short, there was no way I could have him in the house for Yuto's party since I had no desire to pay off any lawsuits when he inevitably latched onto someone's ankle.

The morning of the big event, I hooked him up to his harness and walked him down to Foxx's house. Maui lived in that house for the first few years we were together, so he knew the lay of the land and felt comfortable there. Foxx was home since he'd decided to take the day off from Harry's, so he kept Maui company while I helped Alana prep for the party. Is it weird that I'd want someone to keep my dog company? If you're a dog person, then you'll understand.

Our house was designed for entertaining, which was kind of ironic since we rarely did it. The first floor has a large, open layout, and the back wall is basically one giant window looking out to the ocean.

The company Hani hired to provide the food and drinks for the event installed a temporary bar on the patio, not far from the swimming pool. They also set up a tent in the yard, under which two long tables of food would be available to the guests. The final touch was a three-piece jazz band for live music. I'm sure you can guess that was my contribution to the party.

Alana's best friend, Raine, was the first to arrive, which was by design. Alana wanted her help making sure everything was exactly in the right place. You may be wondering why she didn't rely on me for that. There's an easy answer to that question. She doesn't trust my style when it comes to entertaining, not that she should. I'm not exactly a sophisticated guy. If I'd been placed in charge, I would have put a couple of coolers on the patio and filled them with beer. Of course, there was the jazz band I just mentioned, so I'm not a completely hopeless case.

Alana's mother was the next person to arrive, which for some reason surprised me. I walked down the stairs and almost bumped into her when I rounded the corner. I'd been preoccupied with searching songs on my phone that I wanted to see if the band could play.

"Excuse me, Ms. Hu. I didn't see you there," I said.

"Am I that insignificant?"

"Not at all. I was caught up in something else. May I offer you a drink? The bar is open."

"I'd love a bourbon. Jack Daniels if you have it," Ms. Hu said.

"Of course. However, might I tempt you with a different brand I've been enjoying lately? It's called 1792."

"I'll give it a try."

We walked outside and I ordered two glasses of 1792 Kentucky Straight Bourbon. I handed Ms. Hu her glass and held up mine in a toast.

"To your youngest daughter and her upcoming wedding. May she have a long and wonderful marriage to Yuto."

"Hopefully this one will go better than the last," Ms. Hu groaned, and she took a sip of her bourbon.

I knew what she'd meant. Hani's first engagement had ended with the groom being murdered the night before their wedding. If you've read my tale *Wedding Day Dead*, then you'll know all the details.

"How do you like the bourbon?" I asked.

"It's good. Where's Alana?"

"Upstairs getting dressed."

Ms. Hu turned from me and walked back into the house, presumably to go to Alana. So much for small talk with my mother-in-law.

"What in the world did you say to her?" Foxx asked, and he laughed.

I turned and saw him walking toward me.

"Nothing. She just jumped at the first opportunity to ditch me."

"Consider yourself lucky. What's that you're drinking?" Foxx asked.

"The 1792 bourbon you introduced me to."

"Good choice. I think I'll get myself one."

Foxx walked over to the bar and returned a moment later with a drink in his hand.

"Is Hani here yet?" he asked.

"Not that I know of."

I looked through the sliding glass door and saw that several people had arrived since I'd been on the patio. Yuto and Hani had invited close to fifty people. Of course, who knew how many would actually show. On the other hand, people have a tendency to come out of the woodwork when free food and good booze are involved.

"Edgar, this all looks incredible."

Both Foxx and I turned to see Yuto standing several feet away.

"You and Alana have really outdone yourself," he continued.

"The big day is just a week away. You ready for it?" I asked as Yuto walked up to us.

"People keep asking me if I'm nervous. Should I be?" Yuto asked.

"I think it's normal to be nervous, but I also don't think it's strange not to be," I said.

"Do you drink bourbon, Yuto?" Foxx asked, and I almost fainted when I heard Foxx use Yuto's real name.

Yuto said he did, and Foxx got him a drink from the bar. I'll say this about my best friend. He was really trying to keep the peace treaty going.

"So, what's the big surprise you have planned for Hani?" Foxx asked.

"All will be revealed in due time," Yuto said, and he looked at his watch. "I'll need to leave in a little while to pick it up. Will you both excuse me for a moment? I want to see if Hani's inside."

Yuto walked away and Foxx turned back to me.

"It's a new car, definitely."

"I don't know. Maybe."

Foxx and I spoke for a while about the Eric Ellis murder investigation. I don't think we planned to do that, especially at the party. The next thing I knew, the backyard was filled with partygoers. I was about to go look for Alana when she exited the house. She'd changed into a tight floral print dress that made me want to suggest that we go to the master bedroom so I could get a better look at all of the curves it showcased.

"How did that awkward guy I knew in high school end up with a chick like that?" Foxx asked.

"I'm not going to take any offense at that question."

"That's because you were asking it yourself."

"That's exactly right."

I walked over to the bar and ordered Alana a white wine since I knew that's what she'd want. I carried the wine to Alana, who'd just been joined by Hani. Hani was wearing a short white dress that was even tighter than her sister's outfit. Were the two women competing for hottest lady at the party? Apparently.

"Have you seen Yuto?" Hani asked me.

"No, but he told me a little while ago that he needed to leave to pick up your surprise," I said.

"Really? Huh, I guess I was wrong. I was so sure it was a trip somewhere," Hani said.

"Me too," Alana said.

"He told you, didn't he?" Hani asked me.

"No, nothing."

"Come on, Poe. We know you guys talk to each other," Hani said.

"Nope. Foxx asked Yuto earlier tonight and he wouldn't budge," I said.

"Foxx is here? I didn't see him," Hani said.

"Your fiancé invited him. You remember, don't you?" Alana asked.

"Yes, I remember. But I don't know how I missed the big oaf," Hani said.

"Hani, that's rude," Alana said.

"It's true," Hani said.

"That's the last thing Foxx is," Alana said.

"If you say so," Hani said, and she looked around the yard. "There's Foxx and look who he's with."

I turned and saw Foxx speaking with Ms. Hu by the bar.

"Oh Lord, I better go save him," I said.

"You? Save him from my mother? I'd love to see that," Hani said.

I walked over to the bar and saw a full glass of bourbon in Ms. Hu's hand. Was that her second, third, or fourth? I wondered.

"So, Mr. Foxx, how long do you intend to stay?" Ms. Hu asked, and there was a definite slur to her voice.

I didn't think she was going to stumble and fall into the pool, but she was on her way.

"At the party?" Foxx asked.

"What else would I be talking about?"

"Long enough to see what this surprise is," Foxx said.

"Well, here's what's not a surprise. You blew it," Ms. Hu said.

"I'm sure I'm going to regret asking this, but how did I blow it?" Foxx asked.

"Hani, of course. That could have been you marrying her next week, but thank God for small miracles," Ms. Hu said.

"You can say that again," Foxx said.

"What's that supposed to mean?" Ms. Hu asked.

"It means exactly what you think it means. I dodged a major bullet when I ended things with your daughter," Foxx said.

"How dare you," Ms. Hu said.

"Let's take it down a few notches, both of you. This is supposed to be a celebration," I said.

"Poe's exactly right. It's a celebration that I won't have you as a mother-in-law," Foxx said.

Ms. Hu was about to reply when Yuto suddenly appeared at the back gate.

"Attention everyone. Can I have everyone's attention?" Yuto asked.

The crowd grew silent. Yuto stayed by the gate instead of walking closer to the partygoers, which I found a bit odd.

"First, I'd like to thank everyone for coming. Your presence means a lot to us and we can't wait to see you a week from today when Hani and I officially tie the knot," Yuto said.

The crowd broke out into applause. I looked to Hani. She was still standing beside Alana.

"Hani, you've made me the happiest man in the world, and I wanted to return the favor. I've brought someone here and I know you'll be thrilled to see him again after all of this time," Yuto continued.

He turned from the crowd and signaled the mystery person to appear. Yuto stepped away from the gate and a Japanese man around sixty-five years old walked into the backyard.

"Oh my God," Ms. Hu said.

I turned to her and saw her eyes roll up into her head. She fainted and I managed to catch her right before her head struck the concrete patio.

"Why did you have to be so fast in catching her?" Foxx whispered to me.

"I couldn't let her hit the ground."

"Who do you think that is?"

"I have no idea," I said.

I picked up the unconscious Ms. Hu and carried her into the house past a confused Hani and curious partygoers who watched and murmured to each other. Alana hurried up to me as I placed her mother on the sofa in our living room.

"What happened?" Alana asked.

"A combination of too much bourbon and the shock of seeing whoever that was," I said.

"Is Mom all right?" Hani asked from the open sliding glass door.

"She'll be fine," I said.

Hani stepped into the house and walked over to Alana.

Yuto followed Hani inside and rushed over to Ms. Hu to check on her.

"Do you know who that man is?" Hani asked.

Alana didn't answer her. Instead, she looked past Hani to the older, Japanese man who was standing where Hani had been a second before.

"Is your mother okay?" the man asked Alana.

"She'll be fine," I said a second time.

"Who are you?" Hani asked.

"He's our father," Alana said.

"What the BLANK!" Hani yelled.

Mr. Hu stepped inside the living room.

"What are you doing here?" Alana asked.

"Yuto found me. He wanted to surprise Hani," Alana's father said.

Hani started to sway as well, and she steadied herself by grabbing the back of a chair. Yuto came to her aid.

"Are you all right?" he asked.

He put his arm on her shoulder, but Hani shoved it away.

"Don't touch me," she said.

Alana scowled at her father.

"You're just going to pop back into our lives and do it at a party? Why not jump out of a damn cake?" Alana asked.

"You're right. I should have done it another way, but this is how Yuto wanted it," he said.

"Now you're going to blame Yuto for your bad judgment?" Alana asked.

"I'm sorry. I didn't mean to hurt anyone," Yuto said.

"Shut up, Yuto. No one asked for you to talk," Hani said.

"I understand how mad you are, Alana," her father said.

"No, I don't think you do," Alana said.

"Perhaps you should leave, Mr. Hu," I said.

"Yes, I think you're right," he said, but he didn't immediately leave. Instead, he looked at both Alana and Hani for a few more moments. "Yuto has told me so much about you both. You don't know how happy I am that you've grown into such amazing women."

"Does my husband need to show you the door or can you find it on your own?" Alana asked.

"Come on, Mr. Hu. Let me walk you out," I said.

"As you wish."

I led Mr. Hu through the kitchen and out through the door that led to the open garage.

"Did Yuto drive you here?" I asked.

"Yes, but I can call a taxi to get back to the hotel." He paused a moment. Then he asked, "You're Edgar Rutherford, is that right?"

"Yes, I'm married to Alana."

"Yuto told me a lot about you too. Thank you for loving my daughter and taking such good care of her."

"We take care of each other," I said.

Mr. Hu nodded.

"I'm here on Maui for another two weeks. Please let Alana and Hani know that I'd love to talk to them if they change their mind."

"I will."

Yuto's surprise had been a train wreck of biblical proportions and I feared this might be the end of his relationship with Hani.

By the time I walked back into the house, Ms. Hu was coming around, or at least pretending to come around. You may have found her fainting spell a bit of an exaggeration on my part. It wasn't. I told you the truth about what happened.

That said, I wasn't entirely sure she'd really fainted. Her body hadn't been as limp as I'd expected it to be. Did that mean she'd faked it as a way of not dealing with the reappearance of her ex-husband? It was a possibility.

You may also be wondering why Alana recognized her father and Hani didn't. Hani was quite young when her father abandoned his family and went back to Japan. Alana is a few years older than Hani, old enough to have remembered what their father looked like.

"Are you all right, Mom?" Alana asked.

"What happened?" Ms. Hu asked.

"You fainted. Poe caught you," Alana said.

"Why did I faint?" Ms. Hu asked.

Her ridiculous question convinced me that she'd faked it. I sensed she was now in full-on drama mode, and she was going to attempt to make the evening all about her.

"Dad came back," Hani said.

"Oh my God, I wasn't just dreaming it," Ms. Hu said, and I was surprised she didn't bring the back of her hand up to her forehead and pass out again.

"Are you all right, Hani?" Yuto asked.

I turned and saw him standing several feet from Hani. I didn't blame him for keeping his distance.

Foxx had come into the house by this point and was behind Yuto and off to the side.

"How the hell could you do this?" Hani asked.

"It was supposed to be a surprise," Yuto said, which wasn't the smartest reply for him to have made.

"Do you have any idea what you've done?" Hani asked.

Before Yuto could answer, she picked up an empty highball glass from the table in front of the sofa and hurled it at Yuto. He ducked, which didn't make a difference since her aim was off. Instead, the glass smashed into the floor-to-ceiling window. The highball glass shattered. Fortunately, the thick windowpane did not.

"Stop it, Hani. You could have hurt him," Alana said.

"Good. He deserves to be hurt," Hani said.

"I know you don't mean that," Yuto said.

"Don't be so sure. I'm going home. I suggest you don't follow me," Hani said.

Hani left the house without saying another word, not even to Alana and her mother.

"What do I do?" Yuto asked, but I couldn't tell who he was talking to.

"I suggest you go home too. I wouldn't try calling her for at least twenty-four hours," Foxx said.

Yuto nodded. Then he turned and walked away.

I looked out the window to the backyard. The guests were slowly dispersing. Apparently, a good way to break up a party is to throw a glass against the window. The ironic thing, which was actually quite funny in hindsight, was that the jazz trio was still playing. Our family drama had a soundtrack, so to speak.

Alana turned back to her mother.

"Are you sure you're feeling okay?"

"I think I need to go home," Ms. Hu said.

"Then let us drive you back or else spend the night here. You're in no condition to drive on your own," Alana said.

Ms. Hu looked at me.

"You knew, didn't you?"

"Knew what?" I asked.

"That Yuto had found Sora and was bringing him here."

"How would Poe have known that?" Alana asked.

"Because this is the type of stunt he'd pull," Ms. Hu said.

"How many bourbons did you have?" I asked.

Yes, it was a hurtful thing to say, but it sneaked out of my mouth anyway. I'd also like to point out that there was no way in hell she really thought I'd orchestrated the return of her ex-husband. Ms. Hu may not like me, but she knows I'm not that dumb.

"Don't talk to me like that," Ms. Hu said.

"And don't blame me for something you know I had nothing to do with. We're on the same team. Yuto clearly made a mistake, but no one was killed. You're a strong woman. You'll get over this," I said.

"You have no idea what that man did to me," Ms. Hu said.

"I do. He left you with two small children, but you survived. You did a hell of a job of raising them by yourself. Don't let this man take your power," I said, suddenly feeling like a motivational speaker.

"Poe's right. He took us by surprise. That's all. We don't have to see or talk to him again," Alana said.

"I want to go home. Will you drive me?" Ms. Hu asked Alana.

"Yes. Let me get my car keys. We can go now," Alana said.

"Do you need me to go with you?" I asked.

"No, we'll be fine," Alana said.

She was anything but fine, I thought. But I wasn't going to argue the point.

After Alana and Ms. Hu left, I walked outside and thanked the bartenders and jazz musicians for their work. They'd already been paid in advance, so they made a good deal of money for what amounted to one whole hour of labor. Nevertheless, I still tipped them.

Hawaii is an expensive place to live and work. These gigs are hard to come by and it wasn't their fault the party had ended so quickly. I didn't bother to ask them not to speak about what they'd seen since I knew it wouldn't do any good. There was also the fifty or so guests who were probably already on their phones calling everyone they knew.

I could imagine their comments.

This mystery man showed up. Then an old lady fainted. Then the guest of honor hurled a glass at her fiancé. Do you think the wedding will still happen? I'm sure I don't know.

The good news, if there was any good news, was that I had plenty of that 1792 bourbon left. I grabbed a full bottle and carried it into the house. I poured myself a generous amount and gulped it down. No, I don't normally drink like that, but this party definitely earned me a pass. I was tempted to pour another glass but decided against it.

Instead, I walked down to Foxx's house and retrieved my dog. Foxx and I spoke for about an hour. He was convinced the wedding was off. I didn't agree. I thought Hani would forgive Yuto. Yes, he'd made a stupid decision to bring Sora Hu back to Maui, but I knew Yuto. He was a nice guy to the core. I was sure that his intentions were pure. On the other hand, that might not have meant anything to Hani. She's often not the forgiving type.

After Maui and I got back to the house, I spent another hour cleaning up. Guests had left empty glasses and mini plates all through the house. I even found a half-eaten cracker on the hallway bathroom sink. I made a mental note not to have any more parties for a long time. Did Maui help me clean? Of course not. Instead, he spent that time sniffing every inch of the first floor. He could tell people had invaded his territory and he seemed determined to figure out who they were.

I'd just plopped down on the sofa and turned on the television when Alana walked into the house. She looked around the living room and kitchen.

"You already cleaned everything?"

"It seemed a good way to keep my mind preoccupied," I said.

She walked over to the sofa and sat beside me.

"My mother broke down after we left the neighborhood. She cried all the way to her house. She didn't stop until I got her inside."

"Maybe we should have insisted that she stay with us tonight."

"Sometimes you want to be in your own home," Alana said.

"I understand."

"Thanks for getting him out of the house."

"I didn't really do anything. I just followed him outside."

"Still, you were here. I don't know what I would have done if you weren't."

"I thought you handled yourself well."

"It was so out of the blue. I never imagined it would have gone down like that."

I didn't reply.

"I used to dream about seeing my father again. I don't remember exactly how old I was, maybe thirteen or fourteen, when I finally realized he wasn't ever coming back. I hated him for the longest time, but I think that was a way of getting over him. Then I started feeling sorry for him. What kind of man leaves his own family? Then I just stopped thinking about him all together."

Alana turned to me.

"Did he say anything to you when you were outside?" she asked.

It was a telling question. If she truly had gotten over him, I mean completely over him, she wouldn't have cared if Sora Hu had said anything to me or not. I was reminded of that saying, there's a thin line between love and hate.

"He said he'll be on Maui for two weeks. He asked me to let you and Hani know that. He said he's available to talk should you change your mind."

"I won't."

"Did Hani call you guys after she left?" I asked.

"No, I haven't heard anything from her."

"I spoke to Foxx for a while when I went to pick up Maui. He said he's going to call Yuto tonight."

"You're kidding. Foxx can't stand him."

"That might have been true at one point, but I suspect Yuto gained a lot of respect from Foxx when he stood up to him. Plus, Yuto showed Foxx a lot of compassion after he got hurt. There's one other thing."

"What's that?"

"Foxx knows what it's like being on the receiving end of your sister's wrath."

"Yeah, but you can't blame Hani for this one. Yuto really screwed up."

"I'm not blaming Hani."

"What do you think will happen? Will she call off the wedding?" Alana asked.

"I don't know. If you'd asked me that question an hour ago, I would have said no."

"What changed?"

"I thought back to some of the conversations we had in the last year about those two. We both felt that Hani didn't really love Yuto, at least not at the level that someone should feel before entering into a marriage. Maybe this is an excuse to call things off."

"Hani doesn't need an excuse. She can just say no."

"I understand that, but I'm talking about an excuse in her mind that she won't feel guilty about."

"I don't think you're being fair to her."

"Sorry. Maybe I'm not."

"Did you tell my father who you were?"

"No, he already guessed. He said Yuto told him about me," I said.

"Do me a favor. If he comes to see you, tell him you're not interested in talking. Hold on. First tell him that I have zero interest in a relationship with him. Then tell him to get lost." Alana said, and she stood. "I'm going to bed."

"I'll be up shortly," I said.

She left the living room and walked upstairs to the bedroom.

Let me ask you a question. Was I being unfair to Hani? Or was Alana ignoring the truth of the situation? I didn't know. There was one thing for certain. The next week was going to be one for the history books.

9

JAILHOUSE INTERVIEWS

THE NEXT MORNING, I EXPECTED ALANA TO BRING UP THE RETURN OF her father again and offer any new insights she might have had. She didn't. Instead, she asked me about the Eric Ellis investigation, a sure sign that she didn't want to talk about her father. I told her again about my mixed feelings on whether or not Mele Akamu was guilty. She didn't offer an opinion on the matter. She just listened.

Then Alana informed me that she was going to see her mother and Hani at their mother's house. It was pretty obvious what the topic of conversation would be. She didn't tell me how long she'd be gone, and I didn't press her for any details. This was a Hu family matter and I assumed they'd ask for my opinion or help if they wanted it.

I spent the morning tidying up the backyard since I'd focused all of my cleaning the previous night on the interior of the house. As before, I found bottles, cups, and plates in all sorts of strange places and I couldn't believe such a mess was made in only one hour.

I'd just finished hauling the trash bags to the garbage can when my phone vibrated.

"Hello."

"Mr. Rutherford, this is Henry Mitchell."

"The same Henry Mitchell who called me a liar on the witness stand?"

"I disagree with your account."

"Of course, you would," I said.

"I didn't call you a liar. I said you couldn't accurately remember your conversation with my client."

"Okay, so I'm a drunk with a faulty memory. What do you want?"

"Guy Livingston would like to meet with you. Are you available today?" Mitchell asked.

"Why does he want to meet? So he can tell me I'm an ass for testifying against him?"

"I assure you that's not the reason for the meeting."

"Sorry, but I'm unavailable."

"You owe him, Mr. Rutherford."

"How's that?"

"Your testimony was quite damning. You need to find a way to make this up to him."

"Mr. Mitchell, I say this with all frankness. Either you've hit your head sometime in the past or you have the world's most bizarre way of viewing reality. I spoke the truth on the witness stand. I don't owe Guy Livingston or you anything. It's not my fault your client is guilty."

"That's the thing, though. He's not guilty," Mitchell said.

"What are you basing this on?"

"He told me."

"Well then, let's unlock the jail cell and let Guy Livingston go free. He said he's innocent. He must be."

"I can appreciate a good sarcastic remark as much as anyone, but you've got this all wrong. When you've done this job as long as I have, you start to get pretty good at knowing when people are lying to you."

"Sure, but you weren't there when I told him about his wife's affair. The man was enraged."

"As you would have been if the situation was reversed."

"But I wasn't the one who told his investigator that he was going to shoot his wife. I also wasn't the one who was found beside her dead body a few hours later."

"He was found there because he's the one who discovered the body in their house and called the police."

"You can spin this however you want. The man's getting convicted. Goodbye, Mr. Mitchell, and good luck with your case. You're going to need it," I said.

"I apologize for the way I treated you in court. Is that what you need to hear?"

"No, I don't need your apology."

"Would you just do this for me? Would you meet with Guy today? Hear what he has to say. If you're still convinced that he's guilty, then walk away."

I don't know what convinced me to change my mind. Perhaps it was my desire to fill my head with something that didn't have to do with Sora Hu and Hani and Yuto's wedding, but I agreed to meet Guy Livingston and Henry Mitchell in the early afternoon.

I spent the rest of the morning working out. I doubled the usual length of my swim and run. I took Maui on a long walk and I spent a solid hour doing background research on Gracie Ito, the former girlfriend of the murdered Eric Ellis. I found some social media accounts for her, but there wasn't much of interest in them. I did learn she leaned hard to one political side of the spectrum. Of course, I wouldn't dream of telling you which way since I do my best not to let politics enter these tales.

After a late lunch, I climbed into the BMW convertible and drove to the Maui jail. I'd been there far too many times in the past. I'd even been a guest myself on a few occasions.

I found Henry Mitchell waiting for me in the parking lot. He thanked me for coming and then we entered the building where we were escorted to the visitor area to meet Guy Livingston.

I expected Guy to hurl some insult at me, maybe even threaten me. He didn't. Instead, he thanked me for coming as well.

"I'm really hoping you can get me out of this," Livingston said.

I didn't respond.

"You can't possibly think I did it," Livingston continued.

"The truth is that I don't know for certain what happened. All I know is what you told me."

"And you were right. I did tell you that I wanted to shoot my wife. That doesn't mean I did it. We all say things in anger that we don't actually follow through with."

"Why are you calling me this late in the process? Your trial is almost over," I said.

"Because the other investigator couldn't find anything," Livingston admitted.

"What other investigator?" I asked.

"No offense, but I wasn't going to hire you after I learned what you'd told the police," Livingston said.

"Who did you hire?" I asked.

Guy Livingston looked at his attorney, and Henry Mitchell gave me a name. I won't repeat it here since I don't have anything nice to say about the man.

"He's known for following unfaithful spouses, not conducting a murder investigation," I said.

"You follow unfaithful spouses. That's how you learned that Guy's wife was cheating on him," Mitchell said.

"It's a general rule of mine not to take those kinds of cases. Sometimes I come across adultery during an investigation," I said.

"Will you take my case?" Livingston asked.

"What did your investigator learn? Who did he look at?" I asked.

"He looked more into Bret Hardy's background, but he found nothing," Mitchell said.

"Why would Bret Hardy have killed Mrs. Livingston? They were going to run off together. Plus, he'd just received a lot of money when he pawned her necklace and bracelet. He probably thought he could squeeze her for even more money in the future," I said.

"I'm telling you, I didn't murder my wife," Livingston said.

"She was shot with your gun, a weapon that had your fingerprints all over it," I said.

"Of course it had my fingerprints. I owned it, but I only ever used it at the gun range," Livingston said.

"And there was no gunshot residue on his clothing when he was tested," Mitchell said.

I didn't respond.

"You didn't know that, did you?" Livingston asked.

"No, I didn't. But I also didn't dive into the details of your case. I told the police what I knew about our last one-on-one interaction. That was it," I said.

"After I left your bar, I started to drive home. But I pulled over before I got there. I was so angry," Livingston said.

"You were worried you might hurt her," I said.

"Yes, I was. I know that's a bad thing for me to admit, but it's the truth. My wife not only cheated on me, but she lied about the robbery. She took an anniversary gift from me and she gave it to her lover to pay off his debts. Think about that for a minute," Livingston said.

I didn't have to think about it. It was a pretty horrible thing for her to have done, but it goes without saying that she didn't deserve to die because of the act of betrayal.

"Walk me through what happened when you finally got home," I said.

"I saw her car in front of the house, which surprised me because she didn't usually get home that early," Livingston said.

"Do you have any idea why she was there?" I asked.

"I checked with her manager at the bank. He said Lucy left early that day because she was feeling sick," Mitchell said.

"I'd decided that I was going to tell her to leave," Livingston said. "We both owned the house, but I'd be damned if I'd let her get our home too. I figured she could go live with her lover for all I cared. I went inside and called out to her. I walked directly back to the bedroom when I didn't get a response."

"Why the bedroom?" I asked.

"It's a small house like most homes on Maui. You can see the living room and kitchen from inside the front door. There's only one bedroom, so she had to be back there," Livingston said.

"Where was she exactly?" I asked.

"She was on the floor of the bedroom," Livingston said.

"But where exactly in the bedroom? Was she beside the bed? Near the doorway?" I asked.

"Near the doorway, maybe a few steps inside the room."

"Where on the body was she shot?"

"Twice in the chest," Mitchell answered for his client.

"Who knew you had a gun?" I asked.

"My wife knew, but that's the only person I can think of. I'd always go to the range by myself. I didn't talk about the gun with anyone," Livingston said.

"Where did you keep the gun and was it locked up?" I asked.

"In the nightstand and I didn't keep the drawer locked."

"Why not?"

"Because I wanted quick access to it should someone break into the home. We didn't have any kids, so it wasn't like someone could accidentally get their hands on it," Livingston said.

"When you came into the room and saw your wife, where was the gun?" I asked.

"It was on the carpet near the nightstand. It was like someone had pulled it out of the nightstand, shot my wife, and then dropped it where they stood."

"What did you do next?" I asked.

"I checked to see if she was alive. I felt for a pulse but couldn't find one. Then I called 911."

"Who do you think murdered her?" I asked.

"I don't know. My wife didn't have any enemies that I knew of," Livingston said. He paused a long moment. Then he continued. "I can pay whatever rate you want to take this case."

"It's never about the money."

"I find that hard to believe," Mitchell said.

"Will you take my case?" Livingston asked.

"Look me in the eyes and tell me whether or not you killed your wife," I said.

"I didn't kill her. I swear."

Have I been fooled by clients before? I think you already know the answer to that question. So, why did I agree to take his case? Let's chalk it up to insanity at the moment.

"I'm going to need access to your house," I said.

"That's easy. We have one of those keypads on the front door. The combination is ten-twenty. It's my anniversary date," Livingston said.

"How many people know that code?"

"Just my wife and I."

"You didn't share it with anyone else like a pet sitter?" I asked.

"We don't have any pets and we've never needed a house sitter for anything."

"Could your wife have given the code to someone?"

"She could have, but I don't see why," Livingston said.

"Let me know if there's anything you need from me," Mitchell said.

"I will. I can't promise you two there will be some last-minute rush into the courtroom like they have on those TV shows. This could take days, maybe even weeks to uncover the truth."

Of course, the truth may have already been revealed. Guy Livingston had shot and killed his wife.

"I understand," Livingston said.

I left Guy Livingston and Henry Mitchell sitting at the table. I was almost back to my car when my phone vibrated. I looked at the display and saw the name Yuto Takahashi.

10

THERE'S ALWAYS TWO SIDES

As I mentioned earlier in this tale, Yuto works as the general manager of one of the largest hotels in Kaanapali. He'd told me before that he'd reserved two weeks of vacation time for his honeymoon in Paris. Therefore, he didn't have time to take off the week of the wedding. I say all of this to explain why he asked me to come to his hotel and why he was still working at a time like this.

I could hear the despair in the man's voice when he called, and I agreed to meet him at once. It took about an hour to get back to Kaanapali due to heavy traffic. I didn't listen to any music during the drive. I wanted my mind free of distractions as I tried to figure out what I could say to help Yuto.

When I arrived at the hotel, I left my convertible with the valet and headed into the lobby. Yuto must have told the front desk staff to be on the lookout for me, for one of the women picked up the phone and called him as I walked up to her. She put down the phone a few seconds later and looked up at me.

"Mr. Takahashi is on his way now."

"Thank you," I said.

Yuto arrived in less than one minute. Had the man sprinted to the lobby?

"Thank you for coming, Edgar. Perhaps we can speak in my office so we can have privacy," he suggested.

"Of course. Wherever you like."

I followed Yuto back to his office. It was a small space, much smaller than you'd assume the general manager of a massive hotel would have. I sat down while Yuto walked behind the desk and had a seat on his leather chair.

"I don't know where to start," he said.

There was the obvious question for me to ask. Namely, what in the world were you thinking? But I didn't do that. What was the point?

"Have you spoken with Hani since the party?" I asked.

"No, I tried calling her, but she wouldn't answer. She sent me a text message. She asked me to stop calling and not to text her either."

"You asked her about the wedding, though, didn't you?"

"I did. She didn't respond. I don't think she's going through with it. I asked you here because I don't know what to do. There are over one hundred guests coming. They need to be informed if the wedding is off," Yuto said.

You may be wondering why Yuto seemed more worried about the guests than his relationship with his fiancée. I didn't believe he was, but the man is a general manager. It's in his DNA to make sure things run smoothly.

"There's no need to concern yourself with the guests right now. You can get the word out quickly and you can do it the morning of, if it comes to that. I'm not convinced it will."

"I appreciate your optimism, but I feel it may be misplaced."

"Alana is with Hani and their mother this morning. I'm sure I'll find out later today what Hani is thinking. I'll slip you the information," I said.

"You would do that for me?"

"Alana will understand. She's your friend too."

"I'm sure you're wondering why I did what I did," Yuto said.

"The question crossed my mind a few times."

"Before I answer that, can I ask you a personal question?"

"Of course."

"Does Alana ever talk about her father?"

"When we first started dating, I asked her about her parents. That's when I learned that he'd abandoned them, but she hasn't really brought him up since then. She said she'd gotten over it."

"Do you believe that?"

"No, I don't. But I also know Alana. She buried it deep. His absence isn't important to her anymore."

"Hani isn't the same. I can't tell you how many times she spoke about wanting to see her father again. That was one of her complaints about Douglas. She constantly accused him of being an absentee father like hers was."

"That's ridiculous. Foxx sees Ava all the time. He also completely supports her financially. I'm one of the few people who knows what he pays Hani. The truth is that she wouldn't even have to work if she didn't want to. Foxx's payments are beyond generous," I said.

"I've come to realize that my earlier negative opinions of Douglas were heavily influenced by Hani."

"Foxx is a good guy. He may not have handled his relationship with Hani well, especially the way it ended. But he's not the villain in this story. Neither is Hani. They're simply two people who broke up and couldn't get along."

"He showed me a lot of kindness after what happened at the party. I was surprised."

"You shouldn't have been."

"I know that now."

"You said Hani wanted to see her father again. Did she ever try finding him?" I asked.

"I encouraged her to do it several times. She said she didn't have the courage. As we got closer to the wedding, she told me how sad she was that her father wouldn't be there to walk her down the aisle."

"Hani really said that?"

"At least three or four times. That's why I went looking for him. I knew his name and I knew his family had a successful business. It took me less than a minute to find him online."

"What did you say when you contacted him?" I asked.

"I sent him a long email. I explained who I was and why I was reaching out to him. We emailed each other several times. Then we finally spoke on the phone. It's my fault that he came to the party. He didn't want to reintroduce himself to them that way, but I thought Hani would be thrilled that he would be at the wedding. She'd told me it was what she wanted."

I've never claimed to be the wisest fellow, but there are several truths I've learned over the years. One of them is that you can't always believe people when they say they want something. In fact, I'd wager that you should disbelieve them most of the time. If they wanted something, I mean truly wanted it, then they'd find a way to get it themselves.

"Have you spoken with Sora since the party?" I asked.

"I spoke with him this morning at breakfast."

"He's a guest here at the hotel, isn't he?"

"Yes, I booked him a suite once he agreed to come."

"He told me last night that he'll be here on the island for another two weeks. Is that still correct?"

"I don't know. When we spoke this morning, it sounded like he was going to change his flight and head back to Japan early," Yuto said.

"That makes sense."

"Is there something else you can do for me?"

"What is it?" I asked.

"Can you let Alana know I'm sorry for any hurt that I caused her? I intend to apologize to her in person, but I assume I'm the last person she wants to see right now."

"I'll let her know. Alana knows your heart, Yuto. She understands you're a good person."

"Thank you. I would have been honored to have you as a brother-in-law. I'm sorry it hasn't worked out."

"Don't give up hope. The fat lady hasn't sung yet," I said.

"The fat lady?"

"Sorry, it's probably not polite to use that phrase anymore, but it generally means that the show isn't over until the woman of above-average weight appears on the opera stage to sing the final song. The point is, until you hear from Hani herself, I wouldn't assume anything."

Yuto didn't respond.

"I do have one question," I continued. "What do you think of Sora Hu? Does he seem sorry for what he did?"

"He does. He thanked me for opening the door to a possible reunion with Hani and Alana. You should have seen the look on his face when I picked him up at the airport. It had been over thirty years since he'd been on Maui. All he wants to do is repair his relationship with his children."

I nodded.

"Thank you again for coming here, I appreciate your friendship."

"You're welcome, Yuto. I'll let you know if I hear anything."

Yuto walked me back to the lobby and I got my car out of valet. I thought about driving to Harry's to get something to eat, but then I decided to go home instead. The truth was that I wanted to be alone. It wasn't even night yet, but I was already feeling wiped out.

The alone time was not to be, though. I saw Alana's car in the garage when I got back to the house. I found her sitting on the sofa and watching some trashy reality TV show.

"I was surprised you weren't here when I got home. I was just about to call you," she said.

I sat beside her on the sofa.

"I had a couple of meetings today."

"With who?"

I told Alana about my meeting with Guy Livingston and his attorney. I also broke the news that I'd agreed to look into his case, which was embarrassing to admit. My decision seemed even more ridiculous when I told someone else about it.

"Why are you helping him? I thought you were convinced he was guilty," Alana said.

"No one is more surprised by my actions than I am. I guess I just wanted to keep myself preoccupied."

"And one murder investigation isn't enough?"

"Good point."

"Sorry, I'm not trying to criticize. I'm doing the same thing. I cancelled the rest of my vacation. I go back to work tomorrow."

"Does that mean what I think it does?"

"I'm not sure yet. Hani's still trying to decide what to do about the wedding. What was your second meeting about?" Alana asked, changing the subject.

"I met with Yuto."

"He called you?"

"Yes, right as I was leaving the jailhouse. I drove by the hotel and we talked in his office."

"Let me guess. He wants you to solve his problems and get Hani to take him back."

"Not at all. First, he said Hani won't communicate with him, so he's in the dark as to what she wants to do. Second, he asked me to let you know that he's sorry for any pain he caused you. He says he intends to apologize in person, but he knows you don't want to see him now," I said.

"Well, that's one thing he got right."

"I'm not interested in defending Yuto's actions."

"Then don't."

"But there are two sides to every story."

"I already know his side. He wanted to make Hani happy. That doesn't excuse his stupidity."

"Yes, but did you know that Hani expressed to him many times that she wanted to be reunited with your father? She also told him that it was her wish for your father to walk her down the aisle."

Alana said nothing.

"I figured Hani didn't tell you guys that," I continued.

"So now you're on Yuto's side?"

"No, I just thought you should know that little piece of information. Did you three come to any kind of conclusion today?"

"No, other than the fact that we're going to do everything we can to avoid my father."

"I wouldn't worry about that. Yuto said he's probably going back to Japan early. For all we know, he could be at the airport now."

"Wouldn't that be nice."

I stood.

"I think I'm going to prep for my interview with Eric Ellis' former girlfriend. Foxx and I are going to try to meet with her tomorrow."

"Do me a favor, Poe. Don't try to fix this."

"I'm not. Yuto needed someone to talk to. That's all. He doesn't have family on this island, and I wanted to lend an ear. I didn't commit to anything but listening. As far as your father goes, I recognize that's up to you, Hani, and your mother to work out. I'm here, though, if you need someone to talk to. I'm even available if you need someone to yell at," I said.

"Thank you. I'll do my best not to yell."

"Don't hold back. Sometimes we need to let it out."

Before Alana could respond, Maui walked up to the sofa. He sat by her feet and looked up at her.

"See, even Maui wants to help," I continued.

Alana bent over and scratched him on his head.

"Thanks, Maui."

Alana turned back to me.

"My father is staying at Yuto's hotel, isn't he?"

"I found that out today," I said.

"Did you see him while you were there?"

"No, I didn't. Why do you ask?"

"Just curious."

"I understand."

And I did. Alana was saying more than she realized. She might have told me that she had no interest in seeing Sora, but I didn't believe that. There was still a part of her, somewhere deep inside, that wanted to see him again. Did that mean that I was going to try to create another meeting between them? No. There was no way I was going to do that. Alana would need to make that move on her own.

11

THE GIRLFRIEND

ALANA WAS GONE BY THE TIME I WOKE THE NEXT MORNING. I DOUBTED she was really anxious to get back to work. Rather, it was obvious that she wanted to throw herself into something that would help her mind escape the mess we were all in.

Foxx and I had arranged to meet at Harry's around eleven since Gracie Ito lived in Lahaina. That left me plenty of time to do my morning exercise and take Maui on a walk. I realized during this time that I had a big decision to make.

If Gracie implicated Mele Akamu and offered no other possible suspects, I needed to decide whether to continue with the investigation. I had no desire to work for another guilty client. Yes, I know that makes me a hypocrite since I'd agreed the day before to look into Guy Livingston's case. What can I say? I was possibly off my game as much as Yuto was. Okay, I wasn't that bad.

I drove to Harry's a little early so I could get lunch, which was another ridiculous move on my part since our refrigerator was overflowing with the leftover food from the party. Sometimes, though, you just want a change of scenery, and I was anxious to be around people once again.

Kiana was behind the bar. I said hello and ordered a burger and fries – a guilty indulgence intentionally designed to improve my sour mood. The food was good, as I knew it would be, and I'd almost finished when Foxx arrived. He looked at the remnants of my lunch and turned to me.

"Why didn't you tell me you were getting here early? I've just been hanging out at the house."

"Sorry. I didn't really think about it," I said.

"You ready to go? I'm anxious to get to this interview. I have a feeling this is the one."

"You've really thrown yourself into this case, haven't you?"

"It's fun. I like a challenge."

"Then let's get to it."

We left Harry's and drove about ten minutes to Gracie's apartment. I'd learned from her social media accounts that she worked as a waitress at a nearby hotel. The photos she'd posted indicated that she worked the night shift, so I thought there was a good chance she'd be home. I wasn't wrong.

Gracie cracked open the door and I saw she'd kept the little chain lock engaged.

"Can I help you?" she asked.

"Yes, Ms. Ito, my name is Edgar Rutherford. This is Doug Foxx. We're hoping you could spare us a few minutes of your time. We'd like to talk to you about Eric Ellis."

"You're with the police? I already talked to that detective."

"Yes, Detective Josh Parrish. We're consultants with the Maui Police Department. We spoke with Lee Walters the other day. He told us to say hello."

The Lee Walters comment must have convinced her that we were trustworthy, for she closed the door, unlocked the chain, and then opened the door again.

"Please come in," she said.

Gracie Ito looked a lot like Alana. She was around the same height, maybe five-six, and she had long black hair and dark eyes. She was dressed in a light-blue surfer t-shirt and tan shorts.

We followed Gracie into her apartment. It was typical of Maui apartments, which is to say it was small. Of course, that didn't mean the rent was cheap.

Gracie walked over to a chair and sat down. Foxx and I sat on a sofa beside the chair that probably should have been left on the side of the road where Gracie had probably acquired it. I felt a spring go right up you-know-where, and I assume Foxx did too based on the grunting sound he made.

"What did you want to know about Eric?" Gracie asked.

"You were Eric's girlfriend at the time he went missing, is that correct?" I asked.

"That's right."

"Did you two live together?" Foxx asked.

"Yes, we lived in Eric's house. I moved out after he disappeared. I'm sure the bank foreclosed on the property."

"Another member of his family didn't take over?" I asked.

"Eric's family was poor. It wasn't like they could handle the payments. I certainly couldn't. That's why I left."

"At that time, were you aware that Eric was leaving Mele Akamu's employ?" I asked.

"Eric and I told each other everything. I knew he was unhappy, and he was willing to do anything to get out."

"Does that mean you knew his plan to blackmail the Akamu family?" Foxx asked.

"I told Eric not to do it. I told him to just walk away."

"Do you know why he didn't follow your advice?" I asked.

"He said Mele Akamu would never let him leave. He needed to force her to let him go. That's why he threatened her. It wasn't about the money. It was to let him leave. Eric had changed. He wanted out of the game."

I didn't believe that for a second, nor did I think Gracie believed it. But we all create little fantasies in our mind to protect the images of the ones we love.

"Do you know if Mele Akamu sent Samson to speak with Eric?" I asked.

Gracie laughed.

"Speak with him? Is that what you call it?"

She stood and walked into the kitchen. She grabbed a laptop from a small table and walked back into the living room where she had a seat again. She clicked a few times on the mouse pad and then turned the laptop so we could see the display. It was a photograph of a badly beaten Eric Ellis, at least I assumed that's who it was. The man's eyes were black and blue, and he had bruises and scrapes on his cheeks and chin.

"Does this look like 'speaking' to you?" Gracie asked.

"You took that photo, I assume?" Foxx asked.

"Yes, I came home from work and found him like that. I wanted to call the police, but he wouldn't let me. I took the photo as proof of what they'd done to Eric. I transferred it to my laptop because I couldn't bear to have it on my phone any longer."

"Is it possible for you to email me that photo?" I asked.

"Of course."

I gave her my email address, and a moment later, I heard my phone ping.

"How much time passed between this beating and when Eric disappeared?" I asked.

"Maybe a couple of days. He got a call at night from Mele Akamu. He said he needed to go see her to make peace. Eric never came back."

"Did you call the police then?" Foxx asked.

"I was going to, but then Samson came to see me. He said he'd kill me if I spoke to anyone about Eric, especially the police."

"Did Samson hurt you too?" I asked

"No, he didn't lay a finger on me."

"I'm surprised you stayed on Maui," Foxx said.

"Where was I going to go? My family was here. I didn't have any money."

"We heard that Eric had problems with Tavii Akamu. Do you know anything about that?" I asked.

"Eric hated Tavii. He thought he was spoiled. Plus, Tavii always gave him a hard time."

"Do you know why?" Foxx asked.

"Eric would always say that Tavii took a disliking to him on the first day they met. I think Tavii was jealous of Eric. Mele Akamu always asked Tavii why he couldn't be more ambitious like Eric, at least that's what Eric told me."

"Did Eric have any more enemies other than Tavii and Mele Akamu?" I asked.

"There was one argument I overheard. The same day that Eric went missing, he got into some heated exchange on the phone with someone. I asked him about it afterward, but he told me not to worry about it. He said it would blow over."

"Did he tell you the person's name?" Foxx asked.

"No, but I heard him say Stan on the phone."

"No last name?" Foxx asked.

"No, just Stan, and I don't know anyone by that name," she said.

"And you have no idea what the argument was about? Did they mention money or anything like that?" I asked.

"No, I definitely didn't hear anything about money. I would have remembered that."

"Did you hear Eric say Tavii or Mele's name to this person?" Foxx asked.

"No, I'm sorry, but I don't know what it was about. Eric raised his voice a few times during the call. He usually didn't do that."

"Other than members of the Akamu family and this Stan person, can you think of anyone who would want to hurt Eric?" I asked.

"No, there was no one."

"Thanks, Ms. Ito. We appreciate your time," I said.

"Do you really think you can prove Mele Akamu killed Eric after all of these years?" she asked.

"We're going to do our best to find who killed him," I said.

"What do you mean? We already know it was Mele Akamu."

"It certainly might have been, but we still have to find the evidence," I said.

We stood and Gracie walked us to the door. We thanked her again and made our way back to Foxx's SUV.

"How do you think that went?" Foxx asked as we climbed into his vehicle.

"We got one new lead out of that interview," I said.

He put the SUV in reverse and backed out of the parking space. Then he pulled onto the road and we started the drive back to Harry's.

"Yeah, but a pretty thin one at that. Some guy named Stan, but she had no idea what they were talking about. Do you believe her?"

"Partially. If she was eavesdropping enough to hear the name, then she must have heard something else."

"Especially if Eric raised his voice. She said he hardly did that."

"Whatever she heard, it was important enough for her to remember that phone conversation and that name five years later," I said.

"What do we do now? How in the world do we track down this Stan guy?"

"There might be one person who knows."

"Mele Akamu?"

"I think it's time I see her again. She wanted an update. Perhaps I should give it to her in person," I said.

"Are you going to confront her about her lies?"

"Why not?"

"What about this Samson guy? You want me to come along?"

"I appreciate the offer, but she won't hurt me."

"How are you so sure?"

"For whatever reason, she's decided that I entertain her."

"Okay, but what if she grows tired of the show?" Foxx asked.

"That's a possibility. We're still only in act one, though. We have a long way to go."

Foxx said nothing.

"What did you think of her statement when she said that Eric had changed and that he wanted out of the game?" I asked.

"It contradicted what Lee Walters told us. He said Eric wanted them to go into business for themselves. Sounds to me like Eric was still very much going to be in the game if he got his way."

"Do you think people are capable of change?"

"You don't?" Foxx asked.

"No, I don't."

"I'm surprised to hear you say that."

"Why?"

"Because you of all people should know people can change. Look at you. The guy I knew in Virginia would never go back to someone like Mele Akamu and call her a liar."

"Does that mean the new me is reckless?" I asked.

"Not reckless. Definitely more daring, but not reckless. I have a theory about that."

I laughed.

"I'd love to hear this."

"The way I see it, once you landed a woman who looked like Alana, you realized anything was possible," Foxx said.

"I can't argue with that."

"No, buddy boy, you can't argue with the truth. And just think, you owe all that confidence to me."

"How do you figure?"

"Because you never would have stepped foot on this island if I hadn't practically dragged you out here."

I didn't reply. Why? Because Foxx was right again.

12

THE FATHER-IN-LAW

After getting back to Harry's, Foxx invited me inside to talk more about the case and our interview with Gracie Ito. It felt good to be able to bounce thoughts off of someone else since I usually worked alone.

We'd been at the bar for about thirty minutes when an elderly Japanese man entered. You guessed it. It was Sora Hu. He spotted us in the back-corner booth a few seconds later and walked over.

"Good afternoon."

"Mr. Hu," Foxx said.

I nodded.

"Might I have a seat?" he asked.

"Actually, Mr. Hu, I made a promise to Alana that I wouldn't get involved," I said.

"I understand, but I was actually here to see Mr. Foxx."

That was interesting, I thought, and I chided myself for assuming he'd come to Harry's for me. One could have interpreted his comment as a request for me to leave. I decided to contradict myself for the hundredth time in the past few days, and I slid over so he could sit beside me.

Sora Hu paused a moment. Then he sat down.

"Yuto told me you both owned this bar. He also said Mr. Foxx is here most days," Sora said.

"You wanted to see the father of your granddaughter," I guessed.

"That's right. Yuto never sent me a photo of Ava. I think he believed that should be left to her mother to send," Sora said.

"That's admirable. As Ava's father, I think I also have that right," Foxx said, and he slipped his phone out of his pocket.

He found a photo of Ava and handed Sora the phone.

"That's a photo of us taken last Halloween," Foxx continued.

"She's adorable," Sora said.

"Thank you," Foxx said.

"She looks just like Hani at that age. They could be twins."

"Poe frequently reminds me of how lucky I am that Ava doesn't look like me," Foxx said.

"She got Hani's looks but Foxx's personality," I said.

"You think so?" Foxx asked.

"You don't?" I asked.

Sora smiled and he handed Foxx his phone back.

"Yuto told me you two were good friends."

"What else did he say?' Foxx asked.

"That you and he didn't get along for a while but that your relationship had taken a positive turn recently," Sora said.

"That's right. I guess it has," Foxx said.

Sora turned to me.

"So, Alana asked you not to see me."

"You have to admit your sudden appearance has caught everyone off-guard," I said.

"As I was afraid it might. I thought there was a better way to handle it, but Yuto insisted. I'm certainly not blaming him. He's done so much for me."

"He also said you're leaving earlier than expected for Japan," I said.

"I've decided against that in the hope that Alana and Hani may change their minds."

"I hope you're not here to ask one of us to help with that," I said.

"No, I wanted to meet Ava's father and thank him for taking care of her. I already got the chance to thank you for doing the same with Alana."

"Why did you leave them? I can't imagine ever doing that to Ava," Foxx said.

"I'm not the same man I was. That's not an excuse. What I did can never be forgiven. Luana and I got married way too young and Alana was born before we knew it. My family was against the marriage. They didn't approve of Luana because she isn't Japanese."

It was an ironic statement, I thought, mainly because Ms. Hu had expressed to me recently that she didn't approve of me because I wasn't Japanese or Hawaiian.

"You were still together for several years. You must have loved her," I said.

"I did, but I started drinking because of the pressure my family was putting on me. My drinking got worse, which only made things more difficult between Luana and me."

"She started to resent you because your family didn't like her," Foxx guessed.

"Yes, which was more than understandable. She felt I didn't do enough to stand up for her. The fighting got worse between us."

"And that's when it got physical?" I asked.

"Luana told you about that?"

"A while back. I was surprised she confided in me," I said.

"You don't have a good relationship with Luana?" Sora asked.

Foxx laughed.

"You could say that," he said.

"That's unfortunate. I would have thought she'd understand the importance of the parents supporting the marriage."

"She must have been absent the day that lesson was taught," Foxx said.

"To answer your question, Mr. Rutherford, I struck Luana once when I was intoxicated. The truth is that I don't even remember doing it. She told me about it the next morning and asked me to leave. I did. I went back to Japan with the intention of returning to

Maui once I got myself clean. It took several months, but when I thought that I was ready to reestablish contact with my family, I felt too ashamed. As the years went by, it became harder and harder."

I didn't respond, nor did Foxx. What were we going to say? The man had just admitted to striking his wife or at least being told that he'd done so. There was no excuse for that in my book.

Sora reached into his shirt pocket and removed a business card, which he handed to me.

"This has my personal contact information. Yuto already has one. He said he would give it to Hani. Perhaps you can give this card to Alana should she change her mind."

Sora slid out of the booth and stood.

"You both seem like fine young men."

"Not so young anymore," Foxx said.

Sora smiled.

"It was a pleasure to speak with you both. If we don't see each other again, I wish you tremendous happiness."

He turned and walked out of the bar.

"What do you think of that?" Foxx asked.

"I don't know what to think."

"He doesn't seem the type to have done what he did."

"I know."

"So, he's either a changed man or he's pulling the wool over our eyes."

"What was that you said earlier today? You believe people can change?" I asked.

"Yeah, but how do you know the guy really did? It would be a hell of a thing for Hani and Alana to open up to their father again, only for him to hurt them a second time."

"My thoughts exactly."

"Are you going to tell Alana he came by, especially after she told you to stay out of it?" Foxx asked.

"I have to tell her. I can't keep something like that a secret."

"Good luck, buddy. Let me know when you do that so I can stay here at Harry's."

"I don't blame you one bit."

I said goodbye to Foxx and made the short drive back to Kaana-pali. I'd been at home for about an hour when Alana got back. As soon as she walked through the door, I could tell she was in a foul mood.

"Keeping secrets from me again?" she asked, and she tossed her car keys on the kitchen counter.

I searched my mind for how she might have learned about her father's meeting with me. I didn't think Foxx would have told her, so my brain turned up an empty list of tattletales.

"I'm not sure what to say. Who told you?" I asked.

Alana got this confused look on her face.

Then she asked, "What are you talking about? Josh Parrish told me."

"Josh?"

"You know, about your little meeting with him at the coffee shop. Why didn't you say anything about it?" she asked, and she walked into the living room and sat on the sofa beside me.

"It was when you were deep into the wedding planning. I didn't want to be a distraction. Besides, it didn't seem that big of a deal."

"Not a big deal? He said he told you to butt out of his case."

"If I had a dollar for every time someone told me to butt out," I said.

"It was a bit of a surprise that he'd act like that."

"How so?"

"I've known Josh for a long time. He didn't strike me as the type to get all territorial like that."

"Maybe it's born out of insecurity. He's just starting out as a detec-tive. I was nothing but polite to him. I didn't do my usual pushing back out of respect to your working relationship with him."

"When has that ever stopped you before?" she asked.

"A true statement, but in this case, I am without guilt."

Alana paused a moment.

Then she said, "You didn't think I was going to mention the meeting with Josh. You thought I was talking about something else."

"Not much gets by you, does it?"

I reached into my pocket and produced the business card that Sora had given me. I handed Alana the card.

"I thought we agreed that you wouldn't see him," Alana said.

"Not my fault. He showed up at Harry's to meet Ava's father."

"He wanted to talk to Foxx?"

"Yes, and to thank him for helping to take care of Ava. I happened to be there with Foxx discussing the Eric Ellis case. Your father insisted on telling us why he left. Check that, he explained his shame and embarrassment about his past behavior. He asked me to give you the card. I told him I couldn't be involved."

"But you took the card anyway."

"Yes, I did."

Alana stood and walked back into the kitchen where she deposited the business card into the garbage can. Then she opened the refrigerator and removed a bottle of wine.

"Would you like a glass?" she asked.

"No, thank you."

She poured herself a glass, then put the wine bottle back into the refrigerator and returned to the sofa.

"Any more news on Hani and Yuto?" I asked.

"No, nothing. I don't know how to interpret that other than Hani's still trying to make up her mind."

"Are you going to call her later?"

"Probably. I'll let you know what she says."

Alana stood again.

"I'm going to change out of these work clothes," she continued.

"Sounds good. I was just about to head outside to the pool."

"Maybe I'll join you later."

Alana turned and headed upstairs to the master bedroom.

"Maui, come on boy," I called.

He appeared from under the sofa a moment later.

"Want to get in the pool?"

The dog wagged his tail and he followed me outside. I jumped in the swimming pool and pushed his raft to the edge. The dog took a flying leap and landed on the middle of the raft. His momentum carried the raft across the pool and the dog barked three times, a sure sign of his delight.

We stayed outside for at least two hours, but Alana never joined us. I assumed she was passing the time either speaking with Hani or watching television. When I finally walked inside, I didn't see Alana in the living room or the kitchen. I walked upstairs and found her asleep on the bed. Stress does many things to the body. It can certainly leave you feeling exhausted.

I walked back downstairs and went into the kitchen. I grabbed a Negra Modelo from the refrigerator. I popped the top and opened the trash can to throw it away. The trash bag was full, and I knew I needed to empty it.

There was one thing odd, though, that I noticed. Sora's business card should have been on top of the trash pile. It wasn't. Alana must have retrieved it before going upstairs. I thought her actions, if I was even right about the card, spoke volumes about the turmoil inside her. I wished I could help, but I didn't know what to say or do.

13

I DIDN'T SEE THAT COMING

THE NEXT MORNING, I SENT MARA A TEXT AND ASKED HER TO SET UP A meeting with Mele Akamu. Mrs. Akamu had demanded updates every few days. I figured I might as well give her one in person. It would also allow me to view her reaction when I confronted her about Eric Ellis being beaten half to death by Samson. I was upfront with Mara and told her things could get heated, but she said she still wanted to be there.

You may be wondering if Alana brought up her father in the morning. She didn't, mainly because she didn't get a chance to. She'd gotten up earlier than usual again and had already left for work by the time I climbed out of bed. I did something that I'm not proud of, but I try to always be honest in these tales. I opened the drawer to Alana's nightstand and saw Sora's business card inside, confirming my suspicions that Alana had removed it from the trash.

I completed my morning swim and jog, running an extra mile in an attempt to distract myself from my problems. It didn't work. Mara phoned me right as I was climbing out of the shower and informed me that we had a meeting with Mele Akamu at eleven, the same time as our previous encounter.

As I'm sure you expected, I played more jazz on the drive across

Maui. Sonny Rollins was the artist of choice, and I got through his songs, "St. Thomas," "Namely You," "You Don't Know What Love Is," "Blues for Philly Joe," and "I Want to Be Happy."

I arrived at the Akamu home about ten minutes early. Mara was already there. Anxious, were we?

"Good morning. Sonny Rollins by any chance?" she asked as she climbed out of her car.

"Good morning, Mara. How do you always know what I'm playing?"

I hopped out of my BMW and shut the door.

"I guess I listen to more music than I realized."

"I shall make it my new mission to stump you one of these times. Anything new to report?"

"I was hoping you were going to tell me something new," she said.

"Nothing that helps Mrs. Akamu."

"Do you have the feeling we're working for another guilty client?"

"How have you dealt with that in the past? You've been a lawyer longer than I've been doing this investigative thing. How do you handle it?"

"Everyone deserves the right to the best defense possible."

Yes, it was a cliched answer and I was hoping for something a bit more helpful from Mara. But in hindsight, what else was she going to say?

We walked to the front door and rang the bell. Samson answered a few moments later.

"Good morning, Ms. Winters, Mr. Rutherford. Mrs. Akamu is expecting you."

He led us to the back of the house where we found Mele Akamu in her normal seat by the fire pit. This time Samson stayed within earshot. Was there a reason for that? I didn't know.

"Well, Mr. Rutherford, what do you have to report?" Mrs. Akamu asked in her calm and measured voice.

I could have danced around for a while and told her about my interviews with Lee Walters and Gracie Ito, but what would have been the point? A picture is worth a thousand words, as they like to say.

I removed my phone from my pocket and pulled up the photo Gracie had emailed me. I stepped closer to Mele Akamu and handed her the phone.

"You specifically told me that Samson didn't locate Eric Ellis. It seems that you were wrong. Either Samson lied to you or you lied to me," I said.

Mele Akamu glanced at the phone a moment. Then she handed it back to me. Her expression never altered one bit.

"Would you have taken my case if I'd told you what Samson did to Eric?" Mrs. Akamu asked.

"Probably not."

"Then why are you asking me an insignificant question? I told you what I needed to tell you."

"Sorry, but I'm not buying that as an excuse."

"Who gave you that photo? I assume it was Gracie Ito."

"She told me that Eric had a meeting with you the night he disappeared."

"There was no meeting, I assure you. Eric might have been coming here to see me on his own. He never arrived."

"Forgive me if I have a hard time believing you," I said.

"Let me ask you a question, Mr. Rutherford. Why would I have ordered Eric's death after having him beaten? Why not just kill him from the start?"

"Perhaps he refused to get the message, despite your butler's considerable skills in hurting people."

"A fair argument, but that's not what happened," Mrs. Akamu said.

"Is it possible your grandson ordered his death?"

Mrs. Akamu laughed.

"No one would have followed it. Nothing happens around here without my direction."

"Yes, but Tavii is a member of the Akamu family. He will be the one to inherit the crown, so to speak. Maybe someone wanted to stay on his good side."

"Tavii will only inherit what I allow him to inherit, and no one on my staff would be foolish enough to believe otherwise. That is true today. It was true five years ago."

"Why did you fire Lee Walters but not hurt him too?" I asked.

"You have made some progress interviewing people. Good. I always liked Lee and I didn't think he had anything to do with Eric's plan to blackmail me. Still, one must be careful. I couldn't take the chance by allowing him to continue under my employ. I'm sure you've heard the phrase, cut your losses. Lee made the wise decision that it would be better for him to pursue a new path than try to come after me. I would think that my compassion for Lee would have convinced you that I didn't have Eric killed. If I was that ruthless, why kill one and not the other?"

It was a good point, but I said nothing.

"One more thing," Mrs. Akamu continued. "Allow me to put forth a hypothetical story. Let's suppose that there was another man under my employ who tried to betray me. Let's also assume this happened many years before Eric's disappearance. Perhaps I had one of my men rid me of this betrayer. Maybe I also had them take this individual and deposit him in the ocean several miles from shore. After such a successful endeavor, why would I then be so foolish as to bury Eric's body on the island where it could eventually be found? Do you think that little of me, Mr. Rutherford?"

"Let's move on to something else," I said.

"Good."

"Gracie Ito informed me that she overheard Eric arguing with a man on the phone the day he died. She said Eric called this person Stan, but Eric refused to tell her who he was and what the argument was about. Do you know anyone by that name?" I asked.

I saw Samson look at Mele Akamu out of the corner of my eye. She obviously did know Stan. Would she admit it, though?

"Ms. Ito said nothing else about that phone call?" Mrs. Akamu asked.

"No, only that Eric raised his voice, which she claimed he rarely did."

"That is true. He was always calm, at least around me. It was one of his qualities that I admired," Mrs. Akamu said.

"Do you know this man?" Mara asked, finally getting into the conversation.

"Yes, I know him. His name is Stan Cross. He thinks he's a business competitor of mine," Mrs. Akamu said.

"He thinks? I don't understand," Mara said.

"Stan Cross has been after me for years. He's never gotten close. I always suspected that Eric might have tried to sell the information on my business to him. Mr. Rutherford just confirmed that."

"Yet Eric was arguing with this man. Perhaps he changed his mind about working with Stan Cross," I said.

"Or they were arguing over the price Stan would pay Eric. That's the more likely scenario. Stan is well known for making promises he doesn't intend to keep. I would have thought Eric would have known that," Mrs. Akamu said.

"Is Stan Cross still in business?" I asked.

"Yes," Mrs. Akamu said.

"If Eric originally agreed to sell the information to him but then backed out, it would be a powerful motive for Stan Cross to have killed Eric," I said.

"It could also explain the discrepancies of how the body was disposed of," Mara added.

I was about to ask for Stan Cross' whereabouts when I heard the backdoor to Mrs. Akamu's house open. I turned and saw Detective Josh Parrish and four uniformed police officers walking toward us.

Samson, the elderly butler, started for them. Did he intend to take them all on at once?

"Samson, it's okay. Let's hear what the good detective has to say," Mrs. Akamu said.

Samson stopped in his tracks. Then he walked back to Mrs. Akamu and stood beside her chair. He was loyal, I'll give him that.

"Mr. Rutherford, imagine seeing you here," Detective Parrish said.

"Hello, Detective," I said.

Detective Parrish turned to Mele Akamu.

"Mele Akamu, you and Samson Opunui are under arrest for the murder of Eric Ellis," Detective Parrish said.

He then proceeded to read them their Miranda rights as two of the uniformed officers moved toward them with handcuffs. One of the officers tried to yank Mele Akamu to her feet, only for Samson to level him with a punch to the throat that was so fast I barely saw it. One of the other officers pointed his gun at Samson, while two more restrained him and put him in handcuffs. What was Mele Akamu doing during this struggle? She was smiling.

Mele Akamu stood on her own and turned to Mara.

"Ms. Winters, please contact Ruben Dalton for me and let him know what's happened. Please also tell him that I wish for you to officially join our legal team."

"I will," Mara said.

One of the officers, apparently learning the lesson of his co-worker, politely asked Mrs. Akamu to put her hands behind her back, which she did. He then placed her in handcuffs.

"Cuff him too," Detective Parrish said, and he nodded at me.

"What are the charges?" Mara asked.

"Obstruction of justice," Detective Parrish said, and he walked up to me. "I told you to stay away from my case. Maybe this will show you that I'm not playing games."

I said nothing.

"That charge will never stick," Mara said.

"Maybe not, but he'll still have the pleasure of spending the night in jail."

"I'll have him out within the hour," Mara said.

"Perhaps, but that won't stop me from enjoying hauling his hand-cuffed ass to jail," Detective Parrish said.

You may be wondering if the detective's harsh words enraged me. They didn't. A bully's main desire is to get a reaction out of you, and I was determined not to provide that. Besides, I knew Mara was correct. The charges would be tossed, and it wasn't like this was the first time I'd gone to jail. It probably wouldn't be the last.

"I'll see you shortly, Mr. Rutherford," Mara said.

"Thank you."

"I'll also phone your wife."

"No need. She'll find out soon enough."

The officer tugged at my restraints and practically dragged me back toward the house. I saw Samson in front of me. He was being handled even rougher than I was. The police allowed Mrs. Akamu to walk without keeping a hand on her.

The meeting with Mele Akamu had certainly not gone the way I expected it to. The question was, where did this little adventure go next?

14

MY PROTECTOR

Unfortunately, I can't give you a description of the music I listened to on the way from Maui's upcountry to the police station. The officers refused my request to turn on the radio. Just kidding, I didn't ask that.

I recognized one of the officers from previous cases of mine. I knew he had a couple of kids and I inquired as to how they were doing. He said they were well. All in all, it was about as pleasant of a drive to a booking as one can get.

As we pulled into the parking lot, I saw that Mara hadn't followed my request and had instead phoned Alana. She was waiting for us outside the building. Our three vehicles pulled to a stop. Detective Parrish was in his own car. I was in another with two of the four officers. Mele Akamu and Samson were in the third car with the remaining officers.

Alana bypassed my car and headed straight for Detective Parrish. Fortunately, I heard the exchange since one of the cops pulled me out of the police car before she reached the detective.

"What the hell do you think you're doing?" Alana asked.

"This is a conflict of interest for you. I'm sure you know that."

I won't repeat what Alana said immediately after his comment. I will give you one clue. She told him where he could put his claim of a conflict of interest.

"He has the legal right to talk to whoever he wants," she said.

"I don't see it that way."

Alana turned to the officer beside me.

"Release him," she said.

The cop looked at Detective Parrish.

"Don't even think about it," Detective Parrish said.

Alana stepped closer to him.

"Listen to me, you smug asshole, you have no idea how difficult I can make things for you. Is this really the hill you want to die on?"

Detective Parrish didn't immediately respond.

I started counting in my head. One, two, three, four.

"Release him," Detective Parrish said.

I hadn't thought I'd get past two.

The police officer, the one whose kids I'd asked about, whispered in my ear as he removed the handcuffs.

"Sorry about all this," he said.

"Don't worry about it," I said.

Alana turned from Detective Parrish and walked up to me.

"I assume your car is still at Mele Akamu's house."

"Yes."

"Let's go get it."

We started to leave when Mele Akamu called out to Alana.

"Detective Hu."

Alana stopped and turned to her.

"Yes, Mrs. Akamu."

"It's a pleasure to finally meet Mr. Rutherford's wife. You're everything I heard you were and then some."

"Thank you, ma'am."

Alana looked at Detective Parrish again. For a moment, I thought she was going to extend him the middle finger, maybe even the middle finger from both hands. She didn't. Instead, she gave me a quick, "Let's get out of here."

We walked across the parking lot and climbed into her car. She didn't say a word until we got onto Hana Highway.

"I can't believe that guy. What in the world was he thinking?"

"Interesting question. I've been trying to figure out his angle since that coffee shop meeting," I said.

"Come to any conclusions?"

"He reminds me a bit of a co-worker of mine from the architecture days. The guy always tried to establish dominance from the start. If you pushed back, then you became enemy number one. I always thought it came from a place of insecurity."

"Josh was always such a nice guy. What the hell happened?"

"Give someone a little power and their true personality emerges."

"I can't believe I allowed myself to get that heated. I wanted to punch him. No one locks up my husband but me," she said.

I waited for her to laugh. She didn't.

"No one locks up your husband but you? Are you referencing some type of bedroom bondage act I don't know about?" I asked.

"No, I have no idea what I meant by that."

"Ah, now it makes sense."

"It does? I'd appreciate it if you'd enlighten me."

"I expect you were yelling more at your father than you were at Detective Parrish. You have a lot of feelings bottled up," I said.

"No, you're wrong. I was yelling at them both. They're both jerks."

"Well then, I guess my diagnosis was incorrect."

"Not completely."

"Any idea what damning evidence Detective Parrish has on Mele Akamu and Samson?"

"I made some inquiries after Mara's call. Apparently, Josh found an eyewitness to the murder. I don't know who it is."

Mele Akamu's arrest certainly wasn't a surprise, but I hadn't seen it coming so quickly.

"No comment?" Alana asked.

"Sorry, just processing."

"Looks like your work for her is over. I doubt she'll be able to get herself out of this one."

"She made some compelling points when I spoke with her this morning," I said, and I told Alana about Mele Akamu's argument that she'd never be so dumb as to bury the body on the island.

"She really gave you that hypothetical argument about dumping a man's body at sea?" Alana asked.

"Yes, but she didn't need to. I'd already thought of that idea before, especially since people have tried to get rid of me that same way."

"Poe, you're missing the point. I think she just admitted to committing a murder."

"It's nothing that would hold up, especially without a body."

"I know that, but she still must trust you to tell you that story."

"Trust me? No. She lied to me about her butler from the start. She told me he didn't lay a hand on Eric Ellis and then I found photographic proof that he did."

"Okay, but why is she trying so hard to convince you that she didn't have Eric Ellis killed? She doesn't need you to come up with other suspects. She and her lawyer can name anyone they want."

"We need to find out who that eyewitness is," I said.

"I'll work on it when I get back to the office."

"Why am I back to thinking Mele Akamu might not have done it?"

"Forget what I told you earlier when I said your work for her is done. It sounds like it's just getting started."

"Is there any way you can get me the name of the guy who found Eric Ellis' body?" I asked.

"Ordinarily I would tell you to go through Josh out of respect to him, but not now. I'll have the name by the end of the day."

A pissed-off Detective Alana Hu can be a powerful ally. Detective Parrish, for whatever his reason, had made a bad play.

We were silent for the rest of the drive. Alana was probably consumed with thoughts on her father. Me? I kept flip-flopping on whether or not I thought Mele Akamu was guilty.

By the time we arrived at her house, I decided the only way to know for sure was to continue with my investigation. Was I worried that Detective Parrish would arrest me again? No, I wasn't. I thought my intimidating spouse had put an end to that threat. I made a mental note to buy Alana flowers on the way home. After all, one must show appreciation for anyone who keeps them out of jail.

I thanked Alana for the drive, and we agreed to regroup later in the day. I retrieved my car, selected a playlist of songs by the legendary jazz musician, Charlie Parker, and pointed the little BMW in the direction of Kaanapali and the safe confines of my home. I'd only been driving a few minutes, though, when I decided to make a quick detour to Guy Livingston's abode.

My brief moment under arrest made me think of him. I'd promised to look into his case, and never let it be said that Poe isn't a man of his word. I found his Kihei-based home easily enough. He wasn't kidding when he'd said it was small. That's not a judgment on my part, rather a description of what his place looked like. The tiny home was jammed between two others that didn't look much bigger.

I parked my roadster in front of his house. As I walked to his front door, I saw a blonde-haired teenaged girl, maybe fifteen or sixteen, washing a Toyota pickup truck in her driveway. There was a surfboard leaning against the garage door a few feet away.

"Nice board," I said.

"Do you surf?"

I laughed.

"I've managed to stand up a few times, but I don't think you can call that surfing. My wife on the other hand..."

"I'd ask if you were with the police, but you're not dressed like them," she said.

"No, I'm not. I imagine you've seen a lot of cops coming by lately. How well did you know the Livingstons?"

"I spoke to Mrs. Livingston from time to time, but I didn't know her well."

"What about Guy Livingston?" I asked.

"He seemed nice, but we didn't really say much."

"Any chance you saw anyone go into their house other than them?"

"The cops asked me that after Mrs. Livingston was killed. I never saw anyone over there but them."

"Were you at home when she was killed? Did you hear the gunshots?"

"No, I was at work. My parents own a surfing school."

"You teach tourists how to surf?"

"Try to. It doesn't usually work."

"Well, hopefully the tips are good," I said.

"Sometimes yes, sometimes no."

"Thanks for your help. I'm Poe by the way."

"I'm Kari."

"Pleasure to meet you, Kari."

I excused myself and continued to the house. I punched the four-digit security code into the keypad on the front door. I heard the lock disengage and then let myself into the house.

The layout was as Guy Livingston had described. The front door opened to reveal an open floor plan, which consisted of a small living room and an even smaller kitchen beyond that. There was a sliding glass door at the far end, and I could see a lanai on the other side.

I walked through the living room and proceeded down a short hallway. There was a bathroom on the right side and then a single bedroom after that. The bedroom door was already open. I looked inside and saw a queen-size bed with a nightstand on each side. It was about fifteen feet from the doorway to the nightstand.

If the killer, presumably Guy Livingston, had been standing by the bed, and Mrs. Livingston had been a few paces inside the room, it would have been a shot someone could have made with their eyes closed.

I left the bedroom and walked back to the sliding glass door. The door was locked, and the Livingstons had placed a thick wooden dowel rod between the edge of the door and the wall as a secondary lock. It would have been impossible to get through without breaking the glass. That meant the killer had to have come into the house through a window or the front door. I checked all of the windows next. They were all locked and none looked tampered with.

There were two possibilities. Option one was that Guy Livingston had come home, walked into the bedroom and retrieved his gun. He then shot and killed his wife with it. Possibility number two was that an unknown person came through the front door and headed to the bedroom because they knew a gun was in the nightstand. They then waited for Mrs. Livingston to return so they could kill her.

That also meant the killer knew the code to the keypad. If you'll recall, Guy Livingston said only he and his wife knew the four-digit number.

I know what you're thinking. Things were not looking good for Guy Livingston. You would be right.

15

DOG DAYS

That evening, Alana gave me the name of the man who'd found Eric Ellis while walking his dog. She even got his address for me. The man's name was Daniel Davis and he lived in an apartment complex off Hana Highway in Paia. I would have thought he lived in Haiku since it was closer to the old pineapple fields where the body was buried. But he could have gone for a short ride down the coast and then decided to stop and take his dog for a stroll. It wouldn't be the first time I'd seen that happen. I even did it several times a year with my own dog.

Alana wasn't able to discover the name of the eyewitness who'd pointed to Mele Akamu and Samson for the murder, but she promised that she'd look into it again in the morning. I figured Mara would also be a good resource for that since she was apparently now on Mele Akamu's defense team. The defendant had a right to face his or her accuser. The police would have to name the witness at some point.

You may be wondering if there were fireworks when Alana got back to the station after driving me to my car. There weren't. She said she never came across Detective Parrish since he was busy interrogating his two suspects. Alana did say the office was abuzz with gossip about her argument with her fellow detective over yours truly. I felt a little bad for dragging my wife into my disagreement with Detective Parrish. I made a mental note to reach out to him in a few days and try to broker some kind of peace treaty.

The next morning, I spent about an hour thinking about the nature of eyewitnesses, especially as they pertained to this specific crime. My mental exercise came at the same time as my morning swim and jog. I find those incredibly productive moments to ponder over my investigations.

Most people have heard how eyewitnesses are often unreliable. There have even been university studies done to prove this point. In one particular study I read, ten people witnessed a staged crime and those same ten people gave ten different physical descriptions of the suspect. Some saw him as tall. Others said he was average height. Some saw dark hair while others saw a blonde man. One person even thought that the man was Asian, while the others said he was Caucasian.

There was another problem I had with the idea of an eyewitness to this particular murder. I didn't see how Mele Akamu would be so reckless as to commit the act where others could potentially see her. That brought up two options in my mind.

Option one was that the eyewitness was someone in her inner circle who knew about the murder and had decided, for whatever reason, to come forward now. The second option was that Mele Akamu was innocent and someone was trying to frame her. Again, a likely suspect could have been an inside person who was making a power grab for her throne.

Either way, I didn't see how this could be some random person who accidentally saw the murder, but I've been known to get things wrong from time to time. The bottom line was that I needed the name of that witness.

After spending the morning performing my mental sleuthing exercise, I climbed into my convertible and made the short drive to Harry's where I met Foxx in the parking lot. We got into his Lexus SUV and drove to Paia, one of my favorite little towns on the island. I made Foxx stop so we could grab a shave ice. I selected a tasty blend of grape and strawberry, while Foxx stood off to the side and wondered how a grown man could be so addicted to these things. I don't see how he could question that. They're delicious, and I'm sure you'd say the same thing if you've had one before.

Once my craving was satisfied, we drove all of sixty seconds to the apartment complex. We found one empty parking spot in the back of the lot and climbed out of the Lexus. It was a relatively small apartment building, maybe twelve units in all, with six on the bottom floor and the other half on the second. Alana had also given me the make, model, and license plate for Daniel Davis' car, which I spotted in the lot, a good sign that he was home.

We took the exterior stairway to the second floor and knocked on the door for apartment eight. A tall man, somewhere in height between Foxx and me, answered a few seconds later. I guessed his age at around thirty. He had black hair that was long enough to cover his eyes.

He pushed his hair away from his face after opening the door. I had at least thirty pounds on the fellow. He was so skinny I could easily see his Adam's apple protruding from his neck. He kind of reminded me of Ichabod Crane, the famous literary character who was chased by the Headless Horseman.

"Can I help you?" he asked in a deep voice that didn't seem to match his body.

"Yes, my name is Edgar Rutherford. This is Doug Foxx. We're consultants for the police department. We'd like to ask you a few follow-up questions regarding the man's body you found while walking your dog."

Daniel Davis hesitated a long moment. Then he nodded and stepped back so we could enter.

"I'm not sure what else I can tell you. I told the police everything that happened."

"Understandable, but sometimes certain details can pop into your mind a few days later," I said.

Daniel Davis led us over to the sofa, which was covered with a few surfing magazines and a crinkled bag of pretzels. I looked around the room as he removed the items so we could sit down. I saw a couple of surfboards leaning against a wall. A skateboard was turned upside down and was sitting on the floor beside the surfboards.

The other walls were covered with posters of giant waves, as well as some images of specific surfers who I assumed were on the pro circuit. I didn't recognize any of them, which doesn't mean they aren't famous on the islands. I simply know little to nothing about the surfing community. There was a tiny kitchenette at the back of the apartment and a hallway off to the right, which probably led to the bedroom and bathroom.

There was one thing I didn't see, and that was a dog. Furthermore, I didn't see any items that would indicate a dog even lived in the apartment. There were no dog toys, no dog dish, and no dog bed. I looked on the sofa as I was sitting down, but I didn't see any animal hair. Granted, some dogs, like mine, don't shed.

"Can you tell us again how you found the body?" Foxx asked as he sat beside me.

I must admit that Foxx was really getting the hang of this investigator thing. He was going to give me a run for my money in no time.

"Really? I've gone over this no less than ten times," Davis said.

"If you don't mind, please go over it once more," Foxx said.

"I took my dog for a walk off Pe'ahi Road. He kept tugging on the leash and whining, so I let him go. He ran into the fields and I followed him. That's when he found that guy's body."

"Do you normally let your dog off the leash like that?" Foxx asked.

"Sometimes. He needs his exercise and I like to let him run."

"What kind of dog is it?" I asked.

"I'm not sure. Maybe a lab or something like that."

"Where is the dog now?" I asked.

Daniel Davis paused a moment. It was maybe only a second or two, but it was long enough to get my attention.

"He's at the vet."

"What for?" I asked.

"Surgery. I'm getting him neutered."

"How old is he?" I asked.

"Five. Why all the questions about my dog?"

"We're dog lovers," Foxx said.

"What's his name by the way?" I asked.

"Fred," Davis said.

"Great name. Simple and easy to remember. But you're right. That's more than enough questions about Fred. Let's get back to the unfortunate discovery you made. Has anyone come by to see you since you reported the body to the police?" I asked.

"Just you guys."

"The man's identity was established as Eric Ellis. Did you know him?" Foxx asked.

"Why would I know him?" Davis asked.

"Can you describe what the scene looked like?" I asked.

"What do you mean?"

"Was most of the body uncovered or just some of it?" I asked.

"Just his arm, part of which was in my dog's mouth. To tell you the truth, it was kind of hard to tell what it was. I thought it was an animal bone at first. Then I saw the guy's hand."

"I'm sure that was quite upsetting," I said.

"Yeah, you could say that. I got my dog out of there and then called the cops. Look, I don't know anything more than that."

"Thanks for your time, Mr. Davis, and good luck with your dog's surgery. I'm sure he'll pull through fine," I said.

"Thanks."

We stood and Daniel Davis walked us to the door.

"Thank you again," I said.

We exited the apartment and headed for the stairs.

"Well that was a giant waste of time. Why did you want to see that guy anyway?" Foxx asked.

I ignored his question. We got to the bottom of the staircase and continued toward Foxx's SUV.

"You're not going to answer me?" Foxx asked.

"Sorry, I wanted to get farther from the building. I didn't know what we'd find, but I had an inkling something was up."

"What do you mean?"

"A theory I had this morning. Either Mele Akamu killed Eric Ellis or she didn't. One of those statements must be true and one must be a lie."

"Of course. What's your point?"

"If Mele Akamu didn't do it, then someone is setting her up."

"You mean the eyewitness?" Foxx asked.

"Maybe."

"Daniel Davis doesn't really have a dog, does he?"

"What makes you say that?" I asked.

"I didn't see any sign that a dog lived there. I can't tell you how many times I tripped over your dog's toys when you two lived with me."

"There was something else. He said his dog was getting neutered, but he also said the dog is five. Most people get a male dog neutered when they're much younger."

"Maybe he just adopted the dog," Foxx suggested.

"Maybe. Let's head back to Harry's. The drive will give me time to make some phone calls," I said.

"Who are you calling?"

"You'll see."

We climbed into Foxx's car and I pulled my phone out of my pocket. I googled veterinary clinics and found five that were fairly close to Paia. The first one that came up was called the Maui Veterinary Clinic, not the most original name, but it got the job done. I pressed the phone icon link on the website and a receptionist answered a few moments later.

"Good morning, Maui Veterinary Clinic. This is Teri. How may I help you?"

"Hi, Teri. This is Daniel Davis. I'm calling to check on my dog's surgery. His name is Fred. Is he out yet?" I asked.

"I'm sorry, Mr. Davis. I don't have a dog named Fred for today's surgery. I suspect you called the wrong clinic."

"You're right. I hit the wrong link. My apologies."

"No problem. Have a good day."

"You too," I said, and I ended the call.

"No Fred?" Foxx asked.

"Nope. Let's try the others."

I repeated my gimmick four more times and struck out with each one. I even called two additional clinics that were located on the opposite side of the island. I slipped my phone back into my pocket and turned to Foxx.

"Well, I called every vet clinic on Maui. Unless Daniel Davis is getting some back-alley surgery for his dog, he lied to us."

"If he lied about the dog, then he had to have lied about the way he found the body," Foxx said.

"Here's the next question. Who put him up to it? This helps us focus our investigation. We were looking at who might have killed Eric Ellis. Now we need to discover who benefits the most from Mele Akamu going to prison."

"I don't know, Poe. I don't think this lets Mele Akamu off the hook for killing Eric Ellis."

"No, it doesn't," I said.

"You know, there's a giant hole in your theory."

"What's that?"

"Eric Ellis has been in the ground for five years. If someone was setting Mele Akamu up, then they started the con job years ago. That's a hell of a long game to play."

16

THE WEDDING PLANNER

FOXX AND I DROVE BACK TO HARRY'S. FOXX INVITED ME IN FOR A DRINK and we spent the next hour debating what we'd learned in our interview with Daniel Davis. We both agreed that Daniel had probably lied about owning a dog. Although Foxx thought there was a harmless explanation for the lie, my mind went to more nefarious theories. Who was right? I had no idea.

I was about to drive home when I received a phone call from Hani. She told me that she'd just gotten a phone call from a wedding planner who wanted to view our event space in Wailea. Apparently, her clients were unhappy with the places they'd viewed, and their wedding planner had told them about our venue as a last resort.

I certainly didn't like my business being viewed that way, but I agreed to meet the couple and their planner since Hani said she was still too distraught to leave her house. I made a quick U-turn and pointed the little silver car east.

It gave me an opportunity to listen to Dave Brubeck, another legend in the jazz world. I got through his songs, "Take Five," "St. Louis Blues," "To Us Is Given," "Weep No More," and "Autumn in Washington Square." The last song of his that I listened to, "I May Be Wrong," perfectly summed up how I was feeling about the Eric Ellis case. I was certain of nothing except the fact that I didn't know what in the world was going on.

I eventually pulled into the parking space for my Wailea venue and found the happy couple (actually, they didn't look all that happy) and their surly wedding planner. Was the wedding planner surly because of the couple or was the couple upset because the wedding planner was surly? Perhaps it was both.

The wedding planner, whose name I'm intentionally withholding, greeted me with a curt, "It's about time. Do you know how long we've been waiting?"

I was tempted to answer her by turning around and immediately climbing back into my BMW for the return drive to Kaanapali. But I am a team player, when I want to be, and I didn't want to lose the potential commission for Hani.

The end result of the tour was that the couple seemed to like the space, at least they said they did, but the wedding planner replied, "We can do better."

Again, I was tempted to be nasty right back, but then I looked past her to the ocean in the distance. The water was one of the most gorgeous shades of blue I'd ever seen, and I came to the happy conclusion that there was no way this person was going to ruin my mood.

The couple thanked me for my time. The wedding planner did not, and they headed out the door. I didn't immediately walk for my car too. Instead, I went onto the back deck that overlooked the beach. It was a reliable place to catch a nice breeze, and I decided to hang out for a while and enjoy the weather and the view.

I was about to leave when I heard the door open behind me. I turned and saw Hani walking toward me. She joined me on the deck a moment later.

"Change your mind about meeting the clients?" I asked.

Hani got this nervous look on her face.

"They haven't gotten here yet?"

"They left about ten minutes ago."

"Thank God, I hate dealing with that woman."

"Oh, so you willingly threw me to the wolves?"

"Poe, you deal with murderers all the time. I figured you could handle a grumpy wedding planner. Besides, I'm just not in the mood. Did they book the place?" Hani asked.

"That's a big, fat no. The wedding planner said they could do better than our place."

"She really said that?"

"Yep."

"Well, she can go..."

Yes, I trailed off the words to save you from hearing what my sweet sister-in-law said. But I'm sure you can guess what it was.

"If you didn't come to see the couple, then why are you here?" I asked.

"I need a fresh perspective, one that doesn't belong to my mother or sister."

"I assume this is about your own wedding."

"Partly."

"Then the other part has to be your father."

"You have to promise me that what I'm about to say goes no further than this room. You can't even tell Alana."

"Come on, Hani. You can't ask that of me. I don't want to lie to Alana."

"You don't have to lie to her. Just don't mention anything."

I know I've posed this philosophical question before, but is an omission of a fact also a lie?

"What is it?" I asked.

"Not until you promise me."

"Look, I already know what it is, so let's just start talking about it."

"You can't possibly know."

"You went and saw your father," I said.

Hani looked at me as if I'd just pulled the proverbial rabbit out of the hat.

"How did you know? Did he call you?"

"I guessed because you specifically said a moment ago that you wanted a perspective that didn't involve a Hu woman. Then you asked me to promise not to tell them. What else was it going to be?"

"Why do you always have to be such a know-it-all?"

"Sorry, I wasn't trying to be."

Hani said nothing.

"Well, are you going to tell me the details?" I asked.

"I saw him this morning."

"What made you change your mind?"

"Yuto texted me my father's phone number the day after the party. I called my father late last night. We met at the Whaler's Village in Kaanapali."

It was a crowded place with lots of people so Hani could easily walk away. Had she been worried her father would do something? I didn't know and I didn't ask.

"How did things go?"

"Fine."

"That's it? Just fine?"

"He apologized for staying away for so long. He explained to me why he didn't come back sooner. I don't know, Poe. I don't think there's anything he could have said that would make up for what he did."

"Probably not. Are you going to see him again?" I asked.

"He wants to meet Ava."

"What are you going to do?"

"I'm not sure. There's a part of me that wants Ava to meet her grandfather, but I know it would hurt my mother. She might not ever forgive me."

I didn't think Hani was wrong in that assessment.

"Maybe it's too soon to do that. Perhaps you should work up to it," I suggested.

"I don't know if I'm going to even see him again."

"Do you want to see him again?" I asked.

"That's the problem. That's why I wanted to talk to you. I do think I want to see him again, but I'm scared it will destroy my relationship with Mom and Alana."

"I can't speak for your mother, but I feel pretty confident that I know how Alana would react."

"Yeah, she'd be furious," Hani said.

"I don't agree. I think she'd understand."

"Does Alana want to see him too?"

"I don't know. She said she doesn't, but that might change."

"Is that all she's said?"

"Pretty much. She's avoiding the topic, which I understand. I've tried not to press it."

Hani said nothing.

"You're also feeling guilty about Yuto, aren't you?" I asked.

"Why would I feel guilty about him? He's the one that pulled this stunt, not me."

"Yes, but you also know that he had the best of intentions."

"I thought you were on my side."

"I am. I've never said this before, but I think of you as my younger sister. I'm always going to look out for you."

"But you just said I feel guilty. You must blame me for something," Hani said.

"No, but Yuto told me that you expressed to him more than once that you wished your father could walk you down the aisle. He was trying to make you happy. Yes, he shouldn't have handled things the way he did, but he did his best."

Hani looked around our wedding space.

"I'm supposed to get married here in just a few days."

"Does that mean you're still going through with it?" I asked.

"I haven't decided yet."

"When was the last time you spoke with Yuto?"

"At the party."

"You should call him. It's not fair to keep him in the dark. Talk things out. I'm sure it will help."

"I don't know what to do," she said.

"Do you want to marry Yuto? It's really that simple."

"But it's not. We're talking about doing something that's supposed to last the rest of our lives. How can I go into something like that when I'm still angry with him?"

"Then postpone the wedding. Tell him you need more time to think things through," I said.

"What about the guests?"

"Who cares about them?"

"My father said he met with you and Foxx at Harry's. He actually said he liked Foxx. Can you believe that?"

"Well, that's another giant mark against him in your book, isn't it?" I asked, and I laughed.

"That's not helping."

"It's not such a bad thing, Hani. Better that at least one of Ava's grandparents likes her father. I don't have to tell you how important it is that you guys at least try to get along. Ava's relationship with Foxx is going to help dictate her relationship with every guy she meets. He's her example of how a man is supposed to be."

"God help her."

"I know you don't really mean that. You know she's the most important person in the world to him. You've seen how they act around each other."

"Yeah, he's not such a bad father," Hani admitted. "What did you think of my father?"

It was the one question that I'd hoped she wouldn't ask, but she had.

"I had a similar reaction to you, although I'm sure it was nowhere near as intense. I've also disliked your father for what he did to you three, but the guy I talked to at Harry's didn't seem capable of doing that."

"Was he tricking us?"

"If so, why? If he didn't care, if he wasn't interested in repairing the damage that's been done, he would have stayed in Japan and never gotten on that plane," I said.

"He's here for two weeks. Did you know that?"

"He told me, so did Yuto."

"I guess I have a big decision to make."

"Yes, you do, but I think the other question is the more important one. Will you marry Yuto or not?"

Hani turned away from me and looked out toward the ocean.

"This is one of the most beautiful spots on the island," she said.

"That's the main reason I bought the place."

Hani laughed. Then she turned back to me.

"Your little sister, huh?"

"Yep."

"I've never had a brother. I guess you'll have to do."

"Thanks, I think."

"I remember the first time I met you, Poe. You had this look of shock on your face."

"I thought I was looking at twins."

"That's what everyone says when they see Alana and me together. I don't see it, though."

"I don't know how."

"I guess I better get home. I have some decisions to make."

"Good luck."

"Remember, not a word of this to Alana. Got it?"

"I got it. But keep this in mind. You should tell her yourself. I think you both could help each other get through this. There's no reason to keep it a secret."

"Maybe. I'll think about it."

Hani hugged me, which she almost never did. Then she turned and walked out of the building. I stayed on the deck for a few more minutes and was about to leave when my phone rang again. I looked at the display and saw Alana's name.

"Hey, Alana."

"I ran into Josh Parrish this morning."

"Oh, yeah? How did that go?"

"He semi-apologized."

"Semi-apologized? What does that mean?" I asked.

"He said he regretted how things went down yesterday."

"Did he specifically say that he regretted arresting me?"

"No. He kept things generic. He said he wanted a good working relationship with me and asked if we could start over."

"What did you say?"

"I said yes. No reason to make an enemy."

"Understandable."

"Besides, I thought it would be the perfect opportunity to ask who the eyewitness is. He couldn't very well say no after asking me for a fresh start," she said.

"Smart play. Who is it?"

"Any guesses?"

"It would have to be one of her enemies. Sorry, I know that's an obvious guess."

"Maybe, but it's a wrong guess. Then again, you might be right after what I heard later. The eyewitness is Oleen Akamu, Tavii's wife."

"You said she might be an enemy. What else did you hear?" I asked.

"After Josh gave me that name, I made a phone call to a woman I know in the mayor's office. She's known to be tuned into the gossip. She said the word is that Tavii and Oleen are getting a divorce. I asked her why and she said she's heard several different stories, adultery being the main one. She said she also heard that Oleen already moved out of their house."

"So, Oleen left Tavii and then decided to seek revenge on the Akamu family by turning on Mele Akamu?"

"It would seem so. The question is, is Oleen Akamu telling the truth? Did she really see Mele and Samson murder Eric Ellis?" Alana asked.

"That is the question, isn't it?"

"How did your meeting with Daniel Davis go?"

I gave Alana the rundown on my meeting, including my suspicions that Daniel Davis didn't own a dog.

"Why in the world would he lie about that?" Alana asked.

"I have a crazy theory that he's part of the set-up against Mele Akamu."

"A five-year set-up?"

"Foxx made that exact same point."

"Sorry, Poe, but I'm going to have to side with Foxx on this one. If someone wanted Mele Akamu that badly, they'd have found a way to get her a long time ago."

I didn't respond. Alana and Foxx were probably right, and it didn't make much sense to keep debating the point.

"I expect you'll hear from Mara Winters later," Alana continued. "Mele Akamu and Samson Opunui go before the judge today."

"What's your guess? Will they be granted bail?" I asked.

"No chance. I suspect she'll never see freedom again, especially now that we know who the eyewitness is. A jury is going to have a hard time overlooking that testimony."

"You're probably right."

"Is this the point you back out or are you going to keep going?" Alana asked.

It was a very good question, I thought. Unfortunately, I didn't have a good answer.

17

THE BUTLER

I CALLED FOXX IMMEDIATELY AFTER I GOT OFF THE PHONE WITH ALANA. I recommended that we take a divide and conquer approach to the Eric Ellis investigation. Foxx's mission was to find where Oleen Akamu had moved to. My goal was to meet with Samson.

I'm sure you're wondering why my internal debate on whether or not to continue with the case had lasted all of a few seconds. There's an easy answer to that question. There was an intriguing mystery to solve and I wasn't about to walk away from that.

I realized a while back that I rarely did these cases for the client who hired me. I did them for myself to bring the truth to light. Someone, and I was willing to concede that it might have been Mele Akamu, had murdered Eric Ellis. That person needed to be brought to justice.

I left the wedding venue in Wailea and drove back to the jail in Kahului since visiting hours were about to start. I didn't think I'd get any more useful information from Mele Akamu, but I thought talking with her butler was worth a shot. After all, he doubled as her enforcer.

Yes, it was a long shot at best. I didn't think he'd turn on her for a second, but I also thought I might have a chance at convincing him that I could best serve him and his boss if he gave me more information. What is that I hear? Laughter coming from you? Don't worry. I don't blame you one bit.

The weather was still quite nice, and I enjoyed listening to more music from Dave Brubeck. After arriving at the jail, I was escorted to the visitor area. I was already seated at the table when a guard brought Samson out. I studied him as he approached. He didn't express any sign of surprise when we locked eyes. Was that a good sign? I didn't know.

"Hello, Samson. How are you holding up?"

"I'm fine," he said, and he sat on the other side of the table from me. "Have you seen Mrs. Akamu today?"

"No, are you worried about her?"

"She can handle herself, but it seems strange not being able to serve her."

"How long have you worked for Mrs. Akamu?"

"Maybe fifty years or so."

"How is that possible?"

"Her father hired me to take care of her. She was just a little girl. I wasn't much older."

"Did her father start the business?" I asked.

"He did. Mrs. Akamu took it to new heights."

"I'm not surprised."

"It was no secret that he wanted a son to take over for him one day. He and his wife only had one child, though. You have to remember that this was many years ago. Women were not expected to be able to do the work of a man. Mrs. Akamu proved him wrong."

"Just curious. Did her father ever acknowledge that?"

"I think he did in his own way."

"How many children did Mrs. Akamu have?"

"She had one son. He and his wife died several years ago in a car accident."

"Was Tavii their only child?" I asked.

"He was."

"I'm sure you can guess why I'm here. Things aren't going well for my investigation."

"You're referring to the eyewitness, I assume."

"Your attorney told you about that?"

"No, Mrs. Akamu got word to me earlier today."

Samson had been right. She could handle herself.

"She also told me who the eyewitness is."

"What do you think about that?" I asked.

"It's impossible for her to have seen it since it didn't happen."

"What do you know about Oleen's relationship with Tavii?"

"It's over as far as I know."

"What's the reason?"

"She discovered his affairs. Perhaps I should clarify that. She finally decided that she'd had enough of them. Tavii always assumed that he had her fooled. He didn't," Samson said.

"Did she ever tell you that?"

"She didn't have to. It was obvious."

"Did Mrs. Akamu know about her grandson's affairs?" I asked.

"She knew and it bothered her. She would never have accepted that from her husband, not that she ever had reason to worry. He worshipped her. He never would have strayed."

"Do you think Oleen is saying she saw the murder to get back at the Akamu family?"

"Yes, and it's a brilliant plan."

"What makes it brilliant?" I asked.

"She could have accused Tavii of killing Eric, but she didn't. She went after Mrs. Akamu because she's the more dangerous adversary. With Mrs. Akamu locked up, the business is unprotected. I know you have a basic understanding of Tavii's skills. He's not up to the task."

"So, the company fails under Tavii's leadership and he loses everything."

"He's already lost his political career through his own reckless-ness. There will be nothing left for him."

"And Oleen? What does she get?"

"That's the one part of this that I haven't figured out. Oleen doesn't have her own money. She and Tavii have relied on Mrs. Akamu to essentially run their lives. She will lose everything too," he said.

"Tell me, Samson, who do you think killed Eric Ellis? Was it Lee Walters? That's who Tavii pointed me to."

"Lee offered to kill Eric for Mrs. Akamu. I'm sure he didn't tell you that."

"Why would he make that kind of offer? I thought they were best friends," I said.

"They were, but Lee felt betrayed by Eric. He told Mrs. Akamu that he would kill Eric for her if she let him back in. She refused."

"Do you know why?" I asked.

"She liked Eric, maybe even loved him like a son. I doubt there was anything Eric could have done that would have made her order his death."

"What about you? Did you feel the same way about him?"

"I only have one job and it's the one I was hired for fifty years ago. Protect Mele Akamu. I would have killed Eric had he posed a real threat to her. He didn't."

"I thought he knew intimate details of her business," I said.

"There are many layers to it. Eric only saw what she was comfortable with him seeing, nothing more."

"Did Mrs. Akamu hire me to help keep her from being convicted or because she really wants to know who killed a man she once saw as a son?"

Samson said nothing, which I suspected was an answer on its own. Mele Akamu's plan was straightforward, yet I'd only seen parts of it. I would deliver her the name, if possible, and she would send Samson before the police ever had a chance to arrest the killer.

"Mrs. Akamu has people of her own who can do what I'm doing, but she doesn't trust them. That's why she hired me. She thinks this is an inside job, doesn't she?" I asked.

"She doesn't know, but it's a possibility. I was looking on my own years ago when Eric disappeared. I didn't find anything."

"Did she have you look at Tavii?"

"She would never ask that of me," Samson said.

"But you looked anyway, didn't you?"

"I did. I didn't think he murdered Eric, but now I'm not so sure. Oleen's accusations have changed my mind somewhat."

"Because if Tavii did murder Eric, then she might have known about it."

"It's possible. Oleen is far more observant than Tavii realizes. The man is a fool who somehow thinks he's smarter than everyone else in the room."

"What about Stan Cross, the man who had the argument with Eric the same day he was killed?"

"He's a strong possibility. That's who I would look at if I were you," Samson said.

"Any advice for when I go to talk to him?"

"You can't go at him directly. You'll get nowhere. You may even get yourself killed. I'm sure you know he won't volunteer any information. You'll need to come up with a good reason for him to communicate with you."

"One more thing. If I wanted to pay a visit to Oleen Akamu, where would I find her?" I asked.

"She has an apartment in Kihei," he said, and he gave me the address.

"How did you find that out?"

"Mrs. Akamu sensed Oleen was about to do something. She just didn't know what. She had me follow Oleen. I saw her in the leasing office. She got the keys to the apartment a month ago."

"Why didn't Mrs. Akamu step in and try to keep her from leaving Tavii?" I asked.

"Two reasons. She didn't blame Oleen."

"And the second?"

"She hoped that Oleen's departure would scare Tavii into making changes. She obviously didn't see this murder charge coming."

"Thank you, Samson. You've been of tremendous help."

"There's one more thing. I need you to do something for me."

"What is it?" I asked.

"If and when you find out who committed this murder and framed Mrs. Akamu, I need you to tell me first."

I didn't respond.

"Mrs. Akamu's father gave my family a second chance. We were homeless when he hired me to look out for his daughter," Samson continued.

"How did that happen?"

"I found a young girl being beaten by three boys. I saved her."

"That girl was Mele Akamu."

Samson nodded.

"The boys were sent by one of her father's rivals. It was meant to send him a message."

"What did you do to the boys?" I asked.

"After I helped her get home, Mr. Akamu paid me to find the boys and to put them in the hospital."

"He sent a message of his own."

"I've never left her side since. The Akamu family took care of mine and we were never homeless again. I owe her everything. Someone is trying to destroy her. I can't allow that to happen."

"I understand."

"Do you?"

"I do, but I need to make something clear. I'll get you both out of here if I can, but I can't help you beyond that. I'm not going to be responsible for anyone else getting hurt. If the police ask me about it, then I'll tell them the truth of what I know."

"I think we understand each other well."

I stood.

"Thank you again."

"Thank you, Mr. Rutherford."

I said goodbye to Samson and left the jail. I phoned Foxx on the way to the car.

"Hey, buddy. How did the conversation with the butler go?" he asked.

"I'll fill you in when I see you in Kihei."

"Oh, yeah? Why are we meeting there?"

"Samson told me where Oleen Akamu lives. Apparently, Mele Akamu had him follow her a while back."

"Glad you found her address because I struck out with my contacts."

"Let's meet in a couple of hours. I have another stop I need to make first," I said.

"Where's that?"

"I want to have a quick chat with Bret Hardy."

"The lover in the Guy Livingston case? What makes you think he'll want to talk to you?"

"That's the whole challenge. Most of these guys don't want to talk. I have to come up with a good reason to convince them to change their mind."

"And what reason are you going to use with Bret Hardy?"

"I don't know, but I'll think of something."

18

THE BLAME GAME

I ALREADY KNEW WHERE BRET HARDY LIVED SINCE I'D FOLLOWED HIM for a few days during the original Guy Livingston case. His home wasn't that far from Guy's, which explained one of the reasons they'd become friends. They'd met at a nearby golf course where each of them played. Those games turned into invitations to dinner, which eventually evolved months later to Bret's affair with Lucy Livingston.

I'd also discovered during my investigation that Bret had a bit of a gambling problem. That was one of the sources of his financial difficulties. As I'm sure you know, Maui is an expensive place to live. It's easy to fall behind on your bills and that often leads to people seeking alternative ways to catch up. There are only so many hours a day one can work, though, and most island jobs don't pay enough to dig yourself out of a deep hole. Hence, Bret's turn to gambling.

He was a decent golfer, at least that's what some of the other players at the club told me. He'd wagered with some of the players, betting big money on each hole. Although Bret was talented, he apparently wasn't as good as the guys he'd bet against. I'm sure you can guess what happened next. His money problems got worse, and he turned to Lucy Livingston for help. Lucy allowed him to steal her jewelry, with the word "steal" in obvious quotation marks.

Don't ask me why Lucy would stray from her marriage to be with a man who had such noticeable problems. Forgive me if it sounds like I'm judging the deceased, but it's important to ask as many questions as possible if one is to discover the whole truth. That sometimes involves making indelicate statements about the victims.

Lucy's affair with Bret and her false report to the police were stains on her character. That could have certainly been a sign that she wasn't the angel the prosecutor made her out to be. I don't mean to imply that she deserved to be murdered. Far from it. But there was the possibility that she'd been in more trouble than I knew, and the source of that trouble might have been the true perpetrator of the crime.

Foxx had asked a good question when he'd inquired how I intended to get Bret Hardy to talk. I'd seen him in the courtroom on the day that I'd testified against Guy Livingston. He'd even glared at me in the hallway afterward. What would his reaction be when I knocked on his door? I think you already know the answer to that question.

By the time I parked my car in front of his house, I still didn't know what I was going to say. I climbed out of my car and walked up the driveway to his covered porch, which ran across most of the front of the house. I hoped along the way that a brilliant idea would come to me. It didn't. I knocked on the door anyway, and a moment later, Bret Hardy answered.

Bret is a tall man, maybe just an inch or two shorter than me. I guessed his weight at around two-thirty, which gave him a decent weight advantage on me. He has short, dirty-blonde hair, blue eyes, and tanned skin. He looked like a former surfer who'd turned to golf and gambling and had gotten a bit puffy around the mid-section as a result.

"You! What the hell are you doing here?" he asked.

"Mr. Hardy, my name is Edgar Rutherford. I'm–"

"I know exactly who you are," he said, cutting me off. He stepped onto the porch. "You're responsible for getting Lucy killed."

"How do you–"

Before I could finish my question, Bret threw a punch at me. In hindsight, I should have seen it coming, but I suppose that my brain was so preoccupied with finding some reason for him to talk it never occurred to me that he'd actually assault me.

Fortunately, he was not an accomplished fighter. Most guys aren't. By the time they hit forty, the age I guessed Bret Hardy was, they probably hadn't been in a fistfight for twenty-five years or more. Bottom line, they're out of practice, even though they still think they can take most guys in the room. Blame male arrogance for that over-confidence.

One of the benefits to getting beaten up as much as I have during these investigations is that it makes you more alert to physical attacks. My response time has improved over the years, and I was able to move my head back, and at the same time, put a hand up to deflect Bret's wide and slow swing.

He'd left his midsection wide-open for a counter punch, but I didn't take it. Bret was too enraged to notice my act of kindness, and he took a second swing. This one was more of a lunge combined with a punch. Sorry if that doesn't make much sense, but it was such an off-balanced attack that I wasn't sure what he was doing.

I shifted my weight again, but instead of deflecting the blow as before, I grabbed his wrist and used his own momentum to toss him to the ground. It wasn't the most graceful move on my part, but it did the trick. He tumbled off the front porch and landed belly-first onto the grass.

"Stay down, Bret. I just want to talk."

As I am often a naïve fellow, I assumed that would be the end of his physical assault. It wasn't. I failed to mention this earlier, but there was a portable workbench in the yard with a stack of wood placed on top. There was also a DeWalt circular saw and a rolled-up orange extension cord.

Bret grabbed one of the two-by-fours and walked toward me. I stepped back toward the front door and positioned my body close to one of the wooden columns that supported the roof of the porch. Bret swung the piece of lumber at my head. I jumped back and the wood banged against the column. Before he could take another swing, I moved forward and kicked Bret between the legs. I heard a loud, "Ooff," and he dropped to his knees.

I could give a more detailed account of the positioning of my foot during the kick, but there's no reason to cause phantom pains with male readers. I will mention this for clarification. I played soccer growing up and I could kick a ball well past the mid-point of a sports field. If anything, my leg strength had improved with all of the jogging I'd done while on Maui.

The point of all of this is to say that my kick to Bret's you-know-what was devastating, and it also explained how the man almost lost consciousness. After resting on his knees for a few seconds, he fell forward and rolled onto his back. He instinctively pulled his legs up toward his midsection in an attempt to protect himself from another kick. He needn't have bothered. I wasn't going to hurt him a second time.

His discomfort (yes, I know, that's not nearly a strong enough word for it) gave me more than enough time to grab the orange extension cord from the workbench and tie Bret to one of the front porch columns. I wrapped the cord around his torso several times, then secured it with a triple knot in the back. There was no way he was going anywhere.

It took Bret several minutes to regain some level of composure. I felt a little guilty for the damage I'd done, but the man had tried to bash my head in with a piece of wood. I mean, what would you have done if you were in my position?

"You good to talk now?" I asked.

"You'll pay for this," he said, but he struggled to get the words out.

"Hardly. I record all of my interviews. I had the record app on my phone running when I knocked on your door. It captured you assaulting me. It was a completely unprovoked attack, I might add. If anything, you're going to jail."

You may be wondering if I was making that up. I was, but Bret didn't know that.

"What do you want?" he asked.

"Just a few questions and then I'll be out of your hair. Whose idea was it to pretend to steal the diamond necklace and bracelet?"

"Hers."

"You told her about your money problems, and she volunteered to help you out?"

"Something like that," he said.

"What do you mean 'something like that?' It either was or it wasn't."

"Lucy didn't have any money. The only thing she had of value was the jewelry. The necklace and bracelet were the most expensive items, but she wore them every day. She couldn't very well sell them without Guy noticing."

"She offered them up and also suggested you cook up the fake robbery? Is that what you're saying?"

"Yes."

"Did she know about your little gambling addiction?" I asked.

Bret looked away.

"Oh, you didn't tell her. That's interesting. Bad assumption on my part."

Bret turned back to me.

"Lucy loved me. It wouldn't have mattered."

"I know you don't really believe that. Otherwise, you would have told her. Did she ever tell you about the times Guy hit her?"

I studied Bret for a reaction. I got one, but it wasn't a look of anger. Instead, it was confusion.

"Another interesting reaction. She didn't tell you, which probably means it didn't happen."

"What difference does that make? It doesn't mean he didn't kill her," Bret said.

"No, it doesn't. Still, it's intriguing. I don't know the statistics, but I'd imagine that a man who's willing to shoot his wife might have raised a hand to her sometime before that. Why did she cheat on her husband?"

"What do you mean why? She hated him. She thought I could make her happy."

"Why did she hate him?"

"Because he cheated on her. She told me that he'd had an affair before they moved to the island. They were separated for a year, but then she took him back."

"They lived on the island for a few years. What changed? Did she suspect he was cheating again?" I asked.

"Yes."

"With who?"

"She didn't know. She said she started monitoring his email. She checked his text messages and calls too. She even installed software on his phone so she could track his movements."

"But she still didn't know who he was cheating with? Maybe she was wrong."

"She swore she wasn't," Bret said.

"Okay, so she thought he was cheating, and she jumped right into your bed to get even."

"It wasn't like that."

"Here's what I think happened. She finally came to the conclusion that she'd guessed wrong about the affair and she felt guilty for giving you the jewelry – jewelry that her husband had given her for their wedding anniversary. She came to you and broke off the affair. You got mad and you're the one who killed her."

"That's crazy. I never would have hurt her. We were going to move back to the mainland together. I'd already contacted a real estate agent about selling this house. You can check with the agent if you don't believe me."

I looked around the yard and then turned back to Bret.

"I don't see a 'For Sale' sign anywhere."

"That's because I decided not to go through with it after Lucy was murdered," Bret said.

"Did Lucy give you the four-digit code to her front door?"

"No, why would she do that?"

"Have you ever been in her house?" I asked.

"A few times when they asked me over for dinner."

"Wow, you ate dinner at the man's house, and the entire time, you're sleeping with his wife."

"That was before the affair. I never went back after we started up."

"Was Lucy scared of anyone?"

"What do you mean?" he asked.

"I mean, was she scared of anyone? Did she ever tell you about a fight she had with someone, maybe at work or someplace like that?"

"No, never."

"Were you the only one she ever had an affair with?"

"How should I know? I didn't ask."

"No, but you suspected, didn't you?"

Bret looked away again.

"You know something, Bret, you're not very good at hiding your emotions," I said.

Bret hurled an insult at me, one that I don't intend to mention here since it was so vulgar. I will say that as far as insults go, it was entirely predictable, and I felt a little disappointed that he hadn't come up with something more original. I know, I know, that's strange of me.

I reached behind him and undid the triple knot.

"It may take you a while, but you'll eventually work yourself free," I said, and I stood.

He insulted me again, which was an exact repeat of what he'd said a moment before. I was tempted to mention that, but I managed to restrain myself. My ability to be a smartass does have its limits.

I turned from Bret and walked back to my car. I climbed inside and started the short drive to Oleen Akamu's apartment. With any luck, she wouldn't try to beat me with a piece of lumber.

19

THE ART OF THE BLUFF

I GOT TO OLEEN'S APARTMENT IN KIHEI ABOUT TWENTY MINUTES BEFORE Foxx did. It gave me time to mentally prep for the interview. Like many things in this investigation, it seemed like Oleen's actions came down to two possibilities. She either saw Mele Akamu and Samson murder Eric Ellis or she didn't. You may be inclined to think that I assumed she hadn't seen it. I didn't. The truth is that I didn't know what to believe. I thought there were compelling arguments that could be made for either possibility.

That said, if she was lying about it, then it wasn't hard to figure out her motivation. Tavii had hurt her and she wanted her revenge. Taking out his grandmother and destroying the family business was a good way to do that. She also had to know that he was finished as a politician.

Still, I couldn't stop thinking about something Samson had said to me earlier in the day. He'd told me that Tavii and Oleen relied on Mele Akamu to take care of them. Oleen apparently didn't have money of her own, so Samson couldn't figure out why she was willing to go as far as she apparently was.

It's one thing to be broke in your youth. It's quite another to be willing to walk into poverty in your forties, which was the age I guessed Oleen was. The last thing someone at that age wants to do is live in some crummy apartment when they're used to living in a large, well-appointed house.

None of this is to say that I was surprised that Oleen had left Tavii. I wasn't. If anything, I was shocked that she'd stayed with him as long as she had. On the other hand, I'd come across numerous people during my cases who were more than willing to put money and status above love. According to Samson, Oleen had been willing to look the other way too. I suspected there was a piece of the puzzle I wasn't seeing, though, and I had no idea where to look.

As readers of my last tale will testify, I'm a fan of the game of poker. It relies on multiple things: an understanding of the mathematical odds of the cards being dealt, a courage to risk everything you have, and the ability to tell when your opponent is bluffing.

There is one other thing. You have to know when and how to bluff with your own hand or lack thereof. Bluffing is an art unto itself. You can't come across as too confident because then your opponent will see right through you. If you appear too weak, then your opponent will sense that something is up. It's a delicate balance, which also depends on reading the other person's personality and knowing how to go after them.

Unfortunately, I'd never met Oleen so I had nothing to base my approach on. There was also the inconvenient fact that I was working for Mele Akamu, something that I suspected Oleen already knew. It was highly unlikely that she'd be willing to tell us what we wanted to know, and it wasn't like I could keep going around tying up people with extension cords, no matter how appealing that sounded to my darker side. Come on now, we all have those thoughts. Most of us are just too polite to express them.

Foxx eventually arrived and he parked his SUV behind my car. We both climbed out of our vehicles and met in the street.

"Sorry I'm late. Traffic was heavier than I expected," he said.

"No problem."

"How did your meeting with Bret Hardy go?"

I laughed.

"Would you believe me if I told you that I tied him to a column on his front porch and made him tell me what I wanted to know?"

"Hell no, I wouldn't believe that. So, how did it really go?"

"I just told you. I had to tie him up."

Foxx looked at me like I was crazy, which I understood.

"How do you want to play this next interview?" he asked.

"Let's see what happens when we introduce ourselves."

"I think we already know the answer to that."

We walked up to her apartment building, which wasn't that much larger than Daniel Davis' complex in Paia. I knocked on the door. In the eight to ten seconds that we waited for her, a vague idea popped into my head.

Oleen opened the door. She looked at Foxx first. Then she turned to me.

"You look familiar," she said.

"Hello, ma'am. We're hoping we can speak with you for a few minutes. My name is–" I started to say before she cut me off.

"You're that investigator working for Mele. Get the hell away from me. I've got nothing to say to you."

Oleen slammed the door in our faces. Foxx turned to me just as that vague idea I alluded to a moment ago took better shape. I knocked on the door again.

"We know all about Stan Cross. If you don't open this door right now, we're going straight to the police and telling them everything," I said.

"We do?" Foxx whispered.

I shrugged my shoulders just as the door opened again.

"What do you know?" she asked.

"Really, Mrs. Akamu. Do you expect us to tell you everything now? We haven't even had a chance to ask our questions first," I said.

Oleen didn't respond.

"We have just a few questions. No one wants to go to the police. We sure as hell don't," Foxx said.

Oleen hesitated a long moment. Then she stepped back.

"Come in," she said.

We went into her apartment. There were a handful of cardboard boxes stacked against the wall by the door. There was a small, worn-looking sofa pressed against the opposite wall. What was more interesting, though, is what wasn't there.

There was no television or a coffee table or even a lamp. No table in the kitchen nook. No pots and pans or even a coffee maker on the counter. It looked like Oleen had only started to move in. I suspected she'd taken whatever she could, and those few items were in the boxes. Everything else was probably still at her home with Tavii and she didn't have the money to furnish the rest of the apartment.

"What do you know about Stan?" she asked again, and there was no masking the anxiety in her voice. As far as poker players went, she was a lousy one.

"We know you cut a deal with him, but judging by what I see now, it's obvious he hasn't paid you anything yet, maybe only enough for the deposit on this apartment," I said.

Yes, it was a huge gamble to get so specific, but I still thought it was a solid, educated guess. I must have been correct for she didn't tell me that I was wrong.

"Who approached who first?" I asked.

"You don't know?"

"Our inside man didn't hear," Foxx said.

It was a good line and better than anything I could have come up with at that moment.

"It was Stan's idea," she said.

I studied her expression when she'd said it and I thought she was probably lying.

"How much did he offer you to tell the police that you saw Mele Akamu and Samson shoot Eric Ellis?" I asked.

Oleen didn't respond.

"Okay, here's what we're going to do," I continued. "Our man is going to contact the police and tell them about this little scheme you cooked up. You're going to jail for perjury and making a false report to the police."

"You can't prove anything."

"Can't we? What do you think is going to happen when Stan Cross realizes the police are on to you? He's going to cut you loose, and you'll end up with nothing," I said.

"We understand why you're doing this. We understand what Tavii is like," Foxx said.

"How could you possibly know that?" she asked.

"We were on that yacht with him a while back," Foxx said, referring to our previous case, the one I called *Rich and Dead*.

"You were part of those gambling parties?" she asked.

"Yes, and we saw how Tavii is. The man is reckless and foolish. I can't begin to imagine what it was like to be married to him," I said.

"You have no idea."

"He couldn't have been that way from the start," I said.

"He wasn't, at least I didn't think he was. It wasn't until years later that I realized I just wasn't seeing him for who he really was."

"Don't beat yourself up. I'm guilty of that myself," Foxx said.

"Add me to that list," I said.

If you've read *Aloha Means Goodbye*, then you know exactly who I was talking about. The woman's name was Dorothy and she left me for a used car salesman, although I believe I mentioned that in the first chapter of this tale.

"He thought I didn't know about the affairs, but I did," Oleen said.

"We know why you stayed with him. What were you going to do? You gave the guy everything. He promised to take care of you, but he ended up holding that deal against you. It was a blackmail scheme of sorts. Do what I say. Put up with my garbage or I'll leave you with nothing," I said.

"You know more than I thought you did," she said.

"We need you to come forward and tell the police that you didn't really see Mele Akamu shoot Eric Ellis," I said.

"I can't do that. You don't know what Stan would do to me."

"What do you stand to get in a divorce from Tavii?" I asked.

"Nothing. I get nothing. Mele Akamu made sure of that."

"She made you sign a prenuptial agreement?" Foxx asked.

"Yes, drawn up by that crook of a lawyer of hers, Ruben Dalton," Oleen said.

"I have just one more question. Did you really see Mele Akamu and Samson murder Eric?" I asked.

"What difference does it make? They probably did it, even if I didn't see it," Oleen said.

"You've gotten yourself into a big mess, but we're going to help you get out of it," I said.

"Why?"

"Because we want to discover the truth and you're going to help us with that," I said.

"Why would I be interested in helping that woman? She's treated me like garbage ever since I met her."

"You have more leverage than you think. You have the winning hand against Mele Akamu and your husband. You just made a mistake in how you played that hand," I said.

"What would you have had me do? Threaten Mele Akamu? I would have disappeared and ended up at the bottom of the ocean," she said.

"Let us talk to Tavii for you. We'll make him give you half of everything," I said.

"How can you do that?"

"We can be very persuasive when we need to be," Foxx said.

"And what do I do in return?"

"You go to the police and tell them the truth," I said.

"No, I'm not doing that until I get my money from Tavii," she said.

"You never answered my earlier question. Did you really see them shoot Eric Ellis?" I asked.

"No, I didn't. That doesn't mean they didn't do it, though."

"We'll be in touch soon. Give us a couple of days to convince Tavii to see things your way," I said.

She said nothing.

Foxx and I turned from her and exited the apartment. We were almost to our vehicles when he looked at me.

"Well, she admitted it, but it's ultimately her word against ours that she said it."

"Not quite."

I pulled my phone out of my pocket and stopped the recording app. I moved the cursor to the last minute of the recording and hit play.

"You go to the police and tell them the truth," I said on the recording.

"No, I'm not doing that until I get my money from Tavii," she said.

"You never answered my earlier question. Did you really see them shoot Eric Ellis?" I asked.

"No, I didn't. That doesn't mean they didn't do it, though."

I stopped the recording.

"What made you think to record our conversation with her?" Foxx asked.

"I bluffed Bret Hardy when I told him I was recording my interview with him when I didn't. That made me realize I needed to capture this one in case we got lucky. I started the recording app when you pulled up to the house."

"So we don't need her to admit anything to the police. We have proof of her lie."

"True, but I still want to help her," I said.

"So do it. Tavii is a jerk."

20

YOU GIVE LAWYERS A BAD NAME

I SAID GOODBYE TO FOXX AND CLIMBED BACK INTO MY ROADSTER. IT HAD been a long day and I was anxious to get home. There was a swimming pool with spectacular views with my name on it and I was ready to take a dip. Still, I thought there was one more call I needed to make first. I slipped my phone out of my pocket and dialed Mara's number.

"Hello, Mr. Rutherford. I was just about to call you."

"What did you need?"

"An update on your investigation. As you probably guessed, the judge denied Mele Akamu and Samson Opunui bail. I'm about to leave for a meeting with their attorney."

"How's that going by the way?" I asked.

Mara sighed.

"Not well. It's obvious that he doesn't agree with Mrs. Akamu's desire to have me on the legal team. The man is used to working alone."

"Yes, but her wish has to count for something."

"True, but I suspect she only asked me to further entice you to take her case. I'm sure he assumes the same thing."

"Is it possible for me to give you that update in person? I'd like to speak with Ruben Dalton as well."

"Of course. I'll text you his address in Kahului. His office isn't that far from mine."

"I'm in Kihei now. I'll see you shortly."

My long day was about to get even longer, but I thought a meeting with Mele Akamu's attorney couldn't wait. I'd never met the man, nor had I even heard of him before this investigation. But there was Oleen's opinion of him to give me some clue as to what he was like. She'd called him a crook, which wasn't that far off my estimate of how he'd probably be.

I selected the jazz pianist and vocalist Les McCann for the drive to Kahului. I listened to his songs, "Let Your Learning Be Your Eyes," "With These Hands," "Compared to What," "Willow Weep for Me," and "The Lovers."

I spotted Mara's car when I pulled into the parking lot. I parked a few spots down from her vehicle and climbed out. Ruben Dalton's law office was located in a small group of suites, which also consisted of a dental clinic, an ophthalmologist's office, and a flower shop, which seemed completely out of place.

I entered Dalton's office but didn't see a receptionist. The little bell on the door must have alerted Ruben Dalton, at least the person I assumed was him, for a short man in his sixties entered the lobby a few seconds later. He had tanned skin, which somehow made the deep lines in his forehead seem more prominent. Unfortunately, my eyes went straight to his hair. It was jet-black and I was fairly confident that it was a hairpiece. I don't know about you, but sometimes I have a hard time not staring at those things once I'm convinced that they're fake.

"You must be Edgar Rutherford," he said in a deep voice.

"That's right."

"Mara is already here. Come on back."

I followed him into his private office. It was set up differently than Mara's. Whereas she had a separate area with a comfortable sofa and matching chair for clients, Ruben Dalton had an oversized wooden desk with a large leather chair that somewhat resembled a throne behind it. On the other side of the desk were two wooden chairs that looked about as comfy as something you'd find at a boarding gate in a crowded airport.

Mara was already seated on one of the chairs. I took the other as Ruben Dalton sat on his throne. I already had an instinctive disliking of the man and he'd only said a couple of sentences to me. This wasn't good.

"What do you have to report?" Ruben said.

"I've conducted several interviews already."

"And have you learned anything that can actually help me?" Ruben asked.

"Unfortunately, not much. They all point toward Mrs. Akamu. They also contradicted some things she told Mara and me on our initial meeting, things that Mrs. Akamu ultimately admitted to."

"I don't care about any of that," Ruben said.

"I also met with Oleen Akamu," I said.

"She actually agreed to speak with you?" Mara asked.

"Yes. It turns out she's the eyewitness to the murder, at least that's what she claimed," I said.

"That's nonsense. She's lying," Ruben said.

"Based on what?" Mara asked.

"Based on the fact that I've worked with this family for years. I know these people. You can't believe a word Oleen says."

"Were you able to get anything out of her?" Mara asked me.

"Not much, although I suspect I know a way around that," I said.

"Which is?" Ruben asked.

"Oleen has moved out of her home and into an apartment in Kihei," I said.

"I'm well aware of that. I was also already aware of the fact that she's the eyewitness, so you've told me nothing useful so far. I even drove by her new place yesterday. It's not much to look at," he said.

"She told me that you drew up a pre-nuptial agreement that left her with nothing," I said.

"That's right and that's exactly what she'll get, nothing," Ruben said.

"Might I suggest a different course of action? Convince Tavii to amend the agreement," I said.

"Why would I ever do that?" Ruben asked.

"Because the last thing the Akamus need right now is another enemy. Oleen will be very persuasive on the witness stand," Mara said.

"You don't know her like I do. She'll fall apart under cross-examination," Ruben said.

"You could make her look very sympathetic to the jury if you go at her too hard," Mara said.

"Which is why you'll handle the cross," Ruben said.

"There's no need to get to that point. Make her a deal and she'll recant her testimony," I said.

"No deal. Not now. Not ever. She had her chance to do the right thing," Ruben said.

"With all due respect, Mr. Dalton, Oleen's testimony is the only evidence the police have that connects Mele Akamu to the crime. If that goes away, then everything falls apart," I said.

"Tell me something. Did Mele Akamu place you in charge of her defense and she forgot to tell me?"

I said nothing.

"I thought as much. So keep your mouth shut and let me handle strategy for the courtroom. All I need from you is another plausible suspect," he said.

"You want me to point the finger at someone else to create reasonable doubt?" I asked.

"Exactly. Give me dirt on one or two others, even more if you can."

"And if I can't find anything?" I asked.

"Then make something up. I don't care."

It was the response that I expected him to say, but I still wanted to hear it from his own lips before I made my final decision. It was one that I'd been debating on the way to the meeting. Ruben Dalton's abrasive attitude gave me the not-so-gentle push that I needed to make the final leap.

I stood and turned away from the desk. I'd only made it a few paces when he called out to me.

"Just where do you think you're going?" he asked.

"Home," I said without slowing down my stride.

"I'm not finished with you."

I stopped by the door and turned back to him.

"But I'm finished with you. I find you to be an obnoxious, little man and I have better things to do with my time," I said.

"You can go to hell."

"By the way, you'll have to let me know how things go when you explain to Mele Akamu how you lost her best chance to get out of jail. Enjoy your trial, Mr. Dalton."

I looked at Mara.

"Have a good day, Mara. Sorry I can't stay."

"Hold on a second. I'll go with you," Mara said.

"You're quitting too? Good. I never wanted you on this case," Ruben said.

"You're right. It was a mistake for me to join your team, but it's one I'm correcting now," Mara said.

I was tempted to offer the man some departing advice, mainly that I thought he should buy a better hair piece. But I didn't say it.

Instead, I waited for Mara to catch up with me and then we exited the law office together.

"Sorry I helped get you removed from the case," I said as we walked over to her car.

"No need to apologize. I was looking for a way to bow out anyway. You opened the door for me. What kind of blowback do you think this will get?"

"What is Mele Akamu going to do? She and her enforcer are in jail."

"What made you think to ask Ruben Dalton to tear up the prenuptial agreement?" Mara asked.

"Not here. If it's okay with you, I'd like to head back to your office. I know he can't hear us out here, but I don't want him seeing just how much information I have to tell you. I'd rather keep him guessing," I said.

"Of course."

We climbed into our cars and I followed Mara back to her office. It was late in the day and her assistant had already left. We went into the back and sat on the sofa I mentioned a moment ago.

I told Mara about my various meetings with Lee Walters, Gracie Ito, Tavii Akamu, and Samson Opunui, as well as a detailed account of my conversation with Oleen Akamu and her acknowledgement that she'd lied to the police.

"You even got her on audio?" Mara asked.

"Yes, but Ruben obviously doesn't know that, and I have no intention of telling him."

"I sensed you were holding something back."

"Was it that obvious?"

"No, but I've worked with you enough to know that's how you operate. There's something else I know."

"What's that?" I asked.

"You're not really going to quit the case, are you?"

"No, but I finally realized something today after I met with Oleen."

"Which is?"

"I need to disentangle myself from Mele Akamu. This case is way more complex than I originally thought, and it's time that I renew my partnership with the Maui police, at least one detective in particular."

"The lovely Detective Hu."

"Exactly."

"Just curious. What made you think that Oleen had conspired with Stan Cross?" Mara asked.

"It was something that Samson said. He told me that he was surprised that Oleen would walk away from money. So I assumed she might have had another source of cash lined up. I also assumed she couldn't get money from anyone unless she had something to sell."

"Her false testimony."

"Exactly."

"That leads us to one conclusion. Stan Cross killed him," Mara said.

"I thought about that, but I'm not sure it's correct. Stan Cross could just be an opportunist. I'm sure word got out fast in their circles that Eric's body had been found. It would be easy for him to discover that Oleen was unhappy in her marriage and make her an offer."

"You said this case is more complex than you originally thought. What makes you believe that?"

"A feeling I have and it's all because of a non-existent dog."

"A non-existent dog?"

"Check that. I'm sure the dog is real, but the guy who claimed to own it was never his actual owner. I need to find who convinced him to lie to the police and then I'll find the killer."

"It could still all point back to Stan Cross," Mara said.

"Yes, I expect it does, but I've been wrong before."

"I can't believe you called Ruben Dalton an obnoxious, little man. You have no idea how long I've been wanting to say something like that to him."

"I wanted to think of a more original insult, but nothing came to me."

"I wish someone would tell him to stop wearing that God-awful toupee."

"Ah, you noticed it too," I said.

"It's impossible not to. It looks like an old bird's nest on top of his head."

"We'll have to tell him that the next time we run into him."

Mara smiled.

"Yes, we will. Have a good evening, Mr. Rutherford. It was memorable, as always."

21

A TURN OF EVENTS

THE SUN WAS STARTING TO SET ON THE DRIVE BACK TO KAANAPALI. IT was its usual brilliant mix of reds, oranges, and yellows. There was something spectacular about the way the light looked as it dipped behind the nearby island of Lanai. I didn't think I'd ever grow tired of it.

When I finally arrived at the house, I spotted Alana and Maui on the back patio. The dog had his head buried in a new toy Alana had bought him. It's a bit difficult to describe, but it's a round patch of fake grass. The grass is made of strips of green cloth and the basic premise is to hide treats in it. The dog is supposed to have fun hunting for the treats, which Maui certainly does.

Alana turned when she heard me open the sliding glass door.

"I was wondering when you were getting back. How did the day of interviews go?"

"How can talking to people make you so exhausted?" I asked, and I made the decision to leave out the part of the day where I was attacked with a two-by-four. I would save that story for a later date.

"Happens to me all the time. Learn anything of value?"

"Yes, I'm even more convinced that Mele Akamu didn't kill Eric Ellis," I said.

"Any idea who did?"

"A guy named Stan Cross."

"You picked a good one. He's one nasty piece of work."

"There's something else that happened today. I quit the case. So did Mara."

"You did what?"

I told Alana about my run-in with Ruben Dalton.

"I heard about his reputation. I'm not surprised you two didn't get along," Alana said. "I'm assuming this doesn't mean you're walking away for good, though."

"No, but I'm only going to stay on it if I can convince a third person to join Foxx and me."

"Who's that?"

"I'm looking at her."

"Me?"

"Why not? Detective Parrish isn't going to listen to me, but he needs to be convinced that he's got the wrong people locked up."

"I don't know that you'll ever convince him of that," Alana said.

"Tavii's wife admitted to me that she lied about seeing the murder. I also interviewed the guy who found the body, only to find out that he doesn't actually own a dog."

"How's that?"

"One. We saw no evidence that a dog lived in the apartment. Two. Daniel Davis said his dog was having surgery today, but I called every vet clinic on the island pretending to be Daniel and no one had a record of having his dog. Three. He seemed really nervous about us even asking questions about the dog."

"You have had a productive day, haven't you? Did you try to tell Josh about any of this?" she asked.

"No. I've been too busy, but I'm more than willing to meet with you guys tomorrow."

"He won't have warm feelings about me butting into his case."

"I get that, but better to have his ego bruised than to send the wrong people to prison," I said.

"I don't know, Poe. The dog thing seems like a stretch to me. Why would he lie about that? Maybe he just got rid of the dog and he felt guilty about it."

"Why would he care what I think about that?"

"People can be weird. You know that. That makes more sense to me than some conspiracy theory."

I didn't know how to respond, so I said nothing.

"That thing you said about Oleen lying. Is that just your gut instinct?" Alana asked.

"No, she said it. Foxx was there too."

"How did you get Oleen Akamu to admit to that?"

I told Alana about my hunch that Oleen was involved with Stan Cross and how I'd secretly recorded the conversation. I even played parts of it for her.

"Did you send this recording to Ruben Dalton?" she asked.

"Not yet but I will eventually. I wanted you and Detective Parrish to hear it beforehand so you wouldn't be caught off-guard."

"It certainly makes Stan Cross a likely suspect, unless Oleen went to him first. He might just be taking advantage of the situation. Everyone knows he's Mele Akamu's number one rival. I'm sure Oleen knew that too. I wouldn't be so quick to write off Mele and Samson as the true killers. You know they lied to you already."

It was a good point.

"How did your day go? Sorry I haven't asked you about that until now," I said.

"Well I have big news too. Hani called right before you got home."

My stomach sank as I thought about my morning talk with Hani and how she'd admitted to me that she'd secretly seen her father. I wondered if she'd found the courage to tell Alana that, but then I dismissed that thought. Alana was in too good of a mood for it to have been that. There was only one thing it could be. The wedding was officially back on.

"The wedding is back on," Alana said.

"Good. I wonder what made Hani decide that."

"She said she thought more about it and realized that Yuto's heart was in the right place, even if he had done something really stupid. She isn't willing to throw their relationship away over that."

"I'm happy for them both. It's going to be a hell of a wedding."

"I think so too."

"I'm going inside to get something to eat. Let me know if you want me to call Detective Parrish tomorrow."

"Regarding what Oleen told you, do you think she was being honest with you? Do you think she didn't see anything?" Alana asked.

"I think Oleen will say whatever will make her the most money."

"But that's the point, isn't it? A person like that makes for a horrible witness in court, regardless of whether they're telling the truth or not. If Josh is basing his case on her word, then he's in trouble. He has to be told."

"I agree."

Alana didn't respond. I turned from her and walked back into the house. I made myself a sandwich and had a Negra Modelo. I watched television for about twenty minutes or so before I fell asleep on the sofa. When I woke, it was a few minutes after midnight. Maui was asleep on the floor in front of me. He was snoring, by the way. I managed to drag us both upstairs and immediately fell asleep again once my head hit the pillow.

It was nearly five in the morning when my phone alarm went off, which was weird since I didn't remember setting it. Then I realized that it wasn't my alarm. Rather, it was someone calling me. I opened one eye and glanced at the display. It was Alana.

"Hey, everything all right? I didn't even hear you leave."

"You were out like a light. You didn't even hear when my phone rang earlier. I'm hoping you can do something for me," she said.

"Sure, what is it?"

"I'm in Pe'ahi on the beach. There's been a drowning. Can you come out here and take a look?"

"At a drowning victim? Why?"

"Because I think it might have been murder."

"Okay, I'll be there as soon as I can."

I ended the call and climbed out of bed. I slipped on a t-shirt, shorts, and a ballcap and walked downstairs to my car. I opened the garage door and backed out. The sun hadn't risen yet and the air was cool.

It took me over an hour to get to Pe'ahi. It was a pleasant drive, though, and my senses were heightened by the reason for my early morning drive. There's something about death, especially a sudden death, that makes you feel even more alive and more appreciative of the things you still get to experience.

I thought I might have a bit of trouble finding the exact location of the alleged drowning, which in hindsight had been a foolish thought on my part. I spotted the flashing lights of the ambulance well before the turnoff for the beach. The police officer blocking the area must have been alerted to my impending arrival for he waved me through.

He nodded as I passed, and it was at that moment that I recognized him as the officer who'd put me in handcuffs. What a difference a couple of days makes, huh?

I parked my car on the side of the dirt road and made the long walk down to the beach. I eventually saw Alana standing beside a woman I recognized as one of the department's medical examiners.

The drowning victim was a few feet away on his back. His long, wet hair was partially covering his face. There were several other surfers nearby, and they were being interviewed by two uniformed police officers.

"Hey there," I said.

"Hey, Poe. Thanks for getting here as quickly as you did," Alana said.

"Hey, Doc," I said.

"Good to see you again," she said.

"We keep running into each other in these lousy circumstances, don't we?" I asked, and I smiled.

"Unfortunately, yes," the medical examiner said.

"Do you ladies still think it was an accidental drowning?" I asked.

"We found swelling on the back of the head," the medical examiner said.

"Maybe he hit his head on the surfboard or even a rock in the sand," I said.

"Maybe, but there's also bruising on his neck and shoulders," Alana said.

I turned and looked at the surfers being interviewed.

"Did they see anything?" I asked.

"No, they're the ones who found the body. Take a closer look at him if you don't mind," Alana said.

I kneeled beside the victim and looked at his face. The sun was just starting to rise so it was easier to get a good look at him. I'd met the man before.

"This is Daniel Davis," I said.

"We found his vehicle right before you got here. This is the same man you interviewed yesterday?" Alana asked.

"Yes, that's him," I said, and I stood. "You know he didn't drown. That's why you called me out here."

"No, he drowned all right. The question is, did someone help him," Alana said.

I said nothing. Instead, I stepped away from Alana and the medical examiner. I looked out toward the ocean...an ocean that had just claimed the life of Daniel Davis.

"Are you all right?" Alana asked as she approached me.

"I got him killed, didn't I?"

"How do you figure?"

"He panicked after Foxx and I met with him. He called whoever put him up to pretending to discover the body. They figured it was only a matter of time before the police got him to admit the truth."

"That's all probably true, but this isn't your fault. Daniel Davis put himself in jeopardy when he agreed to lie to the police," Alana said. "But maybe we both have this wrong. Maybe this is just a drowning. It happens all the time."

"The day after I talked to him? Kind of a big coincidence, don't you think?"

"It is, but sometimes these things do occur. It doesn't mean there's a coverup."

"You're going to tell Detective Parrish about this, aren't you?" I asked.

"Of course. I'll let you know what he says."

"Is there anything else I can do here?"

"No."

"I can't just let this go and chalk it up to an accident," I said.

"I know. That's why I got you out here. I better go check on those interviews with the surfers. I'll talk to you later."

I looked back at Daniel Davis once more before making the walk back to my car. I knew in my gut that his death was connected to Eric Ellis. It had to be.

22

MAUI ANIMAL CENTER

IT WAS STILL EARLY IN THE MORNING WHEN I LEFT THE BEACH IN PE'AHI, but it wasn't too early to see an acquaintance of mine. Her name is Apikalia and I'd met her during my interactions with the Maui Animal Center. As a reminder, that's the place where I adopted Maui. I frequently donate the fees for my investigations to the center. I do this for a couple of reasons. The first is that I don't need the money. The second is even more obvious. I want to help the center.

After a particularly large donation, Apikalia, who serves as the director for the center, offered to rename the facility after me. I politely declined. The name The Rutherford Animal Center didn't have a good ring to it. Instead, I asked her to name the place after its more famous former resident, my dog, Maui. So, the facility kept the name the Maui Animal Center. There are only three of us on the island who know who it's truly named after: me, Apikalia, and Alana.

There's a fourth person or living creature – my dog. I told him the facility was named after him once I got home from meeting with Apikalia. The pooch was not impressed. If memory serves, Maui rolled onto his back and went to sleep after I delivered the exciting news. I sensed that he was still offended that someone had decided to drop him off at the center in the first place, although that person's loss was my gain.

I knew from prior conversations with her that Apikalia arrived at work around six in the morning. I phoned her on my way home and asked if I could swing by the center to ask her a few questions. The place had doubled in size since my first visit years before. I was delighted that my donations had made such a significant impact, and I made a mental note to send them another check when I got home.

I swung into the parking lot and was thrilled to see that they'd redone their main sign. It now featured a photo of my dog's face beside the name the Maui Animal Center. I parked my car and walked over to the sign. Then I took a photo of it with my phone and texted it to Alana.

"I was so glad you called earlier. How do you like the new sign?" she asked.

I turned at the sound of Apikalia's voice and saw her standing just outside the main entrance. Apikalia is of Hawaiian descent, which I suppose is obvious given her name. She's around fifty, about Alana's height, and she has black hair that falls just below her shoulders. She was dressed in khaki pants and a dark-blue polo shirt with the name of the animal center on the breast pocket.

"We just got the new sign in earlier this week. I was going to invite you up here for the surprise," she continued.

"It's beautiful. That's why you asked me for a photo of Maui the other day."

Apikalia had told me it was for a mural they wanted to create for the lobby.

"I'm glad you like it," she said.

"I love it."

Mental note number two: Double the size of the check I'd already intended to write, which I realized was the whole point of the sign. Sometimes we're all okay with being blatantly manipulated.

"Not that I mind, but it's a little early for a visit. Your questions must involve one of your investigations," she said.

"Good guess and you're correct."

"Come on inside. We can talk in my office."

I followed Apikalia into the building. She locked the door behind us since the place wasn't officially open for a couple more hours. I could hear a handful of dogs barking in the back.

"I don't know how you get used to being around that much barking all day long," I said.

"You learn how to tune it out, believe it or not."

We walked inside her office, which had a colorful collection of photographs of dogs and cats on the walls. One of the photos was of Maui and it was the same one that was featured on the outdoor sign. Let the manipulation games continue.

"What's this investigation you're working on? I've always been intrigued by them," she said.

"A recently discovered murder that actually occurred several years ago."

"Is this about that body they found on north Maui."

"The one and the same. A man found human remains when he was walking his dog. To be more precise, he told the police that he let his dog off the leash and the dog found the bones. I met with the man yesterday, but I noticed something strange when I went to his apartment."

"What was strange about it?"

"I didn't see any sign that he owned a dog. He also told me that his dog was being neutered, but I called all the vet clinics and none of them have a record of the dog."

"That is odd. Why would he lie about that?"

"Good question. He obviously had the dog at some point since I think the police would have noticed if he didn't have a dog when they interviewed him by the human remains."

"You think he might have dropped the dog here?" she asked.

"That's what I was hoping you could tell me. The man's name was Daniel Davis."

"Was? Did something happen to him?"

It was a slip of the tongue and I instantly regretted saying it.

"He had an accident early this morning. He drowned while surfing."

"That's terrible."

"That's where I was right before I called you. Alana got the call about the drowning. She wanted me to help ID the body since I'd recently met him."

"Let me see if I can find his name in our database," she said, and she rotated her body toward a desktop computer.

I watched as she typed the name Daniel Davis into the search bar.

"Yes, we have a record of him. He adopted a black lab from us about a week ago. He brought the dog back the very next day."

"Do you know why?" I asked.

"No, we don't make a note of that, but I could make a few guesses. Sometimes the dog can be wild, and they don't want to take the time to train it. Maybe the spouse didn't know the person was adopting the animal and they demand they return it. Sometimes they don't check with their landlord first."

"Yes, it could be any of those reasons. Does it say if the dog was neutered or not?"

Apikalia looked at the screen again.

"Yes, he was neutered months ago. I don't know why Mr. Davis would have told you that his dog needed to be."

"What was the date the dog was adopted?"

Apikalia told me and I recognized it as the same day the remains of Eric Ellis had been found.

"Does it say the time of day Daniel returned him?"

"Yes, we log the time and date. It says here he was brought back to the center at eleven-thirty in the morning. So, technically, he had the dog less than twenty-four hours. The dog's still here if you know of a good home for him."

"Not off the top of my head but I'll ask around," I said.

"Is there anything else you need?"

"No, you've been very helpful. Thank you."

"Good, but I'm not sure how that can help with your investigation."

"Believe me when I say that it did."

It was obvious what had happened. Daniel Davis had adopted the dog for the sole purpose of having it find the body the next morning. I wouldn't have been surprised if he'd dragged the dog to the body and shoved Eric's arm bone into the dog's mouth.

I made another mental note to ask Alana to follow up on something for me. Daniel had been enticed to lie for some reason and I assumed that reason was probably money. That meant there would be a paper trail of some sort. Hopefully, it was one that we could follow.

I drove home and completed my morning routine of swimming in the pool and jogging around the neighborhood. Afterward, I took Maui on a long walk and told him that his photo now adorned the sign of the animal center. He reacted the way I thought he would. Total and complete indifference. In fact, he was more interested in a bird that had landed on the road several feet in front of us.

I spent the rest of the day thinking about the Eric Ellis case and going over my notes from the various interviews I'd conducted with Foxx. Speaking of Foxx, I'd texted him after my meeting with Apikalia and informed him of both Daniel Davis' alleged drowning, as well as his one-day adoption of the black lab.

I received a call shortly after lunch from a surprise source. Care to take a guess? It was Detective Josh Parrish. He requested a meeting with me and suggested Harry's as the location. I called Alana after getting off the phone with Detective Parrish.

She told me that she'd informed him of Daniel Davis' death and my suspicions that he'd been paid to find Eric Ellis' body. She said that he didn't have much of a response, including any perceived anger at the fact I'd ignored his orders to stop my investigation.

I left the house around three in the afternoon for the short drive to my bar. Foxx was there, but I asked him not to take part in the meeting with Detective Parrish. I didn't want him to know that I had help with my investigation so Foxx's further movements could hopefully go unnoticed.

Detective Parrish arrived at Harry's around half past three. He spotted me in one of the back booths and walked over.

"Mind if I have a seat?" he asked in a neutral tone.

"Not at all. Can I get you something to drink?"

"No, I'm good," he said, and he sat down. "Let me get right to the point. Detective Hu told me about Daniel Davis. She also told me about your suspicions regarding him."

"What are your thoughts on that?"

"It's basically in line with your way of working, isn't it?"

"I'm not sure what you mean," I said.

"I've heard things about you. You see conspiracies everywhere."

"I disagree. I've never blown an investigation. Not one."

"That's the thing, though. This isn't your investigation. It's mine, but we've already had this conversation a couple of times."

"Is this where you arrest me again?" I asked.

"No. I'll admit that I crossed the line before. This case is a big deal for me, though. It can make or break my career. Put yourself in my shoes for once. How would you feel if some unpredictable investigator were running around the island trying to undo everything you've done?"

"That's not what I'm doing."

"It's not? I have Mele Akamu and Samson Opunui nailed for this crime and you're doing your best to prove they didn't do it. How do you think that's not undermining me?" he asked.

"You do realize your eyewitness is lying, don't you? She admitted it to me."

"I always knew she wasn't enough. The soon-to-be ex-wife of Mele's grandson? No, she's too weak of a witness, but I don't really need her."

He paused, which I assumed was for dramatic effect.

Then he continued, "We found the gun that shot Eric Ellis late yesterday. Detective Hu doesn't even know that yet."

"Where did you find it?" I asked.

"I don't have to share that information with you, but I will. We found it inside a wall safe hidden behind a bookcase in Mele Akamu's house. I had to search the house three times before I found it. There was also a stack of cash and a fake passport for both her and Samson Opunui. So you see, Oleen Akamu can fall apart on the witness stand for all I care. I have the gun and the ballistics report to match it to the bullet we found in Eric Ellis' skull. It's game over. Do yourself a favor and bow out before your perfect record goes bye-bye. No one will blame you one bit. Everyone on this island knows Mele Akamu is a criminal, and soon they'll know she's a murderer."

Detective Parrish slid out of the booth and stood. He looked around the bar and then turned back to me.

"You and your partner have a nice place here. If I was you, I'd stick to slinging cocktails and leave the criminal investigations to the police. You'll probably be a happier man."

He walked away and exited the bar before I had a chance to respond, not that I wanted to say anything anyway.

Foxx approached me a few moments later.

"I didn't expect him to say that."

"No, I didn't either," I said.

Foxx slid onto the seat opposite me. I picked my phone up off my seat and placed it on the table between us. I'd dialed Foxx's number right after seeing Detective Parrish enter Harry's. I could have simply repeated everything the detective had told me, but I wanted to get another opinion on the tone of the conversation. Foxx had listened to it while in the back office.

"A safe hidden behind a bookcase. What made him look there?" Foxx asked.

"I'm guessing Gracie Ito told Detective Parrish the same thing she told us. That Eric had stolen records of Mele Akamu's business dealings. Parrish is obviously an ambitious guy. He's not content to arrest her for murder. He wants to take down her entire business empire."

"Which is why he assumed there had to be a safe somewhere in the house."

"There's one thing that's really bothering me about all of this," I said.

"I know what you're going to say. Why would Mele Akamu be so foolish as to keep the gun? I think I have an answer for that."

"Which is?"

"You heard how long it took Parrish to find the safe. Maybe she thought there was no way anyone would ever locate it, so she didn't see the need to throw away the weapon," Foxx said.

"It's possible. But guns are relatively inexpensive. She could have easily replaced it."

"Maybe there was some sentimental value to it."

"To a gun?"

"You know what we should do? We need to find out who knew about the safe. This could still be a set-up."

I didn't reply.

"I hope you're not letting that guy get to you. Don't let him tell you what to do," Foxx continued.

"It's not Detective Parrish. I'm just doubting my theory."

"That's understandable. Want me to call Tavii and ask him about the safe?"

"No. He'll be calling us soon."

"You think so?"

"As far as he knows, I quit his grandmother's case, and now the police have even more solid evidence against her. He'll be in touch, and when he does, we'll have more of an angle to use as leverage."

"Sounds good to me."

I looked at my watch. It was officially late afternoon and the perfect time for a Manhattan. I knew I could use one.

23

THE PHOTOGRAPHER

AFTER FINISHING MY COCKTAIL, I PHONED HENRY MITCHELL, THE lawyer for Guy Livingston. Despite my contentious interview with Bret Hardy, I still felt like I wasn't giving the case enough attention.

"Mr. Rutherford, please tell me you've made a major breakthrough in the case."

"I wish I could."

"Closing arguments are tomorrow. I've got nothing. Guy is going to prison. There's not a doubt in my mind."

"I'm sorry I don't have better news."

"Have you made any progress?" the lawyer asked

"A little, which is why I'm calling. I was told that Lucy Livingston started her affair after coming to believe that Guy was cheating on her. Do you know anything about that?"

"I heard the same thing, but Guy told me it wasn't true. He admitted to one before they moved to Maui, though."

"Did you believe him?"

"Not about that. I thought he was lying."

"How sure are you?"

"No one can be one hundred percent sure of anything, but I'm about as close as you can get."

"What makes you say that?"

"It's what I told you when we first talked. I've been in this game a long time. I can tell when someone is lying. Guy Livingston may have had an affair, but I still don't think he killed his wife."

"If he did cheat on Lucy, who do you think it was with?" I asked.

"That's an easy one. His photography assistant, Bella Bridges. Once you get a look at her, you'll understand."

"Did your previous investigator speak with Bella?"

"Yes, because I told him to. He said he didn't learn anything useful and he dropped it."

"Can you send me her number? Maybe I can get something out of her," I said.

"Sure thing. I'll text it to you in a minute. Do me a favor and try to meet with her tonight. I need something for my closing."

"I'll do my best."

I ended the call with Henry Mitchell, and the contact listing for Guy's assistant came through a moment later. I phoned her and she told me she had a photography assignment she was leaving for, so we arranged a later time to meet in the lobby of one of the Kaanapali hotels.

I didn't feel like hanging out at Harry's until then. Instead, I said goodbye to Foxx and Kiana and drove home. I took Maui on a long walk and used the time to think about what I'd learned regarding the Eric Ellis case. I still had a hard time believing that Mele Akamu would have held onto the gun, even if the safe were as well-hidden as it seemed to be. Still, I knew people who'd committed far dumber acts and Mele Akamu wasn't perfect.

My meeting time with Bella Bridges approached and I hopped into the car for the short drive to the hotel. I put the car in valet and then entered the lobby. It took all of three seconds to spot her. Her photography kit was an easy tell, and she'd done a good job of describing her attire: red polo shirt, black shorts, and black baseball cap put on backwards. The hat did little to hide the long blonde hair that spilled out past her shoulders. I guessed her age at around forty. She was a real looker.

"Ms. Bridges," I said as I walked up to her.

"You must be Edgar Rutherford."

We shook hands.

"Thanks for taking the time to meet with me. How did your photoshoot go?"

"It went well. We often do these shoots in the early evening as the sun is starting to set."

"I think I caught some of that beautiful light on the drive over here," I said. "Would you mind if we go to an area of the lobby that's a little less crowded?"

"No problem."

We walked to the back of the lobby where we found a small table with a great view of the ocean. The area was relatively quiet, and I assumed most of the hotel guests were in their rooms preparing to go out for dinner.

"I was a little surprised when you called me. I was already interviewed by an investigator," she said.

"I know, and I appreciate your indulgence. I picked up this case rather late in the process. I have just a few questions and won't take up much of your time."

"No problem. What did you want to know?"

"How long did you and Guy work together?" I asked.

"Just shy of three years. He hired me to be his assistant when his work started taking off. I'd been dabbling with photography for a while, but I was nowhere ready to go out on my own."

"Just curious. What did you do before photography?"

"I had a string of restaurant jobs on the island. I don't know if you've ever worked in that industry, but it can really wear you out. I was desperate to start something new."

"I have worked those jobs, and you're right, they're not fun," I said.

"Then you know how taking photos on the beach is a big step up."

"Absolutely. I assume you're now taking over the business."

"That's right. The hotels like our work and our service. They started calling me directly once Guy got arrested."

"How was Guy to work for?"

"He was great. Very patient. He taught me a lot."

"How well did you know his wife, Lucy?" I asked.

"Not well. We only met a couple of times. She never came to the photoshoots and Guy and I liked to keep our personal lives separate."

"Meaning you didn't go to dinner with the couple or things like that?"

"Exactly."

"Was that decision his or yours?"

"His, I guess."

"Did you find that odd?"

"Not really. Some people like to keep work and play separate. I respect that."

"What was your typical workday like?" I asked.

"We'd do photoshoots in the early morning. After that, we'd go back to our office in Lahaina and download all of the footage. We'd select the best photos and run them through Photoshop. If we had a lot of work, we'd stay in the office in the early afternoon. Then we'd go home to rest for a few hours, then meet again for the sunset shoots."

"So your late afternoons were usually open?"

"Almost always. It's hottest during the day then and the light can be harsh."

"Do you know where Guy would go during those hours?"

"I assume he'd go home. We didn't really talk about it."

"Did Guy ever confide in you about his wife's affair? Did he ever tell you his suspicions?" I asked.

"No, never. I think he was caught completely off-guard. He was always in a good mood. I don't think he would have been if he'd thought she was cheating on him."

"I spoke to someone who told me they thought Guy was having an affair of his own. Do you know anything about that?"

"No. Who told you that?" she asked.

"It wasn't the most reliable source, but I feel compelled to check it out anyway."

"Guy loved Lucy. I don't think he would have cheated on her, let alone killed her."

"So you think he's innocent?"

"I do."

"Who do you think did it?" I asked.

"I have no idea. I didn't know Lucy very well. I don't know who would have wanted to hurt her."

"Forgive me for asking such an indelicate question, but did Guy ever hit on you?"

"No. Not once. He was always the perfect gentleman."

"You didn't even catch him looking at you inappropriately, maybe even a fleeting glance?"

"What are you getting at? Our relationship was professional."

"I'm sure it was and I'm sorry if I've offended you in any way," I said.

"Do you have any more questions? I really need to get back to the office and download these photos."

"No, thank you for your time."

Bella Bridges stood and walked away without saying goodbye. It was clear my last few questions had upset her, but there'd been a reason for my forwardness. Guy Livingston had an affair before he and his wife moved to Maui to start over. I found it hard to believe that a man like that wouldn't have stepped over the line even once with a woman as attractive as Bella Bridges.

There were two possibilities. Option one was that he was a reformed man, completely dedicated to his wife. A woman, I might add, who was so convinced he was cheating that she decided to stray herself to get even.

Option two was that Guy hadn't changed at all. That meant one thing. His affair was with someone other than Bella Bridges since I was inclined to believe her denials of an inappropriate relationship with her boss.

My brain started going in a million directions at once, but the ringing of my phone interrupted everything. I looked at the display and saw the name Tavii Akamu. He'd reached out to me sooner than expected.

24

THE SAFE

"Hello, Tavii. What can I do for you?" I asked.

"Is it possible for us to get together, now if you're available?"

"Of course. Where would you like to meet?"

"I'm heading to my grandmother's house now. Can we meet there?"

"Yes, I'll see you shortly."

"Thank you."

I ended the call with Tavii and immediately phoned Foxx. I invited him to tag along, and we met in the parking lot of Harry's so we could switch vehicles. We didn't talk much during the drive to Kula. We both assumed that Tavii would beg me to get back on the case, especially with the recent discovery of the gun that had killed Eric Ellis. Once again, I guessed wrong.

We saw Tavii's car in the turnaround when we arrived at the house. Foxx parked his SUV beside it, and we climbed out. We walked up to the front porch and knocked on the door. Tavii opened it a moment later.

"Thank you for coming so quickly. Please come in," he said.

We entered the house and followed him back to the living room.

The first thing I noticed was that the home had been trashed, presumably during the police's search.

"Can you believe what they did to the place?" Tavii asked.

I continued to look around the room. It seemed as if the police had taken a wrecking ball to the house. Everything, from the flower vases to the paintings, had been thrown on the floor, and much of it was broken beyond repair.

"Someone sure has a grudge against your grandmother," Foxx said.

"I agree. This was more than just a search," I said.

Tavii bent over and picked up a damaged painting of a hula dancer. There was a giant hole in the middle. It looked like someone had put their foot through it.

"My grandmother has made a lot of enemies over the years. I guess that goes without saying."

Tavii turned to me.

"I spoke with Ruben Dalton last night. He said you quit the investigation. I don't blame you," Tavii continued.

"He's not the most pleasant person," I said.

"True, but that's not what I meant. The case is hopeless, at least that's the way it looks to me."

"We assume you've heard about the gun in your grandmother's safe," Foxx said.

"Everyone has heard about it by now."

"Can you show us the safe?" I asked.

"It's in the study. Follow me."

We exited the living room and walked a short distance down the hallway. Tavii led us into a study with a wooden desk that was positioned by a large window. The window offered great views of the valley. The other walls were covered with tall bookcases. Two of those bookcases had been separated to reveal a safe hidden in the wall.

"How in the world did they think to look there?" Foxx said.

"Here's another question. How did they move these bookcases with all the books still on them?" I asked.

Tavii walked over to one of the bookcases. He removed a copy of the book *Treasure Island* by Robert Louis Stevenson.

"There's a switch that activates the system," he said, and he reached to the back of the bookcase and pressed a button.

The two bookcases moved back into place automatically. Tavii then pressed the button again and the bookcases opened back up to reveal the safe.

"My father was the one who had the safe installed, but my grandmother was the only one who used it after he died," Tavii said.

"Who knows the combination to the safe?" I asked.

"Just my grandmother."

"You don't know it?" Foxx asked.

"No. The only reason I know about the safe is because I lived here as a child when it was built. My father would pick me up and let me press the button to open the bookcases. He even put *Treasure Island* in front of it since that was our favorite book to read at night," Tavii said.

"Who else knows about the safe other than you and your grandmother?" I asked.

"I'm sure Samson knows since he lives here."

"Does your wife, Oleen, know about the safe?" Foxx asked.

"Yes. I showed her after we got married."

"Any chance she told someone?" I asked.

"I told her not to, but that doesn't mean she didn't."

"But she doesn't know the combination?" Fox asked.

"No, and there's little to no chance my grandmother told her. She never trusted Oleen."

"Did you know Oleen is the eyewitness to the murder?" I asked.

"She's not an eyewitness. She's lying. Oleen would have told me back then if she'd seen something like that. She wants to hurt my family. That's all this is. You've been involved in a lot of these types of cases. What's your opinion? Will my grandmother get convicted?" Tavii asked.

"Based on the evidence as it is today, almost certainly," I said.

"What about the act of keeping the gun? Can't her attorney say she'd never be foolish enough to hold onto it after murdering Eric Ellis?" Tavii asked.

"He can suggest it. That was our first thought too. But after seeing this safe and how well it's hidden, I think a good argument could be made that she assumed it would never be discovered," I said.

"Unless Oleen told someone like Stan Cross about it and he planted the gun," Foxx suggested.

"Yes, but Oleen didn't know the code, so it wouldn't have mattered," Tavii said.

"I'm actually impressed the police found it," I said, even though I knew Detective Parrish had told me he'd spent three days in the house looking for something like it.

"I'm not," Foxx said.

"Why not?" Tavii asked.

"Look at this room. There's not one book on the floor. Why didn't they trash this room like the living room?" Foxx asked.

"True. You should see the bedrooms. Everything's destroyed. They even turned the mattresses upside down and threw them across the room," Tavii said.

"It's like the cops knew exactly what they were looking for in here," Foxx said.

"It's a sound theory. So how did they know?" I asked.

"Easy. Stan Cross told them. Oleen admitted that she struck a deal with Stan to pay her for being an eyewitness. I bet he planted the gun in the safe once she told him you'd figured things out," Foxx said.

There was also a practical reason the police hadn't thrown the books to the floor. They would have most likely obstructed the automatic movement of the sliding bookcases.

"I think you're giving Stan Cross too much credit," Tavii said.

"How well do you know him?" I asked.

"Well enough. The man's a thug. You're describing someone who carefully planned this out. Stan doesn't do that. He's a bulldozer who threatens to run over people if they don't do what he wants," Tavii said.

"Okay, then who did?" Foxx asked.

"There's only one answer that makes any sense. My grandmother. She had Eric Ellis killed and put the gun in the safe. I didn't want to admit it, but she's guilty," Tavii said.

"And here I thought you brought us here to ask us back on the case," I said.

"I wanted you to see the safe and give me your opinion on the strength of her legal defense. You answered that question for me. She doesn't have a chance," he said.

"You're just giving up?" Foxx asked.

"I'm not giving up. I'm being realistic," Tavii said. "My family's business is under attack, not only from our enemies but also family members. I'll be out of political office in a matter of weeks. I need to start focusing on what can be saved. My grandmother got sloppy and now she's paying the price."

He turned to me.

"Thank you for what you did for her. Please send your invoice for your time to Ruben Dalton. I'll make sure it gets paid," Tavii continued.

"I understand. For what it's worth, I think you're doing the right thing. Your grandmother's most likely guilty, and I'm sorry for what you're going through," I said.

"Thank you."

I turned to Foxx. I could tell he wanted to say something, but he was smart enough to know that Tavii's arguments wouldn't have swayed my opinion so easily.

"Let's leave, Foxx, and allow Tavii to start the clean-up process," I said.

"Good luck," Foxx said.

Tavii nodded.

We left him in the study and walked back through the wreck of a living room. Foxx didn't say anything until we got outside.

"You don't really think she's guilty, do you?"

"She might be," I admitted.

"But now you think Tavii might have done it?"

"The guy could have fooled us."

"I don't buy that he doesn't have the combination to that safe," Foxx said.

"I don't either. Lee Walters said he always suspected that Tavii had killed Eric Ellis. Maybe he did and Tavii's the one who planted the gun in that safe."

"It makes sense and he has more than enough government connections to slip a message to Detective Parrish on how to find the safe."

"It's a solid theory."

We climbed into the SUV, and Foxx drove back onto the road.

"I think it's time we made a run at Stan Cross. He's the only suspect we haven't met with. The hell with this coming up with some creative angle. Let's just go right for him," Foxx said.

"I'm with you."

My phone rang.

"It's Alana," I said, and I answered the call. "Hey there, I have you on speaker mode with Foxx."

"Hey guys. I've been doing a little digging into Daniel Davis. Turns out he made a call to a burner phone after speaking with you guys," Alana said.

"That's interesting. Were you able to account for the other calls in his phone history?" I asked.

"I was. Nothing jumped out at me, though," she said.

"Where did he work?" Foxx asked.

"I spoke with the manager of his apartment complex. He told me Daniel worked at the organic grocery store in Paia. I haven't had a chance to swing by there yet."

"What about Daniel's bank account?" I asked.

"Regular direct deposits from his job but no large payment, if that's what you're getting at. I did go through his apartment but didn't find any cash. If Daniel Davis was paid to lie to the police, then he did a good job of hiding the money," Alana said.

"Maybe he already spent it," Foxx said.

"It's a possibility," Alana said.

"Any more news from the medical examiner?" I asked.

"No. She's scheduled the autopsy for tomorrow morning. I'll check back with her then. What about on your end?" she asked.

I filled Alana in on our meeting with Tavii, including a description of the well-hidden safe, and Tavii's admission that he thought his grandmother was probably guilty.

"I'll see if I can get any updates from Josh. Maybe he'll fill me in on how he found that safe," Alana said.

"Sounds good," I said.

"I gotta go."

"See you, Alana," Foxx said.

"Talk to you guys later," she said, and she ended the call.

"Daniel Davis called a burner phone after we met with him. That's pretty damning," Foxx said.

Yes, it was, but there was no way to discover who owned the phone. We were still in the dark and we still had multiple suspects. There was also the real possibility that the guilty party was already in jail.

25

THE PHOTOS

Foxx and I decided to take another divide and conquer approach. He would work on learning more about Stan Cross, while I would transition back to the Guy Livingston investigation. They'd almost certainly finished closing arguments, and the case had then gone to the jury for final deliberations.

I'd told Guy and his attorney that I wouldn't be rushing into the courtroom at the last minute to reveal the true killer, but I still felt the need to wrap up my investigation soon. I had a theory forming in my mind and I had a vague plan on how to prove it.

I drove home after getting my car from Harry's. I said hello to Maui and retrieved my laptop from my home office. I walked outside to the patio. Maui followed me, of course. He took off sprinting after I'd opened the sliding glass door. He often feels the need to race to the far corners of the yard as if he expects to find some intruder.

I positioned my laptop under the shade of the patio umbrella and logged into my Facebook account. I rarely posted anything to the account. When I did, it was usually photos I'd taken around the island, or more likely shots of Maui...the dog, not the island. I mainly had the account so I could use it to snoop on suspects.

I found the Facebook page for Guy's photography business. It showcased numerous shots of customers. They fell into one of three groups: families, couples, and young females. The family shots were all the same, and I know I've made this observation in past tales. Each family member was dressed identical to the others, which usually consisted of white dress shirts and khaki pants. There's certainly nothing wrong with that, but one does wish for a little more originality from time to time.

The couples weren't dressed like each other, but they definitely fell into patterns. Usually the man would be wearing a button-down, short-sleeve shirt, most likely silk or linen, and the woman would be wearing a flowy dress, sometimes a solid color, but many that had floral designs.

The single female photographs also resembled each other. The women all wore skimpy clothing, including string bikinis. One can only assume these shots were for their Instagram accounts. It was sort of a "Hey-look-at-how-sexy-I-am-on-an-island" vibe.

Faithful readers will know that I consider myself a decent photographer, and I gave Guy Livingston and his partner, Bella Bridges, high marks. The photography was well done. The lighting, locations, and composition were all quite nice too.

After going over his business page, I found Guy Livingston's personal page. There wasn't much there, which didn't surprise me. I imagined it was hard to dedicate time to both pages, and I assumed his attention had been spent more on the business account. That said, I wasn't really interested in his personal postings. Rather, I wanted to look over his list of friends.

It took just a few seconds to find the name Vincent Livingston. I clicked on that name and came to the conclusion that he was Guy's brother. I sent him a direct message and asked him to contact me at once. I also let him know that I was investigating his brother's case.

I didn't know how long it would take for him to get back to me, so I walked into the house and changed into my running gear. I was almost through my three-mile jog when my phone rang. I didn't recognize the number, but I hoped it was Vincent. I wasn't wrong.

"Yes, Mr. Livingston. As I mentioned in my message, your brother hired me to look into his case."

"Have you found anything yet?"

"I have a lead, which I'm hoping you can assist me with," I said.

"Anything to help my brother."

"I know this is a sensitive subject, but do you have any knowledge of your brother's past affair?"

"What in the world does that have to do with this case?"

"The evidence against your brother is pretty damning, I'm sorry to say. But I still think there's the possibility he didn't do it. The only theory I have now is that his lover killed his wife. Your brother's attorney thinks he was having an affair, but your brother denied it."

Vincent said nothing.

"Are you there, Mr. Livingston?" I asked.

"I am."

"This is the only working theory I have, but I can't understand why your brother wouldn't be willing to help me."

Okay, that wasn't entirely true. I did have an idea and I was hoping the brother could be persuaded to confirm it.

"I may know why," he said.

"Which is?"

"Before they moved to Maui, Guy had an affair with a sixteen-year-old girl. Lucy found out about it and left him. I still don't know why she took him back. If she'd known the full truth, I don't think she would have ever spoken to him again," Vincent said.

"The sixteen-year-old girl wasn't the only one," I guessed.

"No, there was one other girl. She was also sixteen or seventeen. I'm not sure. The truth is there could have been more. Those were the only ones Guy admitted to. He meets lots of women of all ages through his photography job. He's always been partial to the young ones."

"He's lucky he didn't go to jail."

"The age of consent in Ohio is sixteen, but the parents of the girls never found out either. We both expected Lucy to tell the one set of parents. She didn't."

"What's your best guess? If Guy was having an affair on Maui, would it be with another young girl?" I asked.

"Probably. He swore to me he would never do it again, but I never believed him. I assumed it was only a matter of time before he cheated again. I wasn't that surprised when he told me that Lucy cheated on him. I guess she'd finally had enough, and she wanted to even the score."

"Do you think your brother is capable of murder?"

"No, I don't. He loved Lucy. He just had a lousy way of showing it."

"I appreciate your help with this. I know it's a tough situation," I said.

"Do you think you can prove my brother's innocence?"

"I wish I could give you an answer, but I can't. I'm sorry."

I ended the call with Vincent Livingston and completed my run. By the time I got back to the house, I had a pretty good idea of what happened the day Lucy Livingston was killed. I just needed to prove it.

I went inside the house and took a quick shower. Then I changed into fresh clothes and walked back outside to my car. It was mid-afternoon by this point, and I thought there was a good chance I'd find Bella Bridges in her Lahaina-based office preparing for her early evening photoshoot. I knew the business address from my Facebook research, and it took me no time to get there.

The photography business was located in a small office complex several blocks from Harry's. I found parking in the back and walked around the building to the front door. The door was locked, so I knocked a few times.

Bella eventually came out to greet me. My investigative career has made me more alert to people's expressions, but even a clueless person would have noticed the change in her demeanor once she realized who I was. For a moment, I thought she might turn around and leave me standing outside. She didn't, though.

"What do you need?" she asked.

"May I come inside? I'd rather not have this conversation in the open."

Bella hesitated for a few seconds. Then she stepped back and allowed me to enter.

"I don't know a gentle way to put this, but I had a conversation with Guy's brother earlier today. He told me that Guy had a couple of affairs when he and Lucy lived in Ohio."

"How's that relevant to what's going on now?" she asked.

"I don't think Guy shot his wife because he found out she was cheating. I think this goes much deeper than that and I'm hoping you can help me prove it."

"How can I do that?"

"Did Lucy ever come to this office?" I asked.

"Maybe once or twice after Guy first rented the place. She didn't seem to have a lot of interest in his photography, though. I know it was a bit of a sore spot for him."

"Did she have a key to the office?"

"No, not that I know of. I can't think of a reason why she would."

"I was told that Lucy suspected Guy was having another affair. She was monitoring his computer at home. She was also checking his phone, but she never found any proof. I think the proof is here in this office."

"What kind of proof? You think he had a second phone or something like that?" she asked.

"No. I think it's most likely photographic proof. What do you do after one of your photoshoots?"

"We back everything up to a portable hard drive. Then we back that up to a second drive. All the drives are numbered, and we have a library program that lists the clients' names on each drive."

"Did you both do the post-production work on the photos?"

"Yes. I would do the basic sorting of the photos. I'd select the best shots and put them in a folder. Guy would then take those shots and do all of the color correction. Then the drive would come back to me and I'd put everything online for client review."

"So you both worked with all of the photographs," I said.

"That's right."

"If Guy wanted to keep a photoshoot hidden from you, where would he have stored those photos?"

"That's easy. On his computer. We each have our own Macs so we can both be working at the same time."

"Do you know the password to his computer?"

"I do. Follow me."

I followed Bella through the small lobby and into a back room. There were two large tables that were placed on opposite walls. One table was covered with photography equipment, including camera bodies, lenses, and two tripods. The other table had two iMac computers with Retina 5K screens. They were a thing of beauty.

Bella walked over to one of the computers and jiggled the mouse to wake it up. Then she typed in the password and the desktop display was revealed. There were dozens of folders on it.

"It could take a while for me to go through these," she said.

"Do you mind if I take a crack at it? I'm sure you have prep work to do for your next shoot."

"Sure. No problem."

I sat down in front of Guy's computer while she sat a few feet away in front of hers. I saw Bella pull up some photos of a young couple and start to sort through them.

I dove into the various desktop folders on Guy's computer, most of which seemed to be dedicated to scheduling and budgeting. If Guy did have the photos that I thought he did, then I assumed they'd be hidden and named something innocuous.

I'd been searching for about forty-five minutes when I finally found them. As predicted, the photographs were labeled in a subfolder called "Lahaina Architecture," which was in another folder called "Investment Project."

I opened up the internet browser and logged into my email account. I then emailed myself several of the photographs.

"Oh my God."

I turned at the sound of Bella's voice and saw her looking over my shoulder at Guy's computer screen.

"I had no idea," she continued.

"People don't generally change who they are."

"Do you know that girl?"

"Yes, I met her once."

"How old is she?"

"Not sure. It's hard to tell, but Guy certainly had no business being anywhere near her."

"That's why you asked me if Guy had ever been inappropriate with me," she said.

"And when you said he hadn't, it occurred to me that you weren't his type."

"Because he likes teenaged girls."

"Exactly."

"I'm sorry I got upset with you. You were just doing your job."

"Not a problem. It's completely understandable," I said.

"What are you going to do now?"

"There's one more move I need to make, and then the truth will be revealed."

26

THREE MANHATTANS AND A SHOT
OF TEQUILA

I WAS SO DISTURBED BY THE PHOTOGRAPHS THAT I DROVE STRAIGHT FOR Harry's after leaving Guy's office. I said hello to Kiana and then promptly ordered a Manhattan. One sips those types of cocktails, but I must admit that I drank mine a bit too quickly. I'd just started my second when Foxx walked out of the back office.

"Oh, hey there, Poe. How long have you been here?" he asked.

"Long enough to be on my second Manhattan."

"What happened since I saw you last?"

I reached into my pocket and pulled up one of the photos I'd emailed myself. I handed the phone to Foxx.

"Oh boy."

"That's one of the tame photos. She still has her clothes on," I said.

"There are nude shots of her?"

"Yep. Another guilty client to add to the list."

"Hence the second stiff drink. I think I'll join you."

Foxx started mixing himself a Manhattan, a drink he doesn't have very often, when the door opened. I looked up at the mirror behind the bar and saw Yuto walking toward us. He didn't look happy.

I turned to greet him as he reached the bar.

"Hey Yuto, what brings you by?" I asked.

Yuto looked at the drink Foxx had just finished making.

"Is that a Manhattan?" he asked.

"Yeah, you want it?" Foxx asked.

"Please."

Foxx slid the cocktail across the bar and Yuto picked it up. He took a long sip.

"Excellent drink," he said.

"Thanks," Foxx said, and he started to make himself another Manhattan.

"Everything okay?" I asked.

Yuto took another sip of the drink.

"Not really," he said.

"I assume you want to talk about it, otherwise you wouldn't be here," I said.

"Can we go in the back?" Yuto asked.

"Sure," I said.

"You too, Douglas. If you don't mind," Yuto said.

"Not at all," Foxx said.

The three of us took our Manhattans and walked into the office behind the bar. Foxx was the last one in and he shut the door behind us. Yuto took another long sip of the drink. He was apparently trying to get drunk as fast as I was.

"The wedding is off," he finally said.

"Hani changed her mind?" Foxx asked.

"No, I did," Yuto said.

"You did?" I asked.

"I found something out this morning. I didn't know how to react at first, but the more I thought about it, the more upset I got," Yuto said.

"What happened?" Foxx asked.

"I ran into Sora Hu by the pool at the hotel. He thanked me for inviting him to Maui and he told me that he's met with Hani a few times since the surprise party. He said that they were getting along really well, and he had high hopes for their future relationship."

"I didn't know they'd met. Did you?" Foxx asked me.

"Hani told me about one meeting. I didn't know there were others," I said.

"Did you tell Alana about it?" Yuto asked.

"No, Hani swore me to secrecy," I said.

"I went to see Hani about an hour ago to discuss the wedding. We got into another argument and she blamed me again for bringing Sora to Maui without talking to her first. She was so angry with me. I asked her if she intended to see her father, and she lied to me and said she still hadn't made up her mind."

"That's not good," Foxx said.

"She likes to play the victim. I've known that about her for a while, but it was something that I thought I could accept. I then asked her if she was sorry that she'd thrown the glass at me, and she said the only thing she regretted was that she'd missed me."

Have you ever been in a situation like that when a person makes a cruel statement that's also pretty funny? Despite the humor I found in Hani's statement, I managed to keep a serious and concerned look on my face.

"What did you say after that?" Foxx asked.

"I told her the wedding was off. It was the strangest thing too because I don't remember even wondering if I should make that decision. I just said it."

"Do you regret saying that? Do you want to get her back?" I asked.

"No, I don't," Yuto said, and he took another drink. "I feel as if a weight has been lifted off me."

"That's your gut telling you that you made the right decision. Listen to it," Foxx said.

"May I ask you a personal question, Douglas?" Yuto asked.

"Ask away."

"How did you know it was the right move to end your relationship with Hani, especially after you'd learned she was pregnant with Ava?"

"It wasn't easy, but then I asked myself what I would do if she wasn't pregnant. It was a quick decision after that," Foxx said.

"But what was it that made you want to end things in the first place?" Yuto asked.

"I'm not sure we should be getting into the details like that. She was your fiancée up until a little while ago. She's Poe's sister-in-law too," Foxx said.

"I'd really like to know," Yuto said.

Foxx looked at me.

"Don't hold back on my account," I said.

He turned back to Yuto.

"I didn't think she'd ever put me first. Hani does whatever she wants to do and everyone else be damned. I knew I couldn't make a relationship work in the long-term with a person like that," Foxx said.

"I understand."

Yuto finished his Manhattan and put the empty glass down on Foxx's desk.

"Thank you both for your time. I wanted you to hear the news from me since I'm sure Hani's version of events will be quite different. I hope we can stay in touch," Yuto said.

"Of course," Foxx said.

"Absolutely, Yuto. We're friends. This doesn't change that," I said.

"Thank you."

Yuto turned from us and exited the office.

I finished my drink and put my glass beside Yuto's.

"I think I need a third Manhattan and a shot of tequila after that news," I said.

"I'll join you."

I stayed at Harry's for another hour and was pretty buzzed from my multiple drinks. I realized I needed to get home and break the news to Alana. You may be assuming that Hani had already told her, but I didn't think that was the case since I would have already gotten a phone call.

I was in no position to drive, so I called a taxi to take me back. When it pulled up to the house, I saw Hani's car and my mother-in-law's in the driveway. So that's why Alana hadn't called, I thought.

I paid the driver and then walked into the house. The three Hu women were in the living room, four if you counted the diminutive Ava, who was on the floor playing with my dog.

Alana looked at me.

"You okay, Poe?" she asked.

I tried to figure out if I'd stumbled into the house. I didn't think I had.

"I'm fine. How are you?"

Yes, it was a dumb question, but my brain was dulled by the Manhattans and tequila shot, which had actually turned into shots, plural.

"Hani has some terrible news," Alana said.

I waited for Hani to say something, but she didn't. It must be noted that she wasn't crying. Instead, she looked furious.

"That idiot called off the wedding," Ms. Hu finally said.

"Yes, I know. I just saw him at Harry's," I said.

"Then why the hell did you ask how we were?" Ms. Hu asked.

"Sorry, you're right. It was a foolish thing to ask," I said.

"Have you been drinking?" Alana asked.

There was no point in denying it, so I decided to spin it in my favor.

"Yes, I got so upset at the news that I had a few drinks," I said.

Hani stepped closer to me.

"What did Yuto say to you?" she asked.

"I'm not sure you want to know," I said.

"Why wouldn't she?" Ms. Hu asked.

I said nothing.

"Out with it," Ms. Hu continued.

"It's a promise I made to your daughter," I said.

Hani looked away and it was obvious she'd figured it out.

"What kind of promise?" Alana asked.

Once again, I said nothing, and the hole I was digging for myself continued to get deeper and deeper.

"Poe, we don't keep secrets from each other," Alana continued.

"Just tell them, Hani," I said.

"Tell us what?" Ms. Hu asked.

"You went to see Dad, didn't you?" Alana guessed.

I expected Hani to deny it. She didn't. Actually, she didn't say anything.

"You saw your father?" Ms. Hu asked.

"Yes, I did. More than once," Hani said.

"How could you?" Ms. Hu asked.

"What does this have to do with Yuto calling off the wedding?" Alana asked.

"We got into an argument about him inviting Dad to Maui. I didn't know Yuto was getting regular updates on my meetings," Hani said.

"You got caught in a lie and Yuto walked. Is that what you're basically saying?" Alana asked.

"I don't know. He didn't even give me an actual reason. He just said the wedding was off and he stormed out," Hani said.

"There's still time to get him back," Ms. Hu said.

"I don't want him back," Hani said.

"It's over, Mom, just accept it," Alana said.

"My daughter will not be humiliated. She's too good for Yuto Takahashi. If anyone is going to call off the wedding, it's Hani," Ms. Hu said.

Too late for that, I thought.

"I'm sorry for what's happened, Hani. Let me know if there's anything I can do," I said.

I didn't get a response, which was fine by me, so I walked upstairs and climbed onto the bed. I was asleep within seconds. I didn't wake up until Alana sat on the side of the bed.

"Are they still here?" I asked.

"They left about an hour ago. How many Manhattans did you have?"

"How did you know I was having Manhattans?"

"Come on, Poe. That's your drink."

"True."

"Did Yuto calling off the wedding really leave you that depressed?" she asked.

"It wasn't just that. It was some photographs I found that my client took. They're of an underage girl."

"You're talking about Guy Livingston?"

"Yes. She's just a child, Alana. I don't know how someone can do something like that."

"I'm sorry you have to deal with this."

"Thanks. I'm ready for you to lay into me over Hani seeing your father. I should have told you," I said.

"I'm not mad. After you left the room, Hani told us everything, at least I think it was everything. You never know with that girl. She put you into an impossible situation."

"Once I heard that the wedding was back on, I didn't want anything to spoil the mood by revealing her secret meetings with your father."

"Mom is furious with Hani. I don't know when she'll speak to her again."

"Hani can't catch a break," I said.

"Now I'm going to ask you to keep a secret."

"What is it?"

"Promise not to tell?"

"I promise."

"I don't blame Yuto. I think he did the right thing."

I sat up in bed.

"I do too. I think he'll be happier in the long run. I didn't say that to him today, but I wanted to."

"Hani seemed to be more upset that Foxx knew Yuto had dumped her. Can you believe that?" Alana asked.

"Unfortunately, I can."

"What was Foxx's reaction when Yuto told you guys?"

"He was compassionate. He really likes Yuto. He'd just never admit it to anyone."

"Let's get back to your case. You need to send me those photos."

"I will, but there's something I need your help with."

"What is it?" she asked.

"Do you think you could get your hands on a boat?"

27

SURF'S UP

WHEN I FIRST MOVED TO MAUI, I HAD DREAMS OF BECOMING A WORLD-class surfer. It was not to be. Despite Alana giving me multiple lessons, it soon became apparent that I lacked the coordination skills necessary to ride the waves. These days, my water activities are restricted to either swimming in the pool or the ocean.

I like to think of myself as a creative fellow, so I decided to turn my weakness into a strength. I booked a surfing lesson with Kari, the next-door neighbor of Guy Livingston. If you'll recall, she'd informed me during our one and only interaction that her family owned a surfing school.

I learned during my follow-up phone call that she was home schooled. She completed her educational curriculum in the early mornings so she could spend the rest of the day working for her parents. I admired the young woman's work ethic, but the truth needed to be confirmed.

Their school was located in Kihei, not far from their home. I caught a taxi from my home in Kaanapali to Lahaina after performing my morning ritual of swimming and jogging. If you recall, I'd left my car at Harry's after consuming too much alcohol the day before. After retrieving my little roadster, I made the pleasant drive along the coast, despite the raging headache that hadn't disappeared, even after vigorous exercise.

I found the surf school easily. There was a small shack on the beach with several longboards leaning against one of the walls. They were all a robin's-egg blue, which I assumed made it easier for students to be located.

After checking in and paying for the lesson, Kari escorted me to a flat surface of the beach where she went over the fundamentals of surfing. She was very pleasant, and I found her positive attitude infectious. The truth is that I felt a little guilty for what I was about to do.

Kari taught me how to stand on the board, which is a fairly simple process that somehow escapes my abilities. For those of you who have never attempted the sport, you lie on your stomach and paddle like crazy as the wave approaches you. Once the board starts to accelerate from the movements of the wave, you pop up with both legs at the same time and stand. Couldn't be easier, right? I wish.

We practiced this pop-up technique several times on dry land. She complimented my form and generally seemed to be authentic in her praise. Finally, she declared me ready to try it on the waves. I stood and carried the board into the ocean. Kari came with me, of course, but she had a small board that was white with two yellow stripes that ran its length. She told me that she'd demonstrate the technique first, which she did. Watching her reminded me of my previous lessons with Alana. Kari was graceful and her form was effortless and smooth.

She rode the wave into the shore. Then she hopped off and made a little splash in the water. She turned around and paddled back to me. I could have confronted her right then and there. Instead, I decided to postpone the discussion and instead made several attempts to surf. I wasn't half bad.

After about ten minutes had passed, I told her that I needed to catch my breath, which was partially true. We sat on the boards, which gently flowed back and forth with the waves, and we looked out toward the deep ocean.

"Guy Livingston's case has gone to the jury. Did you know that?" I asked.

"No, I haven't been following it."

"He asked me to investigate his case."

"I know. You told me when we met outside my house."

"It was an interesting case. Not the most complex one I've done, but I still didn't come to the conclusion I thought it would."

I studied her for a reaction, but I didn't get one. Kari seemed genuinely curious and I began to wonder if she was a borderline sociopath. The girl was only fifteen years old, which I'd discovered when Alana ran her name and had discovered she'd just gotten her learner's permit. She should have been panicked by our discussion.

"Guy originally hired me to find his wife's stolen jewelry, only I learned it wasn't actually stolen. Lucy faked a robbery with her lover and had him sell the necklace and bracelet on another island for quick cash."

"I didn't know that," she said.

"After I told him about the affair, he went home, and his wife was dead just a few hours later. The police assumed it was him, but he swore he didn't do it."

"I'm sure they all say that."

"They do, and most of them are lying. Still, I've had my share of innocent clients falsely accused, which is why I agreed to work with him again."

"Now you think he didn't do it?" Kari asked.

"Oh, I think he did, but not for the reasons that the police think."

"Why did he kill Mrs. Livingston then?"

"You may not know this either, but one of the reasons Guy and Lucy moved to Maui was to start over. He'd had an affair where they used to live, and she left him. He eventually got her back, and that's why he'd given her the necklace and bracelet. It was for their anniversary and it was a celebration of their new love."

"Pretty heartless of her to sell it then."

"I thought so too, and I'm a little embarrassed I didn't question that behavior more. But I was hired to find the jewelry and I did. I think I got so caught up in the fake robbery scheme that I didn't bother to look beyond that. Then Lucy was killed and that changed everything again."

"Why would you need to question her behavior? She did what she did."

"Yes, but Lucy obviously loved Guy. She had to love him enough to overlook the affair and be willing to move thousands of miles away to give their marriage another shot. A woman who would do that isn't likely to then embark on her own affair and sell off a treasured anniversary gift."

Kari didn't respond, so I continued.

"I actually met with Lucy's lover. His name's Bret Hardy and he told me that she suspected Guy was having an affair again. He said that Lucy was so convinced that he was cheating that she started to monitor his phone, his computer, even his credit card bills. But she couldn't find any evidence."

"Maybe she got it wrong."

"That was a possibility, but I decided to explore it anyway. Guy had me convinced that he didn't kill his wife. Actually, let me rephrase that. He opened my mind to the possibility that he didn't do it. The way I saw it, if he didn't kill his wife, then maybe his jealous lover did. So, I decided to find his lover and question her.

"At first, I thought it was this woman named Bella Bridges. She was his business partner. A beautiful woman, but he hadn't expressed any interest in her. She did provide one important piece of information, though. She said that they had their afternoons free since they performed their photoshoots in the early morning and early evening.

"That's when I realized why Lucy hadn't been able to find any evidence of Guy's affair. There was no evidence that she could see. He didn't have anything on his credit card because he never took his lover to a hotel. She came to his house. He also never used his cell phone because there was no reason to. He saw her all the time. The computer was a slightly different story. There was nothing on his home computer, but his work computer had the evidence. Did you know, Kari, that today's cameras store metadata on all the photos you take?"

"I don't really think about it much," she said.

"They do, and that's how I was able to determine that Guy conducted a dozen photo sessions with his lover, all taken on the bed he shared with his wife."

"You saw those, huh?"

"Unfortunately, yes."

"They don't prove anything but the fact that I posed for him."

"Sure. I know that. But here's what I think happened. You and Guy felt safe to conduct your affair during the afternoons since Lucy worked at a bank. Those are about as regular hours as you can get. She left work early the day she was murdered. She told the manager she was sick, but I think she'd figured out what her husband was doing. She went home early to catch him in the act, and she did. She must have been horrified when she realized her husband's lover was an underage girl. He'd already done that before, and she was foolish enough to believe he wouldn't do it again."

Kari paused a long moment.

Then she said, "She threatened to turn him in for statutory rape. He panicked and he grabbed the gun from his nightstand."

"He shot her and then told you to go home."

"The idiot thought he could get away with it. He thought he could tell the cops that he found her like that, and they'd believe him."

"You realize you obstructed justice when you didn't tell the police what you knew."

"What are they going to do to me? I'm a minor. I'm the victim here. Guy took advantage of my innocence."

"Your innocence?"

"None of this matters anyway. He's about to be convicted for murder and it's your word against mine. We're out in the ocean. No witnesses to our conversation," she said.

I pointed to a boat about fifty yards from us.

"See that boat over there?" I asked.

"Yes."

"There's a detective onboard with a parabolic microphone. She's recorded every word we've said. That's why I shifted my board in this direction."

"Nice trick, if it's true."

"Say hello to Alana. She's quite the surfer too. She might even be able to show you a thing or two."

"I doubt that."

"I appreciate the lesson, Kari. I think I'll take the board in now."

Kari said nothing.

I paddled the board back into shore. I didn't attempt to ride the waves. I didn't want to look like a fool after my conversation with Kari.

I walked back to my car and retrieved my phone from the glove compartment. I dialed Alana's number.

"Did you get all of that?" I asked.

"Loud and clear."

"What do you think will happen to her?"

"Tough to say. I'll give this recording to the DA's office and they can decide what to do with it. She's right when she said she'll be viewed as one of the victims, at least that's how her attorney will make it seem."

"You saw the photos I saw. She's not so innocent."

"I agree, but the law's the law. She'll probably skate. Fortunately, the same can't be said for Guy Livingston."

I ended the call with Alana and found a public restroom where I changed into dry clothes. I didn't drive home to Kaanapali. Instead, I phoned Henry Mitchell, the attorney for Guy Livingston. He informed me that word had been sent out that the jury had reached their verdict. I told him that I'd meet him at the courtroom since I'd had a major breakthrough in the case. Yes, it was a cruel thing to give someone false hope, but I was in a cruel mood after having my theory confirmed.

It was an easy drive to Kahului, and I arrived just moments before the jury came out. Guy's eyes lit up when he saw me, apparently believing that I'd found an innocent sap to pin the crime on.

"Hello, Guy. I guess I was wrong before when I said I wouldn't be rushing to the courtroom with last-minute proof."

"What did you find?" Henry Mitchell asked.

I removed my phone from my pocket and opened the photos application. Then I handed the phone to the attorney.

"Looks like you were wrong when you said your client wasn't lying about his innocence," I said.

Henry Mitchell looked at the phone. Then he looked at Guy Livingston.

"What the hell is this?" Mitchell asked, and he showed the phone to Guy.

"I can explain," Guy said.

"You're done, Mr. Livingston. Enjoy your time in prison. You've more than earned it," I said.

I retrieved my phone and then walked to the back of the courtroom. I hung around long enough to hear the jury's verdict: Guilty.

28

THE WAREHOUSE

THE REST OF THE MORNING AND EARLY AFTERNOON WAS SPENT IN A funk. I couldn't shake how I'd allowed myself to get talked into helping Guy Livingston and I wondered if I was making the same mistake with Mele Akamu and her sidekick Samson. It certainly wasn't the first time I'd questioned my involvement with her, and I made a promise to myself that I'd walk away from the investigation if my conversation with Stan Cross didn't amount to much.

I was so depressed that I thought about going upstairs to take a long nap and try to forget I'd ever encountered Guy Livingston and Mele Akamu. Fortunately, Foxx called and offered a welcome distraction. He told me that he'd tracked down Stan Cross and he wanted to know when I was available to interview our last known suspect. I told him I was available immediately, which is how I ended up in the Harry's parking lot shortly thereafter.

Foxx must have been on the lookout for me since he came out of the bar as I pulled into the parking lot. He unlocked his SUV's door with the key fob. As I climbed onto the passenger seat, I saw Foxx pull a Glock out from the back of his pants and place it in the side pocket of the driver's side door.

"You're bringing a gun?" I asked.

"You're not?"

"No, I never bring one."

"Maybe you should start, especially after deciding to meet with a guy like Stan Cross."

Foxx started the vehicle and then backed out of the parking space. We exited the Harry's lot and made our way over to Honoapi-ilani Highway for the drive to the center of the island.

Foxx had learned that Stan Cross operated out of an old sugar-cane plantation warehouse. Of course, that wasn't his actual business. He had a diversified portfolio of illegal activities. Check that, alleged illegal activities since the police had been unable to make anything stick. The only person who seemed to have any kind of edge over him was Mele Akamu, and that advantage was quickly eroding, if it hadn't completely vanished by now.

"How do you want to handle this? I doubt he's going to admit to anything," Foxx said.

"You never know. He probably didn't reach his level of success by being modest and withdrawn. He may want to talk freely and rub our noses in it."

"Rub our noses in it? You mean that we're working for Mele Akamu and he wants us to know he's beaten us?"

"Something like that. But it won't just be about us paying attention to his answers. We also need to observe how he talks. Obvious lies can be just as revealing as someone telling you the truth."

"Good point. Kind of like when a girl I was dating recently asked if I was still seeing other people. I said no, which wasn't exactly accurate," Foxx said.

"What did she do?"

"She picked her purse up off the table and walked out of my house without saying another word."

"Sorry to hear that."

"Don't be. I wasn't that into her. Maybe that's why my little white lie was so unconvincing."

I laughed.

"Are you ever going to settle down, Foxx?"

"That's funny. I'm surprised you'd ask me that, especially after this Hani-Yuto mess. Marriage isn't for me. Too much drama."

"I don't know about that. My good moments with Alana are way more frequent than any fights we might have."

"Yeah, but most of your fights are about her family. You don't just marry the woman, Poe. You marry the whole clan."

"There's a lot of truth to that."

"I know there is. But I've got Ava. I've got friends. I've got a successful business. What more do I really need?" Foxx asked.

I didn't respond since the answer was obvious. Foxx was a happy man. He didn't really need anything else. He'd always been that way, though, at least as far back as I could remember. Foxx is the ultimate optimist and I didn't see that ever changing.

"You know we never got much of a chance to talk about Yuto's bombshell since we went right into drinking mode after he left," Foxx continued.

"Don't remind me. I may have to swear off Manhattans for a while. My head still hurts."

"What did Alana say when you told her the news?"

"I didn't have to. Hani and her mother were already at the house when I got back," I said.

Foxx laughed.

"Why didn't you tell me sooner?"

"I'm glad I can amuse you so easily."

"What did I say, pal? You don't just marry the woman. You marry the family."

"Hani seemed more upset that she was the one who got dumped. My dear old mom-in-law sort of said the same thing. Then there was the news that I'd kept Hani's meetings with her father a secret from Alana," I said.

"Oh boy, I bet that went over well."

"Not nearly as bad as expected. I think Alana was worn out by the whole thing. She cut me some slack."

Foxx laughed again.

"What's so funny?" I asked.

"How can a guy as smart as you be so dumb sometimes?"

"Dumb? What did I say?"

"That Alana cut you some slack. Trust me. She's still angry. She just decided to hold it in reserve until she needs to spring it on you at a later date. I can hear her now. 'Remember that time you didn't tell me what Hani was doing?' It's coming, buddy boy. Just accept it and rehearse your apology speech until then," Foxx said.

"Maybe I should buy her some flowers or something."

"I'd wait for the actual outburst to come. Then get the flowers. Maybe even some chocolates."

Our conversation about how dumb I was regarding women continued for several minutes. It certainly wasn't the first time we'd talked at length on that topic.

We eventually arrived at the warehouse but didn't see any cars. Foxx parked by one of the warehouse doors and we climbed out of the vehicle.

I opened the warehouse door without knocking and walked inside. The interior didn't match the exterior. While the outside looked run down and abandoned, the interior was much nicer with a series of small offices and a large common room that had a billiards table, a large flat-screen television, and several pieces of comfortable-looking leather furniture. It resembled a bachelor's recreation room.

A guy about Foxx's size approached us. He appeared out of nowhere, and he didn't look happy.

"You two lost or something?"

The question had come out as more of a growl. I hoped Foxx had remembered to grab his gun from the SUV before coming inside, but it was too late to ask.

"We're looking for Stan Cross," I said.

Before the burly man could respond, we heard a voice coming from one of the offices behind us.

"You found him."

I turned around and saw a man around fifty-years-old walking toward us. He was about six feet tall, muscular, and he had a thick head of light-brown hair that was gray at the temples. A moment later, two more men emerged from the same office. They were both about the same size as the muscle who'd initially questioned us.

"I'd ask how you found me, but it's not like this place is a secret," Stan Cross continued.

"Then why camouflage it?" Foxx asked.

"I'm not. I just don't see a reason to fix up the outside. We spend all our time in here."

Stan Cross stopped several feet away and sized us up.

"Let me guess. You want to ask me about Mele Akamu," he said.

"That's right," I said.

"Ask away. I've got nothing to hide."

"Do you know anything about Eric Ellis' murder?" Foxx asked.

"I know enough. The kid vanished about five years ago and then his body showed up. The cops arrested Mele Akamu and that thug of hers for the crime."

"We spoke with someone who told us that you were dealing with Eric in the days before he was killed," I said.

"That's right. He came to me and asked for a job. I said no."

"Asked for a job? We heard he called you and offered to sell you information on Mele Akamu's business," I said.

"That's not exactly how it went down," Stan said.

"Then what happened?" Foxx asked.

"He wanted a package deal. He said he'd help take down Mele Akamu by giving me details about her business. He also wanted to come work for me. I'm not a trusting man. I already knew who Eric Ellis was. I also knew everything that Mele Akamu had done for him."

"You thought Mele Akamu put him up to it?" I asked.

"The thought crossed my mind. But if she hadn't, I still didn't want anything to do with the guy. If he'd turn on Mele Akamu, then he'd eventually turn on me too. There was also his woman. I looked into Eric and discovered he was two-timing her. It seemed that he'd turned on everyone in his life. Someone like that can never be trusted, and I can't have guys around me that I can't trust. I told him no."

"How did he react?" I asked.

"How do you think? He was upset. He had no one else to turn to, if his story was to be believed."

"What did you think after he disappeared?" Foxx asked.

"I realized I'd guessed wrong. He really had betrayed Mele Akamu and he got killed for it," Stan said.

"You think she killed him?" I asked.

Stan Cross laughed.

"You don't? Who else would have done it?"

"Maybe someone who wanted to frame her for the murder," Foxx said.

"And they waited five years to make their move? No. There's no chance of that. People in this line of work don't have that kind of patience."

"Oleen Akamu told the police that she saw Mele Akamu murder Eric Ellis, but then she admitted to us that you paid her to say that," I said.

"You boys really need to get your facts straight. She came to me all right. I must admit that I got a great deal of satisfaction out of it too. An Akamu begging for my help. It was priceless. She told me that she knew I'd benefit from having Mele Akamu out of the way. She asked me how much it was worth to me. I asked her what she meant. That's when she told me that she'd claim to be an eyewitness to the murder if I paid her."

"What did you say?" Foxx asked.

"I told her that I'd think about it. She went to the police before I gave her an answer. I guess she thought I'd show my gratitude and give her money. Why would I? The idiot already gave me what I wanted, and I didn't have to pay anything for it."

"She's retracted her testimony," I said, although I wasn't really sure if she'd gotten around to telling the police that she'd lied.

"Does it make a difference? I heard the cops have the gun," Stan said.

"You seem to be well connected," Foxx said.

"Not necessarily. Good news travels fast, and the murder weapon found at Akamu's house is certainly good news. I can't wait to see how she tries to get out of that. Now it's my turn to ask a few questions. I heard Tavii Akamu isn't running for reelection. Is that true?"

"It is," I said.

"Please tell me he's going to take over his grandmother's business," Stan said.

"Is that a question?" Foxx asked.

"I suppose not since I can already figure out the answer. My guess is that he thinks he can pull it off. I look forward to going head to head with him," Stan said.

"One more question. Did you know a man named Daniel Davis?" I asked.

"Never heard of him, but I assume he's dead since you referred to him in the past tense."

"He drowned while surfing, at least that's what it was meant to look like," I said.

"I think we're done here. I've indulged you gentleman long enough."

"Not yet. Your man over here looked away when my friend commented about the drowning," Foxx said, and he nodded toward one of the men who'd followed Stan Cross out of the office.

"A man's not allowed to look away?" Stan asked.

"Of course, he is. My friend was just questioning the timing," I said.

"And I said I'm done with your questions. You can show yourself to the door," Stan said.

Neither Foxx nor I made a move.

"Mr. Cross said to leave," the man who Foxx had accused of looking guilty said, and he pushed Foxx in the chest.

Foxx grabbed the man's wrist and twisted it hard. I wasn't sure if he'd broken it, but the guy yelled and dropped to his knees. The burly man beside him rushed toward Foxx, only for Foxx to kick the man in the side of his knee. He started to go down too, and Foxx encouraged the movement to the floor by punching him in the jaw.

The third bodyguard, the one who'd initially approached us,

pulled a gun and pointed it at Foxx. I moved in front of Foxx and held up my hands.

"That's enough. We're leaving," I said.

"That's good to hear," Stan said. "We wouldn't want the husband of Detective Hu getting hurt."

"You know who I am?" I asked.

"I do my homework, Edgar Rutherford. Or should I call you Poe? Consider yourself fortunate that I always think before I act. Tell your lovely wife that I said hello. I've got nothing but respect for law enforcement. They're our modern-day heroes," Stan said, and he smirked.

"Yeah, I'm sure that's exactly how you feel," Foxx said.

"One more thing before you leave. Give Mele Akamu my best, and please deliver this message for me. Tell her that karma has a long memory, even after a couple of decades," Stan said.

I didn't reply. Instead, I turned to Foxx and nodded.

We managed to get out of the warehouse in one piece. I don't think I breathed a sigh of relief until we were a mile down the road in the safety of Foxx's SUV.

"He knows way too much about the case. He must be guilty," Foxx said.

"I'm inclined to agree with you. By the way, did you bring the gun in with you?"

"Yeah, but then I realized I could handle those guys without it."

"Until they pulled a gun of their own."

"A miscalculation on my part. How do you think he found out who you were? Someone must have told him you took Mele Akamu's case. Who do you think it was?" Foxx asked.

I had no idea and that scared me a little.

29

THE AFFAIR

I LOOKED OUT THE WINDOW AS WE DROVE DOWN THE COAST AND headed toward Lahaina. I didn't think I'd ever get used to the beauty of the island. The truth is, I didn't want to.

Foxx turned on the radio and we heard the song, "Speak to Me," from Pink Floyd's *Dark Side of the Moon* playing.

"Great album," I said without taking my eyes off that gorgeous view.

"One of my favorites. I've lost count of how many times I've listened to it. Hey, what did you think about that comment Stan made about not trusting Eric Ellis?"

"I agree with it. I wouldn't have trusted him either."

"Yeah but does that mean Stan wouldn't have done the deal with Eric? I don't buy that Stan told him to get lost."

"No, he wouldn't have. It would have low risk to hear what Eric had to say. Of course, that didn't mean Stan had to act on it," I said.

"What about that comment that Eric was cheating on Gracie Ito?"

"It's certainly possible. Eric betrayed Mele Akamu. He probably did the same thing to Gracie."

"You realize what that means."

"Yep, we have another suspect. The jealous girlfriend."

"Want to question her about it? Her apartment is on the way back," Foxx said.

"Let's do it."

"Do you think Gracie knew Eric was seeing someone on the side?"

"Without a doubt. Women always know. And if Stan Cross was able to find out so quickly, then I'm sure someone who was living with Eric must have known too."

We got to Gracie's apartment complex in no time. It was late afternoon by this point, and I hoped we'd get lucky and find her home. We did. When she opened the door, I could tell from the look on her face that she wasn't exactly happy to see us again. I didn't blame her. I wouldn't have been either.

"Ms. Ito, do you have time for a few more questions?" I asked.

"Not really. I was just on my way out for an appointment," she said.

Did I believe her? Not in a million years. She was wearing a tank top with a long tear on the bottom, short shorts that would have barely covered a bikini bottom, and no shoes. Did that look like someone who was on their way out the door? Of course, we were on Maui, so it was possible. Still, I assumed she was lying as most everyone else in this investigation was guilty of doing.

"It will just take a moment," I assured her.

She paused for a few seconds. Then she nodded and allowed us to enter.

"We just came from a meeting with Stan Cross," Foxx said.

"He said some interesting things," I said.

"He told us that Eric was cheating on you," Foxx said.

A woman ignorant of her boyfriend's infidelity would have shown surprise, even hurt after all of these years. Gracie did not, but I'm sure you already expected as much. I certainly did.

"You already knew," I said more than asked.

"Yes, I knew," she admitted.

"And you didn't say anything because you knew how it would look," I said.

"No, I didn't say anything because it's irrelevant. I didn't kill Eric."

"When did you learn about his affair?" Foxx asked.

"About a week before he disappeared."

"Did you confront him about it?" I asked.

"No, I wasn't sure how," she said.

"I find that hard to believe," I said.

"Me too. I've had more than one woman tell me what they thought of my cheating. They don't ever have problems expressing themselves," Foxx said.

"Well, I'm not like everyone else," Gracie said.

"I'm sure you're not, Ms. Ito. Perhaps you were afraid to lose what you had," I said.

"And that's exactly what happened when he died. I lost everything," she said.

"People aren't acting rational when they kill, though. They're emotional. They're angry. They're out of control," Foxx said.

"You can say whatever you want, but I didn't hurt him. I loved him."

"Do you know who the other woman was?" I asked.

"Not until the night he vanished. I already told you about the day Eric disappeared. He got that phone call from Stan. Later he said he had to meet with Mele Akamu."

"But you didn't think that was where he was really going," I guessed.

"I didn't know what to think. I followed him after he left. He went to that woman's apartment."

"Did you see her?" Foxx asked.

"Yes, when she opened the door. I thought about letting myself in and catching them in the act. I didn't, though. I waited outside in my car. He never came out," she said.

"How long did you wait?" I asked.

She didn't respond.

"How long?" I repeated

"I'm embarrassed to admit it."

"Please. It's important for us to try to establish a timeline," I said.

"He left the house around eleven. I stayed outside her apartment until a little after two in the morning."

"Did you ever find out who she was?" Foxx asked.

"When Eric didn't come home, I thought he was still with her. I went back to her apartment the next day and saw her coming out the front door. That's when I said something to her."

"What did she say?" I asked.

"She wouldn't talk to me. She ran back inside."

"Was Eric's car still in the parking lot?" Foxx asked.

"No, it was gone."

"Did you ever find out the woman's name?" I asked.

"Yes, it's Tiana Wise."

"How did they meet?" Foxx asked.

"I don't know. I don't really care," she said.

"Is there anything else you didn't tell us?" I asked.

Yes, I know. It was a bit of a dumb question, but I threw it out there anyway.

"You know everything now, not that it matters. I already told you before that Mele Akamu killed him. He may not have gone to see her that night, but he probably went the next morning. He never came back."

"Thank you for talking to us again. We won't keep you from your appointment any longer," I said.

"My what?" she asked.

"You said you were on your way to an appointment when we knocked on the door," I reminded her.

"Oh yeah, that."

I knew she'd been lying before, but I wanted to see how good she was at remembering her lies. Apparently, the answer to that question was not very good. As I've said in the past, there are people who are accomplished at telling tall tales, but most liars are pretty easy to spot. Gracie Ito fit squarely into the latter category.

"Can you tell us where Tiana Wise lived?" Foxx asked.

"I can, but I have no idea if she's still there," Gracie said, and then she gave us the address.

Her statement that she didn't know if Tiana still lived there was another lie, based on her eye movement and body language. I assumed Gracie had swung by the apartment after our initial interview with her.

Tiana Wise might not have been the killer, but Gracie Ito apparently thought she could be. The lover might have had enough of Eric's false promises that he'd leave Gracie one day. Did I think that likely? Not really, but Tiana was one of the last people to see Eric Ellis alive. She had to know something, after all.

We thanked Gracie Ito again and walked back outside to Foxx's SUV. Here's something I didn't point out a few moments ago. After Gracie gave us the address for Tiana's apartment complex, I realized that I'd been there before. And here's the stunner. Tiana lived in the same twelve-unit duplex in Paia where Daniel Davis had lived. Did I think that was a coincidence? Nope.

Foxx picked up on the same thing for he asked me about it when we climbed into his vehicle.

"Hey, isn't the–"

"Yes, the same apartment complex as our mysterious dog owner," I said, cutting him off.

"You got time to head there now?"

"I certainly do."

Foxx reversed course and we headed back toward the northern part of Maui.

"You think she still lives there after all this time?"

"I do," I said, and I told Foxx my theory that Gracie may have driven out there after our previous meeting.

"You think she already confronted her about Eric?" Foxx asked.

"No, but I think she intended to. She probably chickened out again like she did when she went to confront Eric and Tiana over their affair."

We made good time to Paia and before we knew it, we were pulling back into the small parking lot for the apartment complex. There were several cars already there, which was a good sign that Tiana Wise was home.

Gracie had even provided us with the apartment number, and she'd done so without referring to any notes, further bolstering my theory that she'd gone there within the last week. We walked the stairs to the second floor of the complex and knocked on the apartment door for Tiana, which was a few units down from Daniel's.

A woman with short, dirty-blonde hair opened the door. She had hazel eyes, an athlete's physique, and she was dressed similarly to Gracie in a tank top and shorts. They were both beautiful women. Eric Ellis certainly had a way with the female gender.

"Good afternoon, ma'am. My name is Edgar Rutherford. This is my partner, Doug Foxx. We're investigating the death of Eric Ellis."

I waited for a response but didn't get one.

"May we come in, Ms. Wise?" Foxx asked.

"Yes," she said.

We walked into the tiny apartment, which was an exact duplicate of Daniel Davis' place. While Daniel's home had been sparse and uninviting, Tiana's was painted in warm colors. The coffee table in front of the sofa was covered with small stones, crystals, and other supplies used to make necklaces and bracelets.

"Sorry, but the place is a bit of a mess. I'm getting ready for an art show this weekend," she said.

"You sell jewelry?" Foxx asked.

"Among other things. I'm a little surprised to find you here. I didn't think anyone was going to interview me about Eric," she said.

"The police haven't been by?" I asked.

"No, I don't think they know about Eric and me. Gracie must have told you."

"That's right," Foxx said.

"Does she think I killed him?" Tiana asked.

"She didn't say that," Foxx said.

"Ms. Wise, before we get into your relationship with Eric, can you tell me what you know about Daniel Davis?" I asked.

"Who?" she asked a bit too quickly.

"He used to live a few units down from you. He drowned recently."

"I heard something about that. Terrible news, but I didn't know him very well. We'd say hello when we passed on the stairway. I didn't even know his name."

"There's only a handful of apartments here. You really didn't know his name?" Foxx asked.

"People here tend to keep to themselves. What can I say?"

I would have believed that if this were in an apartment complex in New York, Chicago, or some other large metropolitan area. On Maui? Not a chance. The Aloha spirit wouldn't have allowed it. Still, there was no point in arguing with her. As I said to Foxx a while back, obvious lies are just as helpful as the truth, sometimes even more so.

"We're not here to judge you, Ms. Wise, but we're assisting the police in their investigation," I said.

It was a lie of my own since we weren't technically helping Detective Parrish, which you already know. But I wanted to put her at some ease since we were about to dive into her romantic dealings. Was I worried that she'd call the police to verify my claim? I wasn't. If she'd wanted to talk to them, she would have called them days ago. And she obviously knew about Eric Ellis' remains being found since she'd told us that she was surprised that no one had come to speak with her before.

"You were in a relationship with Eric Ellis when he disappeared five years ago. Is that correct?" I asked.

"I was."

"How long had you been with Eric?" I asked.

"A few months. We met at the Paia Fish Market. It was a long line that day. Well, it's almost always a long line in that place. Eric was standing behind me. We got to talking. Then he asked if he could sit at the table with me since it was so crowded. We went out that night."

"Were you aware that he was also dating Gracie Ito?" Foxx asked.

"Not at first, but he eventually told me. He said he was going to leave her," she said.

Yes, she felt the need to repeat that tired, old line. They always promise to leave, and they rarely do.

"Did Eric ever talk about his job?" I asked.

"All the time. I was the one who convinced him to leave that Akamu woman. She didn't appreciate him. I told him he could do better," Tiana said.

"Were you aware that he tried to blackmail Mele Akamu?" Foxx asked.

"It wasn't blackmail. He was getting what he deserved."

Yes, it was a loaded statement, but I didn't point out the irony.

"Gracie told us that he left their home to see Mele Akamu, only Gracie followed him to your apartment. She said she waited outside for a while, but she didn't see him leave. Do you remember when he left your place that night?" I asked.

"Yes, it was around three in the morning. I remember because we were both asleep in bed when he got a phone call. He seemed upset and he said he had to leave. I thought it was his girlfriend, but it wasn't."

"Who was it?" Foxx asked.

"That Akamu woman. She said she wanted to meet with him immediately. I told him to wait until the morning, but he wouldn't."

"Are you positive it was Mele Akamu who called him that night?" Foxx asked.

"I'm sure. He said it was her. We argued a little about it. I told him he shouldn't jump whenever she told him to. It made him upset that I'd say something like that. He should have listened to me, though. He might still be alive."

"Why didn't you go to the police about your suspicions after Eric disappeared?" I asked.

"Because I was scared. Wouldn't you be?" she asked.

"One more question, I know you weren't friends with Daniel Davis, but did you ever see him with anyone?" I asked.

"No, he was always by himself."

"Thank you for your time, Ms. Wise," I said.

"I heard they arrested Mele Akamu. Do you think she'll get convicted? Is that why you're here? To gather more evidence?"

"Exactly," Foxx said.

She didn't respond. Perhaps she was trying to figure out if we had ulterior motives.

We thanked her again and she walked us to the door. I wished Tiana Wise good luck with her art show and we walked back to Foxx's vehicle.

"So, Eric Ellis got two calls the day he disappeared. One from Stan Cross and one from Mele Akamu," Foxx said

"Unless either Gracie or Tiana was lying."

"Maybe both. Maybe Eric just told them that so he'd have an excuse to leave."

"Maybe," I said.

"Do you think Mele Akamu would really want to see him in the middle of the night? I can only think of one reason she'd want to do that."

I already knew what Foxx was thinking. She'd only want to see Eric at three in the morning if she'd wanted to kill him. But Eric must have known that too. So, why did he go, especially since it had been such a foolish decision to do so? On the other hand, he had tried to blackmail her. The guy couldn't have been all that smart.

30

POPCORN

Foxx and I continued to debate the facts of the case when we got back to Harry's. We didn't make any progress since everything was still so unclear. After a couple of Negra Modelos, I decided to head for home since I was mentally exhausted. I thought a few laps in the pool might cheer me up, which they did.

I'd just climbed out of the pool when I saw Maui racing past me. I turned and saw Alana walking out of the sliding glass door. Maui did one of his world-famous rolls onto his back, despite having been running at full speed. It was impossible to ignore the skill level of his acrobatics, which I supposed was a part of his master plan for attention.

Alana kneeled and scratched his belly.

"Good evening to you too, Maui," she said.

The dog wagged his tail even more at the sound of his name.

"How did everything go with you today?" I asked, and I must have hit the words, "with you," a touch harder than I realized.

"Rough day?"

"Are you asking me or are you saying you had a rough day?"

"I'm asking you. I can hear the stress in your voice," she said.

"And here I thought my time in the pool helped calm me down."

"Then you must have been really worked up before. What happened?"

I told Alana about my meetings with Stan Cross, Gracie Ito, and Tiana Wise. I left out the part about Foxx bringing a gun to the interview with Stan. I also intentionally forgot to mention that Foxx took two of Stan's guys out.

"You two actually went to see Stan Cross?" she asked.

"It was a friendly conversation."

"I'm sure. You still think he did it?"

"If I had to make the call tonight, then yes, I think he did it," I said.

"What about this Tiana woman's claim that Mele Akamu called Eric in the middle of the night? Do you believe it?"

"He left for some reason. It might as well have been because of her phone call. I think the more interesting revelation is that she lived three apartments down from Daniel Davis."

"Yes, it does seem that Mr. Davis was up to his eyeballs in this case," Alana said.

"Are you still investigating his death, or have you officially ruled it an accidental drowning?"

"I'm still looking into it."

"What does Detective Parrish have to say?" I asked.

"Not much."

"Are you going to tell him the connection between Daniel Davis and Tiana Wise?"

"Not sure there would be a point to that. He already thinks he has his man – or his man and woman in this case. He may not be wrong. Tiana Wise did tell you that Eric Ellis left in the middle of the night after a call from Mele Akamu. Maybe it's time you accept the fact that she probably did it," Alana said.

I didn't respond.

"I'm going to the food mart in Paia tomorrow morning to talk to some of Daniel's co-workers. Let me know if you want to follow me out there," she continued.

"Sounds good. Any updates on Hani?"

"Only that my mother still isn't talking to her, and don't ask me how long that's going to last because I have no idea."

"Does Hani seeing your father change your mind about anything?"

"If that's your way of asking if I'm going to see him, then the answer is still no. Tell me something, Poe. Why are you so convinced Mele Akamu didn't do it?"

"If I told you that, you'd never trust my instincts again," I said.

"I seriously doubt that. What is it?"

"She reminds me of my grandmother, and before you start laughing, yes I know how sad that sounds."

"You must really miss your grandmother."

"Of course. Outside of you, I don't really have any family left. I was an only child, but you already know that."

"I'm sorry I never got to meet your parents. I would have very much liked to get to know them."

"They would have loved you. What I wouldn't give to talk to them for just one more day."

"Come on inside. I bought some tuna steaks on the way home."

I followed Alana into the house. We made ourselves a fantastic dinner, which was followed by an evening of trashy television.

I got up early the next morning to complete my swim and jog around the neighborhood. Then I hopped into the convertible and followed Alana to Paia. If you've been to the town before, then I'm sure you're familiar with the grocery mart where Daniel Davis worked. The small store is jampacked with organic fruits and vegetables, which made me realize I'd forgotten to bring my canvas bags to do some shopping after the interviews.

We entered the store and found the manager. Alana flashed him her badge and asked to speak to any of the employees who knew Daniel best. The answer was a stocker named Brianna Marks. He led us to the storage rooms in the back where we met the young woman.

I guessed her age to be in her late twenties. She had short, blonde hair like Tiana Wise, but she was considerably smaller than Tiana, maybe only five foot tall at most. We introduced ourselves to Brianna and then walked to the employee break area outside the back of the store since everything was so cramped inside.

We found a shady spot under an avocado tree to get out of the hot sun.

"Thank you for speaking with us, Ms. Marks. How long did you work with Daniel?" Alana asked.

"A little over two years."

"Did you have a friendship outside of work?" Alana asked.

"We did. I'd go to his apartment from time to time to hang out," she said.

"Were you romantically involved with him?" Alana asked.

"No, we were just friends."

"Can you tell us if Daniel was under any kind of stress in the last few weeks?" Alana asked.

"Stress?"

"Yes, was he upset about anything?" Alana asked.

"I don't understand why you're asking me these questions. I thought Daniel drowned. Are you saying he might have taken his own life?"

"That's what we're trying to figure out," Alana said.

"Yes, he was under pressure, but he never would have hurt himself."

"Why was he under pressure?" I asked.

"He owed some guy money."

"A friend?" Alana asked.

"No, a loan shark."

"How much did he owe?" Alana asked.

"Five thousand."

"What was the money for?" I asked.

"I don't know."

"Did Daniel take drugs?" Alana asked.

"He smoked pot, but who doesn't?" she asked.

I could think of a few people, myself included, but I decided not to say anything.

"Did he ever say the name of the loan shark?" Alana asked.

"Yes, but I think he was just making up the name. It didn't make sense," Brianna said.

"What is it?" I asked.

"Daniel said the guy's name is Popcorn."

I caught Alana's expression out of the corner of my eye.

"Do you know the guy?" I asked.

"Unfortunately, yes," Alana said, and she turned back to Brianna. "Ms. Marks, did Daniel ever mention the names Eric Ellis or Mele Akamu?"

"No, I never heard of either of those names."

"What about the name Tiana Wise?" I asked.

"The name Tiana sounds really familiar."

"She lives in the same apartment complex as Daniel did. Short blonde hair like you," I said.

"Oh yeah, she was at his place once when I came over. She didn't stay long," Brianna said.

"She was inside his apartment?" I asked.

"Yes."

"Did Daniel say anything about her after she left?" Alana asked.

"Just that they were neighbors and old friends."

"Thank you, Ms. Marks. You've been very helpful," Alana said.

"You really think Daniel killed himself?"

"No, but we have to follow up on things like this," Alana said.

Brianna nodded, but I wasn't sure she'd accepted Alana's explanation. The truth is that I wasn't watching Brianna very closely at that point. I was concentrating too much on the revelation that Tiana Wise had lied to me about her relationship with Daniel Davis.

We decided not to talk to any other co-workers after Brianna. Alana and I walked back to the front of the store. We headed down the sidewalk to where we'd parked our cars. If you've ever been to Paia, then you know how difficult it can be to find parking. I didn't mind, though. The walk gave us time to talk about the interview with Brianna Marks.

"Surprised that Daniel and Tiana Wise were apparently friends?" Alana asked.

"I shouldn't be, but I can't figure out how the whole thing is connected. What's the deal with this Popcorn guy? How did he get that name?"

"I don't know. I asked him a few times, but he'd never tell me."

"Do you think he might have murdered Daniel Davis over the five-thousand-dollar loan?" I asked.

"Not likely. Popcorn isn't the murdering type. He's a low-level guy, which is why we've never gone out of our way to bust him. Maybe that's changed, though."

We reached our cars and I followed Alana to nearby Kahului. Alana told me that Popcorn worked out of a bar there. It was still morning, though, so I didn't know how likely it was that we'd find him. Alana assured me it wouldn't be an issue. She wasn't wrong. We spotted the diminutive loan shark seated on a stool at the end of the bar. He was of Japanese descent and I guessed his age at around fifty.

"Hello, Popcorn," Alana said, and she sat on the stool beside his.

I stood beside her.

"Who's the tall guy?" Popcorn asked after taking a long look at me.

"My husband."

"That guy?" Popcorn asked in a tone that indicated he didn't believe her.

"Don't worry, Mr. Corn, I get that a lot," I said.

"I'm sure you do."

"Don't get smart. We just have a few questions and then we'll be out of your hair," Alana said.

"Ask away, Detective," Popcorn said.

"Did you lend Daniel Davis five thousand dollars?" Alana asked.

"I certainly did."

"You know he's dead, don't you?" she asked.

"I heard that. Damn shame too. I really liked the kid."

"Do I need to ask if you had anything to do with his death?"

"Me?" Popcorn asked, and he sounded offended.

Alana didn't respond.

"First, it hurts that you'd even consider that I'd be capable of such a thing," Popcorn continued. "Second, how could I get my money back if he was dead? And third and most importantly, Daniel had already paid me back."

"All five thousand?" Alana asked.

"Yep, every last penny."

"How did he get that kind of money stocking shelves at a grocery store?" I asked.

"Daniel had a bit of a gambling problem. I assumed one of his bets finally hit big," Popcorn said.

"Who did he gamble with?" Alana asked.

"You'd have to ask Daniel. Oh, I forgot, you can't."

"Did Daniel ever mention being afraid of anyone?" I asked.

"Why is this guy asking me questions? Is he a detective too?" Popcorn asked Alana.

"Just answer his question. Was someone out to hurt Daniel?" Alana asked.

"Not that I know of. Besides, I have a strict rule. Keep it professional. I don't want to hear about their personal lives. Everyone who comes to me has some sob story."

"I'm sure," Alana said.

"When Daniel came to you, was he alone or did he bring a woman with him? Maybe a woman with short, blonde hair?" I asked.

"No, he was alone."

"Thanks, Popcorn," Alana said, and she stood.

Popcorn looked me up and down again.

"You really married that guy?" he asked.

"Yes, I did," Alana said.

"Huh, he must have a big–"

I shoved him hard and almost knocked him off his stool.

"Watch your mouth around the lady, Popcorn," I said.

"And a bad temper too," he said.

"He can be a tad overprotective sometimes, but I wouldn't press your luck with him," Alana said.

"Sure thing. Have a good day, Detective. You too, Mr. Detective."

"Enjoy your day and try to stay out of trouble," Alana said.

We walked outside the bar and headed for our cars.

"You really think I get overprotective sometimes?" I asked.

"Without question. Don't worry. It's a trait that's always scored points with me."

"That Popcorn sure is a charmer."

"He has a certain humor about him. It's how he keeps himself out of jail. That and the fact he's provided valuable information in the past."

"Now I get it. But you were right about him. He doesn't seem like the murdering type," I said.

"I know. So, we still haven't answered our big question. Who forced Daniel Davis' head under the water? I better be getting into work. You heading home?"

"Not yet. I do have a question for you before you leave. When Detective Parrish opened that safe in Mele Akamu's study, was there someone in your department with the expertise to do that?"

"No, there's a locksmith we bring in for jobs like that. I've never seen a safe he hasn't been able to crack. His office isn't far from here. Why do you ask?"

"Can you give me his name?"

"Of course."

"Also, any chance you can get some birthdates for me?" I asked.

"Birthdates for who?"

"The Akamu family, specifically Mele, her late husband and son, and Tavii."

"Why do you want those?"

"I want to test a theory."

31

THE RULE OF THREE

I SAID GOODBYE TO ALANA AND MADE THE SHORT DRIVE TO THE locksmith. His office wasn't that far from Lee Walters' jewelry store. I found a parking space directly in front and entered his shop. It was a small space filled with various safes, doorknobs and locks, and a large assortment of blank keys hanging from a board behind the counter.

There was no one to be seen, but I heard a grinding noise from a room in the back.

"Hello?" I called out.

The grinding stopped a moment later, and an elderly gentleman with a thin rim of white hair around his head walked into the customer area.

"Hi there. How may I help you?" he asked, and he pressed his black-framed glasses up on his nose.

"Yes, I'm working with Detective Hu on a case and she referred me to you."

"Ah, Alana, how wonderful. She's a delightful person."

"She certainly is. She told me that you help the police when they need to open a safe," I said.

"I do."

"Were you the one who recently opened the safe at Mele Akamu's house? It was that home in the upcountry."

"Yes, I did that one."

"I'm hoping you can answer a few questions for me about that day."

"Of course. What would you like to know?" he asked.

"First off, how difficult was the safe to open?"

"Not hard, if you have the right tools."

"Are those tools easy to find?" I asked.

"Not the ones I use. Some are custom-made by me. That safe was a digital one, high-end and expensive."

"Who else on the island has similar tools?"

"No one that I know of. That doesn't mean there isn't some safe-cracker out there who hasn't been caught yet. Alana would be the better person to ask about that."

"Did you have to drill the safe open?"

"No, that would have destroyed it. My job is to open it without damaging the safe."

"You were able to break the code?" I asked.

The man's eyes lit up.

"What can I say? I'm good at what I do. That's why the police call me."

"Was there any sign the safe had been tampered with?"

"No, it looked brand new. Of course, it would look that way since it was protected behind that bookcase. Very clever hiding space."

"After you opened the safe, did you see what was inside?" I asked.

"I saw a gun sitting on top of some papers and a couple of passports. Then that detective told me to back away."

"You mean Detective Parrish?"

"I believe that was his name. It's the first time I'd worked with him. He wasn't the most pleasant fellow."

"Was there anyone else in the room?"

"There were two other police officers. I don't know their names," he said.

"That's all of my questions. Thank you."

"You're welcome. Say hello to Alana for me."

"I will."

I left the locksmith, marveling once again at how mentioning the name Alana Hu opened doors across the island. Mele Akamu might be known as the godmother of Maui, but Alana was the queen.

I hopped into my car and drove to Mele Akamu's house. I didn't bother calling Tavii or Oleen to let me inside. Instead, I relied on my trusty lock picking kit. I was a bit out of practice, and it took me over three minutes to get past the deadbolt.

I walked past the mess that was the living room and entered the study. The bookshelf was still open. The door to the safe was also open and everything that was inside had been cleaned out. I closed the safe and pressed the lock icon. I then walked over to Mele Akamu's desk, sat down and phoned Alana.

"Hello."

"Your locksmith friend says hello."

"That's nice. He's a great guy. I've never met a lock he couldn't get past."

"He said he made some custom tools to get into safes," I said.

"He'd never admit this, but I'm pretty sure he was a burglar back in the day."

"That makes sense. Hey, I'm at Mele Akamu's house and I was wondering if I could bother you for those birthdates now."

"How did you get inside?" Alana asked.

"The door was unlocked."

"Right. Why did I even bother to ask? What's this theory of yours that requires these birthdates?"

"Your locksmith friend said this is a high-end safe, but I bet I can get inside it in under five minutes."

"I'll take that bet. What does the winner get?"

"Loser pays for dinner at the winner's restaurant of choice," I said.

"Deal. Give me a few minutes and I'll text you the dates."

I ended the call, and true to her word, the birthdates for Mele Akamu, her husband, her son, and Tavii appeared on my phone in short order.

I found a piece of paper on Mele Akamu's desk and wrote out the dates. Most people pick numbers that mean something to them when they devise security codes. So, I took some of the numbers Alana had sent me and combined them with others until I had around thirty possible codes for the safe. For example, I took the month of Mele Akamu's birth and combined it with the month of her husband's birth.

I stood and walked over to the safe. I started typing in code combinations. The safe opened on my fifth attempt. It was Mele's birth year combined with her husband's birth year. As with everything else in this case, things came down to two possibilities. Either Mele Akamu had put the gun in the safe since she and Samson had been the ones to kill Eric Ellis, or the real killer had done it.

I'd just proved that it was possible to figure out the code and I'd done so in under ten minutes. Unfortunately, that also meant I'd lost the bet with Alana, which didn't bother me since I would have insisted on paying for the dinner anyway.

I went back over to the desk and grabbed another piece of paper. In past cases, I'd made a list of things I knew or thought I knew about the case. Sometimes seeing the list in black and white helped my mind process things.

I wrote the headline, "Facts of the Eric Ellis Case," on the top of the paper.

Fact. Eric Ellis worked for Mele Akamu until he decided he wanted more. He tried to blackmail her with information he stole about her business. He then tried to sell that information to a man named Stan Cross.

Fact. Mele Akamu stated that Samson couldn't find Eric, yet Eric's girlfriend, Gracie Ito, contradicted that with a photo of a battered and bruised Eric Ellis. Mele Akamu ultimately admitted that she lied to me about that.

Gracie Ito also claimed Samson threatened her if she went to the police. Was she lying about that?

Oleen Akamu, Tavii's soon-to-be ex-wife, claimed to have been an eyewitness to Eric's murder, only to later admit that she made it up so she could be paid by Stan Cross to help implicate Mele Akamu in the crime.

Tavii Akamu pointed to Lee Walters as a suspect, claiming Lee was mad that Eric blew up their business relationship with the Akamu family.

Tavii seemed happy that his grandmother was in jail since it freed him up to take over the family business, especially after his failed political career. Was this a strong enough motive to have framed his grandmother?

Lee Walters denied hurting Eric Ellis, but he admitted that he wanted to. He pointed to Tavii as a possible suspect and said that he might have gone behind his grandmother's back to order the hit on Eric.

Gracie Ito mentioned that a man named Stan called Eric and that Eric argued with him the day he vanished.

Samson confirmed that Stan Cross was a rival of Mele Akamu and may have killed Eric.

Samson also stated that Lee Walters offered to murder his friend, Eric Ellis, in order to get back on Mele Akamu's good side. What was that saying? There is no honor among thieves?

Daniel Davis found Eric's remains with his dog, yet he'd clearly bought the dog for the purpose of finding the body. Who told him it was there? Or was he the one who buried Eric's body five years ago?

Daniel owed a substantial amount of money to a loan shark, yet he somehow came up with the money to pay it back. Was he paid that money to pretend to find Eric's body? Was he killed because of my interview with him?

Stan Cross said that he turned down Eric's offer because he didn't trust Eric. He was worried that Mele Akamu was setting him up.

Stan revealed that Eric was having an affair. The affair was confirmed by Gracie Ito.

Eric went to see his lover, Tiana Wise, the night he disappeared. He left in the middle of the night after receiving a call from Mele Akamu. Why would he have been so foolish to have done so? Or was the call from someone other than Mele Akamu? If so, why would Tiana lie about that?

Tiana Wise lived down the hall from Daniel Davis, yet she said she didn't know who he was. This was directly contradicted by a co-worker of Daniel's who saw Tiana in his apartment. What is their connection?

The police claimed to have found Mele Akamu's safe on their own, yet they hadn't trashed the study like the rest of the house. It's possible that both Tavii and Oleen Akamu separately told the police in advance about the safe. If so, why had Detective Parrish lied to me about that? Probably because he was bragging about his ability to find the well-hidden safe.

According to the locksmith, the gun was in the safe when he opened it in the presence of Detective Parrish and the other police officers. Did someone figure out the combination to the safe like I had and planted the gun beforehand?

I put the pen down. I then folded the piece of paper and shoved it into my pocket. I had a long list of information, but none of it pointed to a guilty party beyond Mele Akamu and Stan Cross, who had been my main suspects from early in the case.

I was still at a dead end, so I decided to drive home and take a run or a swim, which was another tried and true method to free my mind and think about the case. I was almost home when I received a call from Alana's mother. God only knows what caused me to answer.

"Good morning, Ms. Hu," I said in my best cheery voice.

"I need to see you."

See me and not talk to me? That was weird.

"I'll be home shortly. Is there a specific time and place you'd like to meet?"

"I'm at your house now. I'll see you soon."

She ended the call before I had a chance to fake a medical emergency.

I parked my car on the street so I wouldn't block hers in the drive-way. She was leaning against the outside of her car with her arms folded. This wasn't going to be good, and I tried to figure out what manner of crime she was about to accuse me of.

"Is everything all right?" I asked as I climbed out of the car and walked up to her.

"I don't appreciate you encouraging my daughter to see her father, especially after I confided in you what he did to me."

For those new readers, Ms. Hu had told me a few years back that her husband had beaten her, which was the true reason she'd kicked him out of the house. She asked me to keep our conversation a secret, which I had.

"I didn't know Hani had seen him until she told me," I said.

"Then why didn't you try to talk her out of future meetings?"

"I'm not Hani's caretaker. Besides, I thought she mainly needed someone to listen to her."

"I need you to make me a promise. You need to at least keep Alana away. I can't have both of my daughters brainwashed by that terrible man."

"Ms. Hu, I don't know what to say. I can't stop them from doing anything. It's their decision, not mine."

"Then I guess everyone is turning against me. You got your wish."

"What wish is that?" I asked.

"You won."

"I won what?"

"You've always tried to compete with me to be number one in Alana's life. You see this as an opportunity to push me out."

"Ma'am, I know you're under a lot of stress. I also know that seeing Sora has put you in a bad place, but I'm not conspiring against you. I want to help you."

"No, you don't. You just told me that you won't forbid Alana from seeing her father," she said.

I wasn't tempted to laugh at the notion of me forbidding Alana from doing anything. Here's a question for the male readers. You think you could forbid your wife from doing anything? I didn't think so. I can also now hear all the wives laughing at that question.

"You have no idea how fragile Hani is right now. Getting dumped a few days before her wedding by that pipsqueak."

"Yuto isn't a pipsqueak," I said.

"If you say so."

Ms. Hu opened her car door.

"I don't care what preposterous story Sora gives my girls. There's nothing he can do that makes up for the pain he caused, even if it was decades ago."

She climbed in the car, started the engine, and then raced onto the street at a speed that would make a Hollywood stuntman cringe with worry. I could only stand there and shake my head.

I turned and walked into the house. Maui greeted me by the door like he usually does. He performed a little happy dance for me and then rolled onto his back. After scratching his belly, I walked to the refrigerator and grabbed a Negra Modelo. I then picked up my iPad and walked outside with Maui hot on my heels. I thought what my brain needed was a little diversion, so I logged onto an entertainment website and started reading the celebrity news.

I know, with all the drama going on in the world, who cares about celebrities? But Alana's tendency to distract herself with meaningless gossip had rubbed off on me. I was shocked to see that a particular actor had died, which marked the third celebrity death during this particular week.

I'm sure you've heard of the Rule of Three, which states that bad things often happen in groups of three. In this case, it was specifically referred to as the Celebrity Death Rule of Three. Do I believe in such nonsense? Of course, not. But the mind often looks for patterns in things, and it's not hard to create them even when they don't exist.

That said, something popped into my head as I read about the latest celebrity to die. I had my own set of threes, but I'd missed it because I was too busy trying to figure out who was lying to me and about what. Almost every person I'd met with had told me at least one lie or had omitted an important piece of information.

Mele Akamu had told me a lie on our first meeting when she'd stated that Samson had been unable to find Eric Ellis. Gracie Ito had failed to disclose her knowledge of Eric's affair with Tiana, and Tiana had lied about knowing Daniel Davis.

Daniel had lied about owning a dog. Lee Walters had conveniently left out the part about his offer to kill his best friend to get back in good graces with Mele Akamu. Stan Cross had most likely lied about not being willing to work with Eric Ellis because he didn't trust him. Oleen Akamu had lied about seeing the murder, and even Detective Parrish had lied about how he'd found the safe behind the bookcase.

The only people who'd actually told me the truth were Daniel's grocery store co-worker, the locksmith, and the loan shark with the unfortunate name of Popcorn. But none of those things accounted for my reference to the Rule of Three. That was specifically three comments that three different people had made to me.

Mele Akamu told me a story about a hypothetical death that had occurred two decades ago. Stan Cross said that Mele Akamu couldn't escape her crimes, even if they were decades old, and Luana Hu said her ex-husband would never be forgiven for his transgressions even though they'd been committed decades ago.

Three references to crimes or misdeeds made decades ago. The Rule of Three. I placed the iPad on the patio table and stood. I knew who I needed to speak to next.

32

TOUGH CASES

THE MURDER OF ERIC ELLIS WAS A PARTICULARLY DIFFICULT CASE TO solve, mainly because there were so many possible suspects. There was also the fact that the murder was five years old. People's memories were surely affected by the passage of time, and of course there's all the lies I mentioned a moment ago. I'd quickly reached the point where I didn't know who or what to believe. Granted, this was nothing new, but I hoped my wild theory about this case dating back farther than anyone realized would pay off.

I'm sure you're getting whiplash by reading about my multiple journeys across Maui, but such is the case when conducting a murder investigation. Fortunately, I had good timing on my side, and I was able to get to the Maui jail before visiting hours were concluded. After entering the building, I asked to speak with Mele Akamu, our favorite godmother of Maui.

As before, I was already seated at the table in the visitor area when they brought her out. I expected her to look worried or even angry with me for having left her employ and not speaking to her about it. She didn't.

"Hello, Mr. Rutherford, imagine my surprise at seeing you here. I was told you quit my case," she said, and she sat opposite me.

"Not entirely."

"I thought that might be the situation. I didn't think you'd care for Ruben. He has a tendency to rub people the wrong way."

"Yes, there is that. Might I suggest you hire another attorney?" I asked.

"Your friend, Ms. Winters, perhaps? Didn't she quit my case too?"

"One can only take so much verbal abuse."

"How may I help you?" she asked, ignoring my statement. "I assume you've learned some things that you want to run by me."

"Just a few. Does either Tavii or Oleen know the security code to your safe?"

"No. They have no need. Samson doesn't even know it."

"You're the only one?" I asked.

"That's right."

"I figured it out, by the way. Your birth year combined with your late husband's."

"My, you are resourceful. It seems I erred in not coming up with a more original code. Is that how someone else was able to plant the gun or are you confessing to me that you did it?" she asked, and then she smiled.

"You seem to be in remarkably good spirits despite the gravity of the situation."

"I have faith in you."

"I hope that faith isn't misplaced," I said.

"My instincts about people are usually right."

"The night Eric was killed, did you or Samson call him around three in the morning?"

"No. I'm sure I was asleep at that time. If I'd wanted him dead, then I would have shot him at a more reasonable hour. Who told you I called him at that time?"

"Eric's lover."

"Ah, so I wasn't the only one he betrayed," she said.

"Last question. In one of our earlier conversations, you referred to a hypothetical killing where a body and the weapon were dumped in the ocean. Hypothetically speaking, what might have been the name of that hypothetical person?" I asked.

Mele Akamu said nothing.

"It's important. I wouldn't be asking otherwise," I continued.

Mele Akamu leaned forward and whispered in my ear.

"Ronan Huff. His name was Ronan Huff."

"Thank you."

"How's my grandson doing by the way?" she asked.

"He's fine. I saw him the other day."

"And his lovely wife, the one who's trying to make sure I stay in here?"

"I believe she's struggling to find her way after leaving Tavii," I said.

"I think what you meant to say was she's struggling after I stopped paying her bills."

"There is that."

"Thank you as always, Mr. Rutherford. I wish you good luck," she said, and she stood.

I left the jail and walked back to my car. Imagine my surprise when I saw Detective Parrish sitting in the front seat of my convertible.

"Tell me, Poe, how do you like driving this car? That is what your friends call you, isn't it, Poe?"

"I didn't realize we were friends now."

"Oh, I think we are. We came to an understanding last time. We're both working for the same team, after all."

"Why do you think it's okay to sit in my car?" I asked.

"I've always wanted to try one of these out. It's a bit cramped in here, especially for someone of your height."

"Driving with the top down seems to make up for it."

"Yes, I bet you feel rather special cruising around the island in your fancy car," he said.

"Do you intend to get out or do I need to ask you to get out?"

Detective Parrish opened the door and climbed out.

"I'm surprised you leave the top down. Someone can get in your car so easily, maybe even plant something."

"I keep the glove compartment and the trunk locked," I said.

"Good idea. So, did you come here to see your client?"

"Former client. I swung by to officially let her know that I'd left her investigation."

"May I ask why you dropped her case?"

"Three reasons. I don't like being lied to. I don't like her attorney, and I don't want to work for someone who's obviously guilty."

"You've finally admitted the truth? What convinced you?" he asked.

"The gun in the safe behind the bookcase. I spoke to the locksmith today. His information confirmed everything for me."

"Didn't believe what I had to say?"

"No, not especially."

"Maybe we aren't friends, after all."

"No, I've decided that we won't be, but that doesn't mean you're wrong about Mele Akamu. What I couldn't figure out before is why she'd hire me to find the killer when she already knew who'd done it. It finally occurred to me that she likes playing games."

"That's it? She likes playing games?" he asked.

"That was part of it. The other part is that I was the wildcard. She wanted someone driving around the island and getting in the way. The more confusion I could cause, the more it would help her."

"Maybe you're not as arrogant as I thought you were."

"Oh, I wouldn't go that far."

I walked past Detective Parrish and climbed into my car.

"Have a good day, Detective. Now if you'll excuse me, I need to drive home in my fancy car."

I started the engine and backed out of the parking space. Detective Parrish watched me the entire way until I turned out of the lot and made my way down the road. I drove a short distance and then turned into the parking lot for a coffee shop that I'd frequented with Alana. I parked the BMW in the shade of a tree and pulled out my phone. I dialed Alana and she answered immediately.

"Hey, there," she said.

"Can you do me a favor? Can you find out everything there is to know about Ronan Huff and his disappearance? But be quiet about it. Don't let anyone know you're looking."

"Who is he?"

"Mele Akamu had him killed around twenty years ago. He's connected to Eric Ellis' murder somehow."

Alana promised me she'd look into the case, so I put the car in gear again and drove home. I spent the rest of the day not doing much of anything. It was nearing five in the afternoon when Alana called me.

"What are you doing?" she asked.

"Sitting by the pool and listening to your dog snore under my chair."

"Can you make it up to Harry's in a couple of hours. There's someone I want you to meet."

"Who?"

"His name's Nathan Buckley. He's a retired detective. We overlapped by a couple of years at the department. He retired well before I made detective."

"He investigated the Ronan Huff case?" I asked.

"Yes, and I promised him free drinks at your bar if he told us what he knew. Nathan is one of the good guys. If there was anything to find regarding Ronan Huff, then I guarantee you he found it."

"I'll see you there at seven, and I'll tell Foxx to break out the best bottle of scotch."

"Sounds good."

I got to the bar about thirty minutes early and brought Foxx up to speed on my conversation with Daniel Davis' co-worker, the loan shark named Popcorn, and my ability to get into Mele Akamu's safe. I also told him about my still-forming theory that the motive for the Eric Ellis murder had started years before.

Alana arrived right at seven, followed by retired Detective Nathan Buckley a few minutes after that. I guessed his age at around eighty. He was of average height and weight, which I was sure was because most people on the island eat healthy food. That's not hard to do given all of the delicious fresh fruit to be found.

Alana greeted Detective Buckley at the door and led him over to the bar.

"Poe, Foxx, this is Nathan Buckley, one of the department's most distinguished detectives," Alana said.

"I don't know about that," he said, and he shook our hands.

"What can I get you to drink, Detective?" Foxx asked.

"Please call me Nathan, and is it possible for you to make me a Manhattan?" Nathan asked.

"You just became Poe's new friend. That's his drink too," Alana said.

"No wonder you married the guy. He has good tastes," Nathan said.

"I try my best," I said.

"What would you like, Alana?" Foxx asked.

"How about a dirty martini?" she asked.

"A dirty martini it is," Foxx said, and he started mixing our drinks. Nathan Buckley turned to me.

"Alana says you have an interest in an old case of mine."

"That's right. The Ronan Huff investigation. What do you remember about it?" I asked.

"I remember everything, especially since I reviewed my old files after Alana called."

"First, who reported him missing?" I asked.

"A neighbor of his. She was babysitting Ronan's son and she called the police when Ronan didn't come home."

"Where was Ronan's wife?" Alana asked.

"She'd died in a car accident a few weeks before. It was all very tragic," Nathan said.

"Did you have any suspects?" Foxx asked, and he handed Nathan his Manhattan.

"We had one, a very good one. Mele Akamu," Nathan said, and then he took a sip of his drink. "Excellent Manhattan."

"Thank you."

Foxx slid Alana the dirty martini. Then he handed me my Manhattan.

"Thanks, Foxx," I said.

"Let me guess, you weren't able to pin anything on Mele Akamu because she had a solid alibi," Alana said.

"Her son swore she was with him, but we never thought she did it herself. She had plenty of people who would do her dirty work for her," Nathan said.

"Was there a reason why she would have wanted to kill Ronan Huff?" I asked.

"Word on the street was that he'd stolen from her."

"But no body, no case," Alana said.

"It wasn't hard to guess what happened to him. Ronan Huff and the murder weapon were dumped in the ocean," Nathan said. "That's what makes this new charge so strange. Why would she have buried that other guy in a field, especially after she'd gotten away with the other murder?"

"We share your suspicions," Foxx said.

"This man, Ronan Huff, was he associated with Stan Cross in any way?" I asked.

"Not that I know of. Stan wasn't much of a player back in those days," Nathan said.

"The boy that Ronan left behind, what became of him?" I asked.

"He didn't have any other relatives, so he got put in the foster care system. I kept in touch with him for a few years because I felt so bad for him. He got lucky and got adopted by a family."

"What was the boy's name?" I asked.

Nathan told us.

I turned to Alana.

"Now we know who killed Eric Ellis," I said.

33

YOUR HONOR – PART 2

I'M SURE YOU'VE HEARD THE SAYING, "THERE ARE THINGS YOU KNOW and there are things you can prove." That's a line that's been uttered in many cop shows and it fit my situation perfectly. Although I felt satisfied that I knew who'd killed Eric Ellis and why, I couldn't prove it. Everything was circumstantial evidence. I also didn't think there was any way I'd be able to trick the killer into revealing themselves as I had in past cases. So, I decided to steal a play from the killer's playbook, and I went into long-game mode.

Six months had passed since my meeting with Alana and the retired detective, Nathan Buckley, and I found myself once again driving to the courthouse in my little roadster. Mele Akamu's case had finally gone to trial. I hadn't attended any of the court sessions, but Mara had been kind enough to give me regular updates.

Despite the perfect weather for my commute into Kahului, I felt a nervousness in the pit of my stomach. I didn't like appearing in court, which I believe I mentioned at the beginning of this tale. But it was time to put on the show, and one must find a way to rise to the occasion when an innocent person's life is on the line. Of course, I didn't believe Mele Akamu was all that innocent, especially in regard to the death of Ronan Huff, but I knew that she hadn't murdered Eric Ellis.

When I walked into the courtroom, I saw Alana sitting near Detective Josh Parrish in the crowded gallery. Neither was to appear on the witness stand on this day, but I assumed they were both wondering what I had to say.

Perhaps I should clarify that. Alana already knew my testimony since she'd helped me rehearse it the night before. That had come after a handful of practice sessions with Mara. What did I think was Detective Parrish's attitude regarding my courtroom appearance? I'm sure he was curious, perhaps even a little worried. He had labeled me as unpredictable, after all. This was the case of a lifetime for him and he didn't want me screwing it up.

I said hello to Mara, who was seated beside a confident-looking Mele Akamu. I then said hello to Mrs. Akamu. Mara had taken over the legal case after Mrs. Akamu had dismissed her longtime attorney, Ruben Dalton. In full disclosure, she'd done so at my recommendation. I'd told her that I didn't believe Mr. Dalton had the temperament needed for a murder trial, and I suggested that Mara could do a better job of connecting with the jury.

The prosecution, led by the always reliable Piper Lane, had concluded their case the day before, and I was to be the first witness called by the defense. After the judge and jury came into the courtroom, Alana gave me a slight smile. She knew what was coming next.

"The defense calls Edgar Rutherford to the stand," Mara said.

I walked behind the witness stand and the bailiff approached me with the Bible. I put my left hand on the Good Book and raised my right hand.

"Do you swear that the evidence you are about to give is the truth, the whole truth, and nothing but the truth, so help you God?" the bailiff asked.

"I do," I said.

"Have a seat, Mr. Rutherford," the judge said.

Mara walked to the witness stand as I sat down. She was dressed in a navy-blue business suit and her red hair was pulled back in a tight bun. The woman radiated a cool and collected attitude. I glanced at the jury. I could tell they liked her.

"Good morning, Mr. Rutherford."

"Good morning, Ms. Winters."

"Mr. Rutherford, in what capacity did you work for Mele Akamu?"

"She hired me to investigate the murder of Eric Ellis, a long-time associate of hers."

"At the time she approached you, did she give a reason as to why she wanted this murder solved?" Mara asked.

"Yes. She said she thought the police might think she was guilty of the crime because of her association with Mr. Ellis and the bad way it had ended."

"Did you take her case, Mr. Rutherford?" Mara asked.

"I did."

"During your investigation, how many people did you interview?" Mara asked.

"I don't remember the exact number. It was several people, though."

"Does the name Stan Cross mean anything to you?"

"Yes, his name came up during a few of the initial interviews I conducted."

"What is Mr. Cross' relationship to Mrs. Akamu?"

"They're business competitors."

"You said that his name came up during these interviews. For what reason was he mentioned?"

"I always ask people who they think had motive for the murder. His name was mentioned in that capacity by more than one person," I said.

"As you progressed with your case, did you start to form a theory regarding Mr. Cross?"

"Yes, for a while I thought that Mr. Cross might have killed Eric Ellis and then tried to frame Mrs. Akamu."

"Do you still believe that?"

"No, I don't. I think Mr. Cross became aware of the murder and he tried to take advantage of Mrs. Akamu's legal predicament."

"Why do you believe this to be the case?" Mara asked.

"Because Mr. Cross told me that when I eventually met with him."

"Mr. Rutherford, was there anything else you learned during your interview with Mr. Cross?" Mara asked.

"Yes, he provided two big breaks in the investigation."

"Let's get back to those in a minute. Let's talk about the gun that the police found in Mrs. Akamu's safe. The prosecution has stated that it's definitive proof that my client killed Eric Ellis. Do you believe that?"

"No, I don't."

"Why not?"

"For a couple of reasons. The first is the knowledge of the existence of the safe."

"What do you mean by that?" Mara asked.

"The safe was well-hidden behind a bookshelf. It would take a wild stroke of luck to locate it."

"Yet the police still found it."

"Yes, but that's because they were told about it," I said.

"How do you know this?"

"Well, I'm going to get accused of hearsay, but Oleen Akamu told me that she had informed the police."

"Objection. Hearsay, your honor," Piper Lane said.

"See," I said, and I smiled at Mara.

"Sustained. And Mr. Rutherford, don't get cute in my courtroom," the judge said.

"My apologies, your Honor."

"Oleen Akamu's statement aside, was there another reason you believed the police already knew where the safe was hidden?" Mara asked.

"Yes, when I went to Mrs. Akamu's house, I noticed that the place had been trashed during the police's search. The study was not. All of the books were on the shelves. The switch that caused the bookcase to move and reveal the safe was behind a copy of the book *Treasure Island*. It was my belief the police knew exactly where to look."

"If that's the case, then why was the rest of the house trashed?"

"You'd have to ask the police that question."

"Regardless of how the hidden safe was located, the gun that killed Eric Ellis was still found inside the locked safe. Why is that not damning to my client?" Mara asked.

"Someone else put it there."

"How? The safe is state-of-the-art. How could they get in?"

"Because I figured out the combination in less than ten minutes," I said.

"How did you do that?"

"Most people use numbers they can easily remember, like a birthday or an anniversary. The code for Mrs. Akamu's safe was the year of her birth followed by the year of her late husband's birth."

"Why didn't you just ask Mrs. Akamu for the correct code?"

"Because I wanted to see if I could break it myself. I assumed that if I could do it, then someone else could too. It's my belief that the gun was planted in the safe before the locksmith opened the safe in the presence of the police," I said.

"Mr. Rutherford, who is Daniel Davis?"

"He's the man who found the skeletal remains of Eric Ellis in a field near the north shore."

"Did you interview Mr. Davis during the course of your investigation?"

"I did. I went to his apartment in Paia."

"And what did you learn during this interview?" Mara asked.

"Mr. Davis had told the police that his dog had found human bones during their walk. However, I saw no evidence of a dog in the apartment. I went to the Maui Animal Center and learned that Mr. Davis had adopted the dog, only to return it the next day."

"So, on this one and only day that Mr. Davis owned a dog, the dog found the remains of Eric Ellis?" Mara asked.

"That's correct."

"Did you conduct a follow-up interview with Mr. Davis?"

"I wanted to, but I didn't get the chance."

"Why not?"

"He drowned while surfing, at least that was the official cause of death."

"You don't think he died that way?"

"No, he drowned, but I believe he was helped. I saw the body after it was recovered on the beach, and Mr. Davis had substantial bruising on the neck and shoulders."

"You believe he was forcibly held under the waves?" Mara asked.

"That's right."

"Objection, your Honor. Mr. Rutherford is not a licensed medical examiner," Piper Lane said.

"You don't have to be a medical examiner to see bruises on a body," Mara said.

"Overruled, Ms. Lane. Mr. Rutherford is entitled to his opinion," the judge said.

"Since you were suspicious of Mr. Davis' death, did you look into it more?" Mara asked.

"I did. I learned that Mr. Davis was five thousand dollars in debt to a loan shark. He had a gambling problem."

"Let's get back to Stan Cross' interview. Earlier you said that he provided you two breaks. What was the first one?" Mara asked.

"He informed me that Eric Ellis was having an affair with a woman named Tiana Wise. This was at the same time that he was in a long-term relationship with another woman."

"Why is this significant to this case?"

"Because Tiana Wise may have been the last person to see Eric Ellis before he was killed. He was at her apartment the night he died."

"Walk us through that night if you can," Mara said.

"Eric Ellis left his girlfriend under the guise of going to see Mele Akamu. Instead, he went to see his lover. In the middle of the night, he received a phone call from Stan Cross."

"Stan Cross and not my client?"

"That's correct," I said.

"How do you know this?"

"Phone records. Eric Ellis got the call from Mr. Cross at three ten in the morning, not from Mele Akamu."

As before, she handed one of the copies to Piper Lane and the other to the judge.

Mara held the third copy up so that I could see it.

"Do you recognize this photograph, Mr. Rutherford?"

"I do."

"Whose car is this?"

"It belonged to Detective Josh Parrish," I said.

"Belonged? As in past tense?"

"Yes, he sold it about eight months ago."

"Objection, your Honor. How is Detective Parrish's automobile relevant?" Piper Lane asked.

"I'm about to get to that, your Honor," Mara said.

"Overruled," the judge said.

"Mr. Rutherford, why is this Honda Accord important to this case?" Mara asked.

"Detective Parrish sold it after he got a car from the Maui Police Department. They provide sedans for the detectives."

"How much did he sell it for?"

"Five thousand dollars," I said.

"That's interesting. The same amount of money that his old friend, Daniel Davis, owed to a loan shark. This is the same Daniel Davis who found Eric Ellis' body with his non-existent dog."

"Objection, your Honor. Ms. Winters and Mr. Rutherford are trying to besmirch the good name of a member of our law enforcement community," Piper Lane said.

"Sustained. Tread carefully, Ms. Winters," the judge said.

"Yes, your Honor," Mara said, and she turned back to me. "Mr. Rutherford, earlier you mentioned that Stan Cross provided you two breakthroughs. The first was the revelation of Eric Ellis' affair with Tiana Wise. What was the second?"

"He alluded to karma coming back to bite Mele Akamu," I said.

"Why is that significant?" Mara asked.

"Yes, I think we'd all like to know," Piper Lane said, and there was no hiding the sarcasm in her voice.

"Is there an objection coming, counselor?" the judge asked.

"No, your Honor. My apologies," Piper Lane said.

"Let's get back to my question, Mr. Rutherford. Why did you believe Mr. Cross' comment about karma was significant?" Mara asked.

"I believed he was referring to a man who disappeared twenty years ago. That man's name was Ronan Huff," I said.

"Why is this important to the murder of Eric Ellis?"

"I believe they're connected. Ronan Huff was working for Mele Akamu around the time he disappeared. His body was never found."

"Was my client suspected in Mr. Huff's disappearance?"

"Yes, according to the detective who originally looked into it twenty years ago."

"Twenty years is a long time. Were you able to talk to any of Mr. Huff's family about the case?" Mara asked.

"Mr. Huff had one young son at the time he disappeared. It took a bit of an effort to find the man because he changed his last name after he was adopted by his foster family. I haven't had a chance to talk to the man yet."

"Who is that man?"

"Detective Josh Parrish," I said.

"No further questions, your Honor."

34

KARMA

HERE'S AN INTERESTING PIECE OF LEGAL HISTORY FOR YOU. IN RAMOS versus Louisiana, the Supreme Court ruled that a jury must be unanimous in its decision to convict a person in a criminal case. A man named Evangelisto Ramos had been convicted of murder in the state of Louisiana by a ten to two jury vote.

He appealed his conviction and said that the non-unanimous verdict was the result of a Jim Crow law that allowed for racial discrimination by juries. The Louisiana Court of Appeals disagreed with him, and they upheld his conviction. The Supreme Court did not. They said it violated his Sixth Amendment rights, which gives someone the right to a speedy and public trial by an impartial jury.

So, how does this relate to Mele Akamu? It meant that Mara only needed to convince one juror of her client's innocence. Actually, let's not even take it that far. Mara just needed one juror to feel the prosecution hadn't proven the charge of murder beyond a reasonable doubt.

Mara convinced all twelve.

About a week after my courtroom appearance, Mele Akamu was pronounced "Not Guilty" and released from jail. Samson Opunui had the charges against him dropped a few days later. Mara had assured

Piper Lane that she could expect a repeat performance by yours truly and there was no reason for Ms. Lane to suffer another public defeat. In fairness to Piper Lane, I don't think she dropped the charges against Samson because she didn't want to lose the case and embarrass herself. I think she realized the real killer was hiding behind a badge.

Shortly after both Mele Akamu and her butler were freed, I was summoned to the Akamu estate. My jazz phase was starting to ease up, so I made a switch in musical styles and listened to the Pet Shop Boys, the English duo formed in the early 80s. I got through their songs, "It's a Sin," "Always on My Mind," "Love Comes Quickly," and their smash hit, "West End Girls," during the drive to Maui's upcountry.

Mount Haleakala was covered in clouds as it often is, but the temperature was nice, and there was a cool breeze blowing in my face for most of the drive. It was the official conclusion of the Mele Akamu case, at least I thought it was, and I was anxious to put it behind me and move on to less urgent matters.

There were tropical drinks to be drunk. Dogs to be walked. Pools to be swam in, and waves to be surfed. Granted, Alana would have to handle that last activity on her own. I would be content to sit in the sand and snap photos of her surfing prowess with my Canon camera.

I pushed down harder on the accelerator as I hit the upcountry's curvy roads. The little car was quite adept at handling the hairpin turns, and it was always a thrill to push the roadster to its limits. I know, I know. That doesn't sound very safe, but one must have a little bit of danger in one's life.

I eventually parked my BMW convertible in the turnaround in front of the Akamu house and Samson Opunui opened the front door as I approached.

"Good morning, Samson. I'm glad to hear the charges were dropped," I said.

"Thanks to you. I am in your debt, Mr. Rutherford."

"You're more than welcome, but you're not in my debt."

Samson nodded.

"Mrs. Akamu is in the back. I'll take you to her."

I followed Samson through the house. Everything was back in its proper place, unlike my last trip there. The elderly butler led me out the rear sliding glass door where I saw Mele Akamu sitting in her normal seat beside the fire pit. I thought she might rise to greet me after everything I'd done for her. I thought wrong.

"Mr. Rutherford is here to see you, ma'am," Samson said.

"Thank you, Samson. You may leave us."

"Yes, ma'am."

Mele Akamu waited for Samson to walk away. Why? I'm not sure.

"How may I be of service, Mrs. Akamu?" I asked.

"I want to continue your questioning. Ms. Winters is a good attorney, but there were a great number of questions she left unasked in the courtroom."

"I disagree. She asked the appropriate number. You are free, after all."

"Tell me, when did you realize it was Josh Parrish who'd murdered Eric Ellis and framed me?"

"It was something Stan Cross said. I didn't really catch it at first, but it came to me later. He told me that no one in his line of work would have the patience to play such a long game against you. But it was the comment that he made about karma that did it. He mentioned something about you paying for your sins, even if it had been decades. I finally realized that he was talking about a specific event and then I remembered the conversation we had earlier about a hypothetical killing at sea. There was also the mystery as to why Detective Parrish came at me so hard in the beginning."

"Perhaps he's simply a man who likes to maintain the illusion that he's in control," Mrs. Akamu said.

"I thought so at first, but then he shifted gears and tried a different tactic. I realized he was playing a game, so I played one of my own."

"Which was?"

"I pretended to back off and concede the race."

"It worked."

"I have something for you," I said, and I handed Mele Akamu an eight-by-ten envelope I'd brought with me from the car.

She opened the envelope and looked at several incriminating photographs of Detective Parrish in bed with Tiana Wise.

"I hired an associate of mine to follow Detective Parrish for a few weeks before your trial started. She's very adept at tailing people without them knowing," I continued.

"She's also quite the photographer. Does Josh Parrish's wife know about his affair?"

"Not yet. I assumed you'd want to do the honors."

"Thank you. I believe I will."

"Tiana was in love with Detective Parrish. I suspect she would have done anything for him. She helped him set up Eric Ellis. I suspect she also helped convince Eric to turn against you."

"You said she was in love with him. Has something changed?"

"Keep looking through the photos," I said.

She continued to flip through the photographs until she got to the last one. It was an image of Tiana with a black eye and swollen lip.

"That photograph was taken by me. Her injuries were sustained on the same day of my appearance at your trial," I continued.

"Josh Parrish's handiwork, I presume."

"I had the same thought, but Tiana refused to admit it. My wife has a copy of the photo and she's on her way now to speak with Ms. Wise. She hopes to convince her to press assault charges."

"Will the DA arrest Josh Parrish for what he did to Eric?"

"I don't know. I gave them all the evidence I have. I put the odds at fifty-fifty," I said.

"They protect their own. I wouldn't be surprised if he walks."

I didn't reply.

"So, are you ever going to ask me if I did it?"

"Did what?" I asked.

"Killed Josh's father, Ronan Huff."

"Would you like me to ask you?"

She waved her hand, as if dismissing my question.

"No need, but here's something you may not know. I hired

Ronan years ago because of his wife. She and I were friends, and they were seeing hard times. Ronan was a good employee until he wasn't."

"You mean when he stole from you," I said.

"Samson found out. I let Ronan go."

"Forgive me, but I find that hard to believe."

"You wouldn't if you'd known the depth of my friendship with his wife. She died shortly after that incident. Ronan blamed her for what happened. He was convinced she'd told me about the theft."

"You think he killed her? I thought she died in a car accident?"

"I had Samson look into it because I didn't think the police would give it the attention it deserved. It was no accident. So, you can see the irony of Josh Parrish wanting to avenge the man who'd murdered his mother."

"That's why you had Ronan Huff killed," I said.

"He murdered my friend, an innocent woman and a mother. He got what he deserved. Then his son grew up to become a murderer in his own right. Like father, like son."

"Did you know that Detective Parrish was Ronan's son?"

"No. If I had, he wouldn't have been here to cause all of this mischief."

"Does that mean what I think it does?" I asked.

"I'll give the police the chance to do the right thing. If they don't, then I will. And yes, I realize the foolishness of admitting such a thing to the husband of a homicide detective."

It was certainly a moral dilemma for me, but I decided to debate it another day. There was still time to let the Maui Police Department do their thing.

"There's something else. I know I said at the beginning of this investigation that I wouldn't find the documents that Eric stole from you, but I can give you an update on them. I met with Gracie Ito a third time since I had another hunch. It turns out that Eric left the documents with her and she destroyed them after he disappeared," I said.

"Do you believe her?"

ROBERT W. STEPHENS

"I do. Besides, it's been five years. If she still had them and wanted to hurt you, she would have used them by now."

"I have one more question for you," she said.

"Of course."

"I heard there were others besides Stan Cross who saw an opportunity in my incarceration," she said.

"Who are you referring to?"

"My grandson. I have it on good authority that Oleen wasn't the only one who told the police about my safe hidden behind my bookcase."

"Tavii told them too?" I asked.

She nodded.

"He and Oleen weren't talking at that point, but they both tried the same tactic on me."

"What exactly is your question?"

"Did you personally witness Tavii conspiring against me?"

"I think you should ask him that question yourself."

"I will and thank you for giving me the answer. I think it's time my grandson learned how to make his own way," she said. "I know you officially quit working for me after meeting with my former attorney. However, I also realize you continued with your investigation in the spirit of seeing justice done. I'd like to pay you for your time."

I heard the back door open and Samson walked through, further convincing me that he had a microphone hidden somewhere near the firepit.

"How is Detective Hu doing, by the way? I heard you had an unwelcome visitor at a party months ago," she continued.

"My wife is fine, and yes, we did have a visitor, although I don't know how unwelcome he is these days."

"Please give her my best. And don't do anything to screw up that relationship of yours. A woman like that is hard to find."

"I know, and I will do my best to hold on to her."

Samson arrived a second later and he handed me an envelope. I didn't bother looking at the check then and there. That would have been tacky.

I was about halfway between the Maui Animal Center and the airport in Kahului when I noticed a dark sedan quickly approaching from behind. A moment later, red and blue lights flashed on the front grill of the car. The lights were accompanied by a loud whooping sound. I pulled off to the side of the road. I'll give you one guess as to who it was.

I pulled out my phone and opened a recording application. I was about to hit the little red button when Detective Parrish snatched the phone out of my hand. He dropped it on the street and then smashed it with the heel of his shoe.

"Should I report you for police brutality against my phone?" I asked.

"Do you always have a joke for everything?"

"Just where it concerns you."

"I guess you've already collected your blood money from Mele Akamu now that she's out of jail," he said.

"My blood money?"

"You helped a killer go free. What would you call what she paid you?"

"I think you and I can stop playing games now. We both know she didn't kill Eric Ellis."

"No, but she killed my father. Doesn't she deserve to go to jail for that?"

"My answer may surprise you. Yes, I think she should go to jail," I said.

Detective Parrish said nothing.

"And what about Eric Ellis? He had nothing to do with your father's death. Why did he deserve to die?" I asked.

"Sometimes people have to be sacrificed for the greater good. Besides, you don't think Eric Ellis would have eventually turned out worse than Mele Akamu? Whoever killed him probably did the world a favor."

"There was something I didn't mention during the trial, nor did I tell Mrs. Akamu earlier today. I know you didn't act alone. You had Stan Cross' help."

"Why would you say something like that?"

"He helped you lure Eric Ellis to his death. The phone records prove that. He also got rid of Daniel Davis once you two realized that I'd discovered the truth about Daniel's fake dog."

"That fool never should have gotten rid of that dog so quickly," Detective Parrish said.

"It was an ingenious plan. You killed Eric right after you became a cop and then you had the body discovered weeks after you made detective. How did you guarantee that you'd get the case, though?"

Detective Parrish smiled but said nothing.

"By the way, I got Mele Akamu's safe open on my fifth attempt. How many did it take you?" I asked.

"Three."

"Aren't you worried?"

"About what?"

"About Stan Cross. He knows the pressure is on you, especially after the story I told in court. He may think you're going to cut a deal and flip on him."

"If anything, Stan Cross should be worried about me. You should too. Just ask Eric Ellis," he said.

"Oh, I don't take your threats lightly. Have a good day. Maybe we can work your next case together."

"A word of warning, Rutherford. When the end arrives for you, and it will soon, you'll never see it coming."

Detective Parrish kicked the broken pieces of my cell phone and then walked back to his sedan. I waited for him to drive off before starting my car.

I always played my music through my phone, so there was to be no more Pet Shop Boys for the remainder of the drive to the airport.

I parked my convertible in airport parking and walked to the arrivals area. I found the flight information and walked to the appropriate baggage claim. It took me another ten minutes to find the person I was meeting.

"There you are," I said.

Sora Hu slipped his phone back into his pocket.

"I tried calling you a couple of times, but it went straight to voicemail."

"Sorry about that. I had a little accident with my phone on the way here."

I looked at the small roller suitcase at his feet.

"Is that all of your luggage?" I asked.

"Yes, I like to travel light."

"Good, then we won't need to smother it in grease to fit it in the trunk of my car."

"Is Alana outside?" he asked.

"No, she's going to meet us at Harry's."

"What about Hani?"

"She can't make it tonight. She has two meetings at our event space in Wailea. Shall we head for the car?"

"Yes, of course."

We walked into the parking lot and climbed into the convertible.

"Nice car," Sora said.

"Thanks. I bought it off of Foxx when I first moved to the island."

I started the engine and put the car in gear. I turned out of the parking lot, and we started the drive for Lahaina.

"Yuto asked me to tell you that a suite opened up at his hotel, so he upgraded you."

"That's nice of him. How are things between Hani and Yuto?"

"Nonexistent, I'm afraid. Hani has thrown herself into her work, so has Yuto."

"They're not talking at all?"

"Not that I know of. I think they've both moved on. I feel a little bad for saying this, but I think it's probably for the best. There was a little too much drama going on between the two of them," I said.

"All caused by me, I'm sure."

"Not at all. I think your presence was the kick they needed to have a hard look at their relationship."

"Maybe time will bring them back together."

"I doubt that."

"Why do you say that?"

I laughed.

"Because I know your daughter. She'll never forgive Yuto for ending things with her."

"You're probably right."

I watched as Sora looked off to the ocean as we made our way down Honoapiilani Highway.

"I never get tired of that view," I said.

"How do you like living on Maui?"

"I love it. Should have done it years ago. How about you? Do you miss it?"

"Yes, which is why I've got a meeting lined up with a realtor tomorrow. She's going to show me some condos."

"Wonderful. Do Alana and Hani know about that?" I asked.

"I mentioned it to Alana in our last email."

He paused a moment.

Then he continued, "You don't know how surprised I was when I got Alana's first email a few months ago. I thought she'd written me off for good, especially when she refused to see me on my last trip here."

"It surprised me too."

"What do you think made her change her mind?" he asked.

"I think it was a conversation we had about my parents. They're both deceased, and I mentioned that I would give anything to have one more conversation with them."

"Thank you for that."

"You're welcome, but in all honesty, I did it for her."

"I understand. What about Luana? How is she taking all of this?"

"Not well. She hasn't spoken to Alana or Hani in weeks. I'm sure she'll come around, especially since I know she wants to see her granddaughter."

"She's been ignoring Ava too?"

"Ava and Hani are a package deal, so yes, she hasn't seen Ava either," I said.

"Hani said she would introduce me to Ava on this trip. I can't tell you how much I'm looking forward to it."

"I'm sure. She's a special little girl. Smart as can be and energy to spare. I have trouble keeping up with her."

We drove in silence for a few moments. Then Sora turned to me.

"I know I don't deserve this second chance with my daughters, and I'm sure you're worried for them. I want you to know that I don't take this opportunity for granted. I'm a changed man and I'm going to prove that to all of you."

"Good. I look forward to seeing that," I said.

"It's not just them, Poe. I want to get to know you better too. You should hear some of the things Alana wrote about you in her emails."

"Don't believe any of it," I said, and I laughed.

"She thinks the world of you. I want to get to know that man."

"There's Harry's up ahead," I said, ignoring his comment.

I hadn't decided yet how well I wanted to get to know Sora. I still had a hard time processing how a man could abandon his family. But everyone deserves a second chance, or so I've heard. Still, I was content to sit on the sidelines and observe his growing relationship with Alana and Hani. Once they accepted him, or not, then I'd make my own decision.

I parked the BMW under the shade of a tree, and we walked into Harry's. I spotted Alana sitting in a back booth by herself. We walked over to her and stopped at the edge of the table.

"Hello, Alana," Sora said.

Alana stood, but she didn't move to hug him, not that I expected her to.

"Why don't we have a seat and talk," she said.

"I'll send Kiana over to get your drink order," I said.

"You don't want to join us?" Alana asked, and I could hear a hint of nervousness in her voice.

"In a little while. There's something I need to talk to Foxx about first. It will just take me a few minutes."

I walked to the bar and asked Kiana to get anything Alana and Sora wanted. Then I nodded to Foxx and asked him to join me in our office. We walked into the back and I shut the door behind us.

"What's up, buddy?" he asked.

"Since you were my partner in crime on this investigation, I want you to be the first to hear."

"Hear what?"

I reached into my pocket and pulled out a small digital audio recorder.

"Detective Parrish pulled me over on the way to the airport. I made a point of showing him the audio recorder on my phone. I figured he'd grab it from me, which he did. He owes me a new phone, by the way."

"Meanwhile you had the audio recorder running in your pocket the whole time," Foxx guessed.

"I've been carrying it with me ever since my courtroom appearance. I figured it was only a matter of time before he found me."

I pressed play on the recorder.

"If anything, Stan Cross should be worried about me. You should too. Just ask Eric Ellis," Detective Parrish said on the recorder.

"Oh, I don't take your threats lightly. Have a good day. Maybe we can work your next case together."

"A word of warning, Rutherford. When the end arrives for you, and it will soon, you'll never see it coming."

I stopped the audio recorder.

"He basically admitted to killing Eric Ellis," Foxx said.

"There's more. Earlier he admitted that he broke into Mele Akamu's safe."

"Did you play Alana the recording?"

"Not yet. She's all amped up about seeing her father. I'll play her the audio later tonight. I suspect Detective Parrish will be in handcuffs soon after that."

Foxx slapped me on my back and almost knocked me over.

"We got him, Poe. We got him."

"Yes, we did," I said, and I smiled.

THE END

～

Are you ready for more in the Murder on Maui Mystery series?

Poe's next mystery, **Poe's Justice**, is available now!

An American TV treasure found murdered. A surprising slew of Tinseltown enemies. Can this islander investigator shine the spotlight on the killer?

Maui, Hawaii. PI Edgar Allan "Poe" Rutherford has the perfect gift for his wife's birthday. Arranging a Zoom call with her favorite childhood actor, Poe is thrilled when his surprise is a hit. But when the well-loved celebrity is discovered dead in his home a few days later, the private eye travels to LA to find the truth.

With the grieving daughter suspicious of her famous father's death, the detective dives deep into the star's life to investigate possible foul play. And as he uncovers the victim's shady past, Poe's expert sleuthing leads him to a shocking motive for the crime.

Will he catch a Hollywood hitman before the guilty party tears up the script?

Poe's Justice is the thrilling fourteenth book in the Murder on Maui mystery series. If you like shrewd heroes, unexpected twists, and slippery criminals, then you'll love Robert W. Stephens' captivating whodunit.

ALSO BY ROBERT W. STEPHENS

Murder on Maui Mystery Series

If you like charismatic characters, artistic whodunnits, and twists you won't see coming, then you'll love this captivating mystery series.

Aloha Means Goodbye (Poe Book 1)

Wedding Day Dead (Poe Book 2)

Blood like the Setting Sun (Poe Book 3)

Hot Sun Cold Killer (Poe Book 4)

Choice to Kill (Poe Book 5)

Sunset Dead (Poe Book 6)

Ocean of Guilt (Poe Book 7)

The Tequila Killings (Poe Book 8)

Wave of Deception (Poe Book 9)

The Last Kill (Poe Book 10)

Mountain of Lies (Poe Book 11)

Rich and Dead (Poe Book 12)

Poe's First Law (Poe Book 13)

Poe's Justice (Poe Book 14)

Poe's Rules (Poe Book 15)

Alex Penfield Supernatural Mystery Thriller Series

If you like supernatural whodunnits, gripping actions, and heroes with a troubled past, then you'll love this series.

Ruckman Road (Penfield Book 1)

Dead Rise (Penfield Book 2)

The Eternal (Penfield Book 3)

Nature of Darkness (Penfield Book 4)

The Eighth Order (Penfield Book 5)

Ruckman Road

To solve an eerie murder, one detective must break a cardinal rule: never let the case get personal...

Alex Penfield's gunshot wounds have healed, but the shock remains raw. Working the beat could be just what the detective needs to clear his head. But when a corpse washes up on the Chesapeake Bay, Penfield's first case back could send him spiraling...

As Penfield and his partner examine the dead man's fortress of a house, an army of surveillance cameras takes the mystery to another level. When the detective sees gruesome visions that the cameras fail to capture, he begins to wonder if his past has caught up with him. To solve the murder, Penfield makes a call on a psychic who may or may not be out to kill him...

His desperate attempt to catch a killer may solve the case, but will he lose his sanity in the process?

Ruckman Road is the start of a new paranormal mystery series featuring Detective Alex Penfield. If you like supernatural whodunnits, gripping action, and heroes with a troubled past, then you'll love Robert W. Stephens' twisted tale.

Standalone Dark Thrillers

Nature of Evil

Rome, 1948. Italy reels in the aftermath of World War II. Twenty women are brutally murdered, their throats slit and their faces removed with surgical precision. Then the murders stop as abruptly as they started, and the horrifying crimes and their victims are lost to history. Now over sixty years later, the killings have begun again. This time in America. It's up to homicide detectives Marcus Carter and Angela Darden to stop the crimes, but how can they catch a serial killer who leaves no traces of evidence and no apparent motive other than the unquenchable thirst for murder?

The Drayton Diaries

He can heal people with the touch of his hand, so why does a mysterious group want Jon Drayton dead? A voice from the past sends Drayton on a desperate journey to the ruins of King's Shadow, a 17th century plantation house in Virginia that was once the home of Henry King, the wealthiest and most powerful man in North America and who has now been lost to time. There, Drayton meets the beautiful archaeologist Laura Girard, who has discovered a 400-year-old manuscript in the ruins. For Drayton, this partial journal written by a slave may somehow hold the answers to his life's mysteries

ABOUT THE AUTHOR

Robert W. Stephens is the author of the Murder on Maui series, the Alex Penfield supernatural thriller series, and the standalone dark thrillers The Drayton Diaries and Nature of Evil.

You can find more about the author at robertwstephens.com.

Visit him on Facebook at facebook.com/robertwaynestephens

ACKNOWLEDGMENTS

Thanks to you readers for investing your time in reading my story. I hope you enjoyed it. Poe, Alana, Foxx, and Maui will return.

.

Made in the USA
Las Vegas, NV
12 March 2023

68974617R00157